Witch of the Midnight Shadow

Witch of the Midnight Shadow

DAWN OF THE BLOOD WITCH BOOK 7

Maria DeVivo

4 Horsemen
Publications, Inc.

Witch of the Midnight Shadow
Copyright © 2026 Maria DeVivo. All rights reserved.

4 Horsemen
Publications, Inc.

Published By: 4 Horsemen Publications, Inc.

4 Horsemen Publications, Inc.
PO Box 417
Sylva, NC 28779
4horsemenpublications.com
info@4horsemenpublications.com

Cover & Typesetting by Autumn Skye
Edited by Jen Paquette

All rights to the work within are reserved to the author and publisher. No part of this publication may be reproduced, stored in a retrieval system, or transmitted in any form or by any means, electronic, mechanical, photocopying, recording, scanning, or otherwise, except as permitted under Section 107 or 108 of the 1976 International Copyright Act, without prior written permission except in brief quotations embodied in critical articles and reviews. Please contact either the Publisher or Author to gain permission.

All characters, organizations, and events portrayed in this novel are either products of the author's imagination or are used fictitiously.

All brands, quotes, and cited work respectfully belongs to the original rights holders and bear no affiliation to the authors or publisher.

Library of Congress Control Number: 2025948347

Paperback ISBN-13: 979-8-8232-1036-2
Hardcover ISBN-13: 979-8-8232-1037-9
Ebook ISBN-13: 979-8-8232-1038-6

Dedication:

For Alex, Cathy, Donna, Erika, Frankie, Joe, Joel, Mark, Morgan, Scott, Ty, and Wendy—You know what you did… and it was magic. I cannot thank you enough for being a part of my crazy journey.

Table of Contents

Chapter One	1
Chapter Two	14
Chapter Three	31
Chapter Four	52
Chapter Five	68
Chapter Six	83
Chapter Seven	101
Chapter Eight	119
Chapter Nine	136
Chapter Ten	149
Chapter Eleven	168
Chapter Twelve	190
Chapter Thirteen	210
Chapter Fourteen	229
Chapter Fifteen	250
Chapter Sixteen	268
Chapter Seventeen	280
Chapter Eighteen	305
Book Club Questions	321
Author Bio	323

Chapter One

Friday, May 12th 1944
Alice Baker's House
1100 Pelton Avenue
Staten Island, New York
Afternoon of the Waning Gibbous Moon

My hand shook something fierce as I reached out to press the buzzer by the door. For the life of me, I couldn't shake the jitters, and it sure wasn't the cool spring breeze that had me trembling. It was somethin' deeper—fear, plain and simple. If someone had told me four years ago, when I left this place, that I'd end up back here like this, I would've keeled over laughin'. But here I was, and none of it was funny.

The white paint on the front door had chipped away even more since I'd last seen it. Dark wood peeked through in patches, making it look worn and tired—kinda like how I felt. Everything seemed splintered and cracked, like the story of my life. I hated that "woe-is-me" feeling, but to be honest, I was at the end of my rope. If there had been anyplace else I could go, somewhere safe, I sure wouldn't have come back here. But life handed me a basket of lemons, and I was still tryin' to make it sweet. And right then, I was also stuck with Althea wrapped around my neck, holding on tight. So, I quit my hesitatin', rang the doorbell, and tried to gently pry her off.

The dogs barked their fool heads off. Momma's glorious beasts. The three outside heard the three inside, and they went wild, too. Althea tightened her grip around my neck, afraid of the howling noises that filled the air around us. "It's okay, Baby," I coaxed. "They're just big puppies who are excited to meet you!" She relaxed a little, satisfied by my comforting words.

Momma always kept big dogs, ever since I was a little kid. Said it was an insurance policy for not having a husband. "Dogs are more loyal than any man! Remember that, Tildy!" she'd preach often. But what did she know? Momma was only fourteen when she had me. And what did *I* know? I was twenty when I took off with *him*, so…

Momma yelled at them to settle down, and Althea tensed up again.

"Shhh…" I said, petting her hair.

I often wondered what the mind of my three-year-old was like. What did she think about? How did she perceive the world? Me? Her reliance on me was all she knew, and that must have been so frightening for her. Like living in darkness with no control over anything. I didn't want to be three again. I shuddered to think such thoughts.

Chapter One

I looked over my shoulder again, anxious that it was taking Momma so long to answer the g-d door. I did that a lot back then... look over my shoulder. I had to. Ever since I had fled with Althea from England six months prior, I hadn't stopped... looking over my shoulder. I had been lucky enough to get a head start on the goons who had been hunting us down, but I knew my time was up. I knew they were too close for comfort. I'd seen it in my dreams and in the cards. And I had felt it. I knew *they* knew where we were. And being back at Momma's house put the three of us in danger, but I was out of options. I needed help. Serious help. And if there's anyone on this planet who could have helped me figure this out... well... it was Momma.

"C'mon..." I said under my breath, willing my mother to hurry to the door. Althea eyed me with a look of dread, but I smiled the biggest, fakest smile I could muster, and she again relaxed in my arms. I stifled a laugh at how easily the child was placated.

And then the door swung open, and I swear the way Momma's jaw hit the floor almost burst my stifled laugh into a symphony of glee. Momma's three massive German Shepherds crowded behind her, barking at their perceived intruders because that's what they had been trained to do. Althea buried her face in my neck, and I handed Momma my overnight bag so I could wrap both arms around my girl. I glanced cautiously down the street one last time and quickly pushed our way into the foyer.

Momma stepped aside, and I slammed the door behind us. Aside from shushing the dogs, she was practically speechless, and she fumbled with the words in her throat. "Tildy? Althea? Wha… wha… what are you doing here?" Confusion darkened her face, and her perfect green eyes appeared tired and weary. Was it my absence that did that to her?

"No, ma'am," I said firmly with authority as I turned my head and looked out of the small window cut out in the front door. "I think you've confused us with someone else."

Momma narrowed her eyes suspiciously. "Til…"

Lady, the largest of the Shepherds, immediately came up to my leg. She rubbed her snout against my knee and curiously sniffed Althea's shoes. "See, Nancy," I whispered to my girl, "this is Lady. She won't hurt you. She just wants to smell you before she plays with you." I reached down to rub the back of Lady's ear to show the child that it was okay—the dog was safe and wouldn't hurt her.

"Nancy? Who's Nancy?" Momma roared.

I didn't respond. Althea mimicked me and put her hand out to reach for Lady. The other two dogs, Bear and Moose, came up and started sniffing as well. "That one is Bear," I said pointing to the gray one. "And that one is Moose," I said pointing to the black one.

Chapter One

Their tails wagged happily, and they playfully licked Althea's little hand. She squealed with delight at their affection, so I gently eased her onto the floor. The second she hit the ground, the three of them surrounded her, all sniffing, licking her face, and practically knocking her over with excitement. "Oh, doggies!" she exclaimed.

"Tell them to go easy, Nancy," I commanded.

"Easy, doggies!" She giggled.

I hadn't seen her that happy in months, and for that brief moment, my heart was filled with something wonderful and tingly in my chest.

But the moment was only fleeting as I could feel Momma's eyes boring holes deep into my body as each second passed. "Nancy? Matilda Jane Baker! Just what is going on? Where have you been? Why haven't I heard from you in six months! You know I thought you were dead and…"

Althea looked at me sharply as Momma said the word "dead." I shook my head at the child, and she went back to playing with the dogs. I pressed a finger to my lips in hopes of silencing Momma, but that proved to be fruitless. Her eyes narrowed, her hand flew to her hip, and she wildly tapped her foot on the wooden plank floor. No, not tap, more like *stomp*. She stomped so violently I thought she was going to stomp a hole right into the basement!

"S-p-e-l-l," I spelled out, indicating to Momma that we needed to shield Althea from any scary words. "It's just Jane, Alice," I said calmly and quietly. "Jane and Nancy Crowe."

"*Crowe*? Really? Oh, heavens, child! What in God's green apple Earth did you do?"

"Can we please go inside? I promise I'll explain everything."

Momma stared at me for a moment. It was the hard, longing stare of a parent who was conflicted. One part of her wanted to cry tears of joy that I was home, one part wanted to fall to her knees and thank Jesus I was alive, and one part wanted to strangle me for having left in the first place! My insides clenched, 'cause with Momma, you never knew just how she was going to react to something. Finally, she handed me my bag and sighed. "C'mon," she relented, and she bent down to pick up Althea from the floor. Althea made a grunt of displeasure from being torn away from her new playmates, but Momma hushed her, and Althea complied.

Momma paused and took a long look at my girl like she was absorbing every feature of her countenance. "Her pictures don't do her justice," she said to me, but her eyes were trained on Althea. "I'm your grandma. Do you know that?"

Althea nodded and her dirty-blonde curls bounced around her face.

"C'mon, kiddo," Momma continued, "I need a little cuddle time before your mother whisks you away from me."

I arched an eyebrow at Momma, letting her know I didn't approve of her statement. But she

Chapter One

was one hundred percent right. My time was limited, so I knew I needed to give her as much "grandma-time" as she wanted.

Momma glided into the kitchen with Althea on her hip and the three dogs at her heel. I exhaled loudly and dropped the bag to the floor. The living room was off the foyer, and I eyed the three-panel window with concern. From the street, anyone would have an unobstructed, straight-line view of the living room leading well into the kitchen. But I feared it was already too late—that they'd seen me enter the house and were just lying in wait. I knew I couldn't stay there long. A night at most, if that.

Slowly, I crouched down a little bit, sneaked my way over to the side of the curtain, and jerked it across the rod, shutting out all the natural light. A line of dust descended from the floral pattern fabric. I sneezed once. I sneezed twice. I sneezed a third time until Momma finally called out, "Jesus! Bless you!" in an aggravated tone.

I grunted back and wiped underneath my nose with the end of my sleeve. I would have taken a tissue from the box on the coffee table, but the layer of dust on top gave me pause. Had I taken a tissue, there would have been at least ten more consecutive sneezes! And as I surveyed the room, I quickly noticed that while this was the physical house of my childhood, it had become a shell of the former home I once lived in.

"*Janey*? Are you coming?" Momma called from the kitchen. Of course, in true Momma-fashion, she had derived an obnoxious nickname for me without hearing my side of the story.

I exhaled loudly and quipped back, "Coming, Alice!"

The kitchen was exactly as I remembered it, but much like the front door, the white paint on the cupboards peeled something awful. It was depressing to see how she'd let the house get to such a lowly state. A stack of dishes piled out of the side of the basin sink like the Leaning Tower of Pisa! Momma would never leave the kitchen in such a mess. Heck, she even threatened me with the switch if I didn't keep things spic and span. An unsettling feeling worked its way into my chest, and I realized that Momma had just as much to explain to me as I did to her.

Althea sat on top of a stack of books so she could reach the tabletop. A small glass of milk and a plate of cookies were just within her grasp, and I sighed. "Really, Momma? We haven't eaten lunch yet!"

"Oh hush, you!" she barked back. "How long has it been since this sweetie pie had some real, homemade treats? She'll be fine." She arched her eyebrow and glared at me knowingly. "Besides, you got other things you should be worrying about, don't you?"

"Alice, I..."

"...am home," she finished for me as her tone softened with the gentle lilt of a loving mother's concern.

Chapter One

I gave a small smile and plopped down in the chair across from the baby. The dogs huddled underneath the table and eagerly snatched at the bits of cookie she tossed at them. She derived a game of "one for them, one for me," and she sang merrily, "One for Moose" and dropped a piece on the floor for him. "One for Nancy" and popped a piece into her mouth. She did the same for Lady and Bear, and on the third time of her saying "Nancy," the warmth in Momma's demeanor transformed on her face in the manner of a hard scowl.

"Nancy?" she spat. "The child has a beautiful name, and you go and call her *Nancy*?"

"What's wrong with Nancy? It's a pretty name."

"Her real one is pretty, too—Althea Aisling Circe Baker."

"*Crowley*," I corrected.

She rolled her eyes and huffed. "But for some reason you don't seem to be acknowledging it. And yours for that matter. Care to tell me why?"

"It's a long story. Very long and very complicated."

Momma put a plate of corned beef and cabbage in front of me and nodded her head for me to eat. I touched the side of the white China, and it was cold. I surmised the food on it was cold too, so I pushed it an inch away. "But you said you didn't eat lunch yet," she said.

"Her," I said and nodded at Althea. "I'm not hungry. She needs to be fed, though. And not corned beef."

Momma put her hand on her hip and groaned. "Well, what then? What does she eat? Jesus Christ, Til, she's my granddaughter, and I have no idea what kinds of foods she likes!"

I wanted to blurt out, "I'm your *daughter* and you never knew what *I* liked," but I refrained. "Peanut butter and jelly. She'll eat peanut butter and jelly."

Momma went to the fridge to fix Althea a sandwich. Althea's eyes widened with ravenous delight at the mention of PB&J. She nodded and kicked her little legs wildly off the side of the book stack. I swear, if she could, that kiddo would eat PB and J's for breakfast, lunch, and dinner! The dogs underneath her were roused by her excitement. Their tails brushed back and forth across the linoleum floor as their tongues wagged happily from their mouths.

"They like her," Momma said.

"Most animals do. They're drawn to her light."

"Her *light*?" she questioned with a disgusted tone. "Please don't tell me you're instilling your cockamamie ideas on this poor thing."

"No. Nothing like that. Besides, she doesn't have it... Nancy's not ... *gifted* in that way."

"What do you mean, *not gifted*? She's a smart little cookie! And cute as a button! How dare you say she's not gifted!"

"Oh no! Nancy is the smartest little thing you ever did see! You misunderstand. She doesn't have the *sight*. There's no... no... *essence*."

Chapter One

"There it is! It took all of ten minutes to start in with the crazy talk."

"It's not crazy, Alice. If you'd just listen to me for more than ten seconds without dismissing…"

"*You* dismissed *me* when you left four years ago. Left for a man old enough to be your grandfather, for Christ's sake. You took off to another country, no less, have his baby whom I'm just meeting now for the very first time, by the way. Then, you disappear for six months—not a phone call, letter, postcard… nothing! And now you show up at my doorstep with new names and being extremely secretive. So, you tell me, what part of that doesn't sound crazy?"

I exhaled, blowing strands of hair from my face as my shoulders slumped forward. I was exhausted. Beaten down. I didn't have the energy to explain everything to her. "It's not that simple."

"Don't feed this to the dogs," she said to Althea sweetly as she placed the sandwich in front of her. "They don't like jelly." Then she sat down next to the baby and reached out to touch my hand. "So, try to make me understand," she said gently, lovingly. I swear, her hot-and-cold attitude was enough to drive me mad. But ultimately, I knew I deserved it and probably worse. I couldn't deny her. When she put it like she did, it did sound a little insane.

I bit my lower lip and looked at Althea. She was so involved with her sandwich and the dogs that I realized I could speak freely without her overhearing or really paying attention. "We have nowhere else to go, Momma," I said in a hushed tone.

"Baby, this is your home. You know you can stay as long as you like. I would never turn you and that beautiful little one away."

"I... We... we can't though." I leaned across the table so I could get closer to her. "The people following us are catching up. We can't stay here, but I need to get far away and fast."

"Followed? What do you mean, *followed*?"

"More like h-u-n-t-e-d," I spelled out as I kept my gaze on Althea. She looked over at me when she heard me spelling out a word, and her face got all screwy. But when Lady licked her ankle again, she turned her attention back to her new furry friends.

Momma gasped a little in her throat. "Tildy! You can't be serious!"

"We've been in hiding for six months, but they've finally caught up to us."

"They? Who's *they*?"

I paused and inhaled deeply.

"It's Crowley's people, isn't it," she blurted.

"Shhh..." I admonished. "You shouldn't..."

"Why is he after you?"

"Well... I... I took something of his."

Momma threw her hands in the air in exasperation. "Can I say it now? Can I say, 'I told ya so'?"

"Please, don't be so dramat..."

"As God as my witness, I knew this day would come. I told you, Matilda Jane! I knew nothing

Chapter One

good would come out of all that. But you insisted on running off with the old man and..."

"Stop! Please!" I begged. "You don't understand. You never understood. And look... *one* good thing came out of it." I paused and looked at Althea again. My sweet and innocent little girl. The love and light of my life. She was everything I wished I could be and more. I would do anything for her...

Momma's eyes widened, and a knowing look lit up in her green pupils. She knew my fierce love for my daughter, for she felt the same way about me. "Althea," she whispered. "He wants her too?"

I nodded. "That's why I need to get away from them. I need to keep her s-a-f-e."

Momma side-eyed Althea the same way I had. "They mean to do her h-a-r-m?"

I exhaled slowly and closed my eyes. The thought bubbled in my chest and made my head pound at the temples. "No, Momma, they mean to k-i-l-l."

Chapter Two

Saturday, May 13th 1944
Alice Baker's House
1100 Pelton Avenue
Staten Island, New York
Morning of the Waning Gibbous Moon

I always knew I was born out of something awful. I might've been as young as three when I started asking about my daddy. Momma never said the word "rape," not directly, but even as a kid, I could sense there was no happy story behind my parents like the other kids had. There was always a shadow over it, something dark and dangerous, something violent about how I came into this world.

And Momma had nothing to hide when it came to the topic; in fact, I think she wore that moment in her life like a badge of honor in some demented way. (But who am I to say it's demented? My innocence wasn't violently stolen from me when *I* was fourteen, so there's no real tellin' how I'd feel or how I'd handle it.) I know Momma did the best she could with the cards she

Chapter Two

was dealt, and she never let herself feel ashamed for what happened to her. Well, at least that's how she masked herself to the world. And to me...

My early life was fraught with confusion—with Momma being so young and close in age to me, I had at one time thought she was my sister, or my grandmother's niece, or a friend of the family. And when I was old enough to realize my friends had fathers, and there was clearly no male figure present (except for my grandfather), I started asking questions to which my child ears heard words they couldn't *fully* comprehend.

April 1919. It had been dark. It had been late. He was a stranger. She was walking home from a friend's house after Bible study. She was alone. She knew he was following her. She ran as fast as she could. He caught her. There were scars all over his stomach. He smelled like hay. He had a large, bushy mustache and rotten teeth. He bit her neck and drew blood. She kicked and screamed as much as she could, but he overpowered her and did what he did. He was old. When he pulled up his britches, he told her he liked her and wasn't going to kill her. At the time, she wished he had. She dragged herself home and didn't tell nobody. She never wore a dress again. Nine months later, I made my way into the world, and she was grateful he hadn't killed her.

There really wasn't much for me to say to any of that. It was easy enough to understand as a little girl and easier to internalize as a young adult. And that was where the discussion of my paternal line stopped.

Until that day...

It was Friday, January 17, 1936. The day after my sixteenth birthday. It was a cold morning—the kind of cold that gets in your bones and doesn't let go no matter how many layers of long johns you put on. I had been up late listening to *Death Valley Days* on the radio, and I really didn't want to go to school. I was moping around the house procrastinating like a slow-poke, and when I had finally sat down at the breakfast table, Momma slapped a copy of *The New York Times* in front of me. I looked up at her, puzzled as she turned open the pages and tapped her long, slender finger on a headline.

"Your daddy is dead," she had said, matter-of-factly.

I looked at the headline that she drummed upon. "'Slayer of Budd Girl Dies in Electric Chair?'" I read out loud.

"Keep readin'," she commanded.

"'Albert Fish, 65 years old, of 55 East 128th Street, Manhattan, a housepainter who murdered Grace Budd, 6, after attacking her in a Westchester farmhouse in 1928, was put to death tonight in the electric chair at Sing prison.'" I brought the paper to my chest and inhaled. My rising bosom pressed against the paper as if there was something inside me that wanted to feel the words, be one with them, to make a connection to a dead man who was supposedly my father. There was no picture accompanying the article, but I pressed the paper harder into me and closed my eyes. A

Chapter Two

vision struck me so deeply, and a face began to take form in my mind—a haggard old man with white stubble across his chin and cheeks and a bushy white mustache. His blue eyes were like two pieces of frozen ice staring at me, into me, and through me. His eyes were like a mirror in which I saw my own reflection, for my eyes were just as blue and icy as his. I dared not tell Momma of this vision because she hated it when I spoke of such things. She hated it when I told her of my visions and premonitions or how I could hear the crows in the backyard talking to me.

I breathed out, angrily. "Albert Fish? Are you saying this psycho was my…"

"Yep," she said, cutting me off, but I already knew the truth. Just having her verbal confirmation was oddly satisfying.

"And he was executed yesterday?"

"Yep," she responded. "He was a bad man who did bad things, Tildy. He hurt many, many people." She paused to reflect, and I saw a strange darkness come into her eyes accompanied by a weird, faraway look. "*Kids*," she finally said with great emphasis. "He did bad things to kids. And now he's dead, Tildy. He's dead and gone, so you don't have to ask about him no more." She sighed and paused for a moment. "You come from a long line of broken people, Matilda Jane. Don't you ever forget that." Then she snatched the paper away before I could read the rest of the article.

I felt gutted from the inside out. I couldn't remember the last time I had asked about my father. It might have been when I was eight or nine. But the fact that she was instructing me to forget about him once and for all was telling. So, I let it go. I had his name, and that was more than enough. I didn't need to know what he looked like, nor did I have any desire to bond with his memory. I didn't need to know what he'd done to the Budd girl. I didn't need to know what he'd done to anyone else, for that matter. I knew what he did to Momma, and that was enough to know he was better off in the grave. He couldn't hurt anyone else from six feet under. And yeah, he may have helped give me life, but being his offspring was not something I was particularly proud of.

So, it made sense when Momma objected to my fascination with Aleister Crowley... *the* Aleister Crowley—world-renowned-practitioner-of-the-dark-arts-Aleister Crowley. Momma had likened him to Fish and forbade me to speak of him in her presence. But I couldn't help myself. There was something magnetic about Aleister's life story and his life's work that I immersed myself in his teachings—read every book I could get my hands on! His teaching spoke to my soul and awakened something magical within me—something that had always been there but was jolted awake as I read his sacred texts.

In 1940, I joined a group based in New York City who were devout followers, and soon they had organized a trip to go to England on a week-long retreat to meet him. News of his failing health made it a necessity to meet him before he

Chapter Two

passed, like a mecca to the holy land. As it turned out, Aleister did not die during that time period, and I ended up staying at his compound—first as a house keeper, and then as the secret woman who shared his bed. One time was all it took, one time was all he needed, because at 66 years of age, it was supposed to be a magical time for him to procreate. When I found out I was pregnant, I decided to stay at the compound. Well, it's not like I had much of a choice in the matter. Had I left with Aleister's unborn child, I'm not sure what they would have done to me. It was a happy time, though. I enjoyed the attention and the top-notch care I received. And then Althea was born, and Aleister held her at arm's length with a look of disgust on his face.

"Vuota," the midwife said to him in Italian, and he nodded at her.

"Sunyata," the nurse said to him in Hindu, and he nodded again, shoved the babe back in my arms and walked out of the room.

Vuota. Sunyata. Both words for "void." *Empty.* And that's the moment I knew things were going to go downhill and fast. I had disappointed my Master by bearing him an empty-souled child when he had been anticipating the most magickal human to have ever been created.

So, as the saying goes: things don't always go as planned, and circumstances both within and beyond my control brought me right back to where I started—in my old room with my old canine companions at the side of my bed like watchful guards. Lady and Moose always slept by my bedside while Bear preferred to stay in Momma's room. The deep, huffing noises they made in their slumber always comforted me, and as I laid in my old bed staring at the cracks in the ceiling just how I used to do when I was a child, I thought about how this time I had my *own* child snoring peacefully next to me. *Huffing beside, and huffing beneath.*

Still, in the early morning, I could not sleep. It didn't surprise me much because all my nights had been endlessly restless for as long as I could remember, so I continued to stare long and hard at the ceiling. It was surreal how the cracks looked thicker and more pronounced than I had remembered. Out of each scar, little spiderweb-like cracks multiplied and spread across the surface, and as the sun started to rise and the daylight began to filter in from the spaces between the dusty curtains, I noticed the ceiling was marred with circular brown stains in each corner.

I thought, *Jeez, Momma's gotta get the roof looked at soon!* But the thought didn't stick around too long because my internal lamenting was soon interrupted by the barking of the "outside" dogs in the backyard. It started so faintly in the background that I scarcely realized it was happening, but when Lady and Moose simultaneously lifted their heads with a curious moan, I shifted in the bed and paid attention as well. The pitch and timbre of the barks indicated Hudson, Murray, and Bug were doing more than just messing

Chapter Two

around with some random squirrel or sewer cat. I even thought I heard one of them growl. Moose shot up and joined Lady on her side of the bed closest to the door, and I pulled Althea to me.

Momma's footsteps on the hardwood floor were like a second heartbeat in my chest. She opened my bedroom door, and it creaked so loudly, I thought Althea was going to wake up. Even in the dimly lit room, I could see terror had washed over Momma's face. Her eyes bulged out of their sockets, and I knew I needed to take swift and cautious action. Quickly, I snaked my body around Althea's and slowly dragged her, and the duvet cover, to the floor with me. She stirred and groaned awake, but I shushed her and crept with her underneath the bed, wrapping the blanket around us.

"Mommy?" Althea mumbled with her eyes still shut tight.

"It's okay, Baby. Grandma wants to play Hide and Seek. We have to be very quiet. Can you do that?" I whispered.

"Mmmhmm," she said sleepily. She closed her eyes and nestled her body against mine.

"Rest, my love," I whispered. "The game will be over soon."

"I win?" she asked.

"Only if you're quiet."

The dogs outside went wild again, their barks alerting to a clear and present danger while Lady and Moose sat like sentries guarding the side of the bed. Bear paced back and forth in the hallway;

his nails clicked loudly on the wood, and I could see his massive shadow moving back and forth from underneath the doorway like an apparition. Across the hall, Momma fussed in the kitchen like it was a normal day—she slammed pans onto the stovetop, filled the coffee pot with water, and hummed a song— "That Old Black Magic." If that wasn't a message to me, I didn't know what was. The dogs outside continued their baying when Momma stuck her head out the back door and yelled, "Quit yer hollerin'!" Following her command, the dogs eased up a bit, but I could still hear their uneasiness as their barking and howling simmered to a low rumbling in their throats. I know Momma used that moment not only to hush the animals, but she twisted and turned her head around in all directions to see what was causing them to act that way. And when she sang a line of the song out loud, "I should stay away, but what can I do?" I knew it was her way of letting me know something awful was lurking out there.

I pulled the blanket up over our heads but left enough room for my eyes to peek out. *They've found us*, I thought. *This is it*.

Suddenly, there was furious knocking at the front door that made me jolt with fear. Althea squirmed against me and made a small gasp, but I reached my hand up to cover her mouth. "Shhh," I said softly, trying to calm her, but I knew it was no use—I knew she could feel me shaking on the

Chapter Two

inside. Lady and Moose sat up at attention, and I heard Bear race to the front door.

There was more knocking, and the intensity grew wilder, more frantic. Bear howled, and Momma slammed a pan against the sink in mock aggravation. "Hold on, hold on!" she yelled down the hallway, but her shadow was right outside the bedroom door, hovering. I knew she was contemplating how to handle the situation because she gave a quick, audible sigh before walking toward the front door.

"I'm coming!" she said with an annoyed tone. The door's normal creaky sound was cut short, and I surmised she had only opened it enough to stick her head out.

"Ms. Baker?" a female voice asked.

"What can I do for you?" Momma responded.

"We're looking for your daughter, Tildy, and your granddaughter, Althea."

"I... I don't know what you're talking about... I..." Momma stammered, but someone shoved the door open. Momma gasped and there was what sounded like a struggle in the entryway. I shut my eyes tight and placed my hands around Althea's ears to block out the sounds.

Please don't hurt Momma. Please don't hurt Momma, I thought over and over to myself.

"Look, Ms. Baker, we're not gonna hurt you," another voice said as if he had read my mind. It was the voice of Paul Kendrick. He had just recently joined the group in England about a month before I left. It was not a surprise they would send him on this mission to find us.

Bear growled, and I heard a low *click* like the sound a pistol makes when the hammer is cocked back. I panicked a little at the thought of someone pulling a gun on Momma! But she just sighed and admonished Bear to behave. She spoke calmly to him so he would think everything was okay. He obeyed her, but I knew he was still on guard. And I also knew that Lady and Moose were paying very close attention to what was happening in the other room.

"You won't need that," Momma said matter-of-factly. She was as cool as a cucumber, and I admired her poise in the face of this unexpected threat. "I'm not gonna give you any trouble."

The front door eased shut, and soon I was able to ascertain there were only two others in the house—Paul, and the female whose voice I didn't recognize.

"She took something of ours," Paul said. "We just want it back, is all."

"Like I said, I don't…"

"Don't lie to us, Ms. Baker. We know she's here. Call her out and let us talk to her. No one will get hurt, we promise," the woman said.

There was another shuffle, as if they had advanced into the house. Bear growled again, echoing my internal sentiment of fear and anger.

"It's okay, Baby Bear. It's okay. Easy."

"You call that a *baby*?" Paul exclaimed.

Chapter Two

"Shut up, Paul!" the woman snapped. "Ms. Baker, it's extremely important that we speak to Tildy. We need to get Althea back to her father. Your daughter is not well. She needs help. Althea is not safe with her, and her father misses her very much."

Momma exhaled loudly. "Oh, what did she do *this* time?"

My heart stopped at hearing Momma's accusatory tone. I knew she was just acting to put on a front to keep me and Althea safe, but there was a hint of truth in her exaggerated pitch.

"Much," the woman answered. "Too much."

"Well, come on in," Momma said, exasperated.

What? No! Don't let them in!

Momma led them down the hallway and made her way to the kitchen. Bear was behind her, putting some distance between herself and the intruders. The dogs in the backyard had ceased their barking, and I concluded there wasn't anyone else lurking about that I needed to worry about.

Chair legs screeched against the floor, and I heard Momma go to the cupboard to pull out mugs. "I just made coffee. Can I get you a cup?"

"Ye..." Paul began.

"No," the woman interrupted sternly. "No, thank you."

"So, are you going to tell me what my *dear* daughter has done or not?" Momma said sarcastically.

"Well, quite frankly, Ms. Baker, it's none of your business what she's done," the woman said.

"Look, I told you, Tildy ain't here," Momma said matter-of-factly.

An uncomfortable silence filled the kitchen, and I could only imagine the looks they were giving Momma.

"But she *was* here," Momma continued. "She came by yesterday with the baby."

Just as I had suspected, Althea had been listening to the entire exchange as well because she muttered, "I not a baby," in her pixie voice. I put my hand back over her mouth to quiet her.

"Oh?" the woman asked.

"Yep. I hadn't heard from her in months, and she just pops up on my doorstep. I coulda killed her for scaring the life outta me. She said she was just passing through. Said she was gonna stay a few days and head down south. Florida. But when I woke up this morning, they had already left. And now here you are telling me she's in some sort of trouble... Well... now it all makes sense."

"What makes sense?" Paul asked.

"All the things she was saying."

"Like what? What did she say?" the woman pressed, and there was an eagerness, an almost desperation in her voice.

"Oh, if you know Tildy, you know what I mean." Momma laughed, but it was her fake chuckle, the one she did when she talked to the women at the market or at the Bingo hall. It was

Chapter Two

the "I-don't-like-you-but-I-have-to-be-socially-nice-to-you" kind of laugh.

Althea squirmed against me. Moose sensed her agitation, turned his head, and stuck his snout underneath the bed. He gave a little snort, like a warning of sorts, and she winced. "He wants you to be quiet," I whispered. She nodded and tucked her face into the crook of my arm.

"Did she tell you why she was back?" Paul asked.

"Uh-uh," Momma replied. "Visiting, I guess."

"And what was it she said about Florida?" the woman asked.

"Oh, I don't know. Something about taking the baby to some aquarium in Key West."

"I *not* a baby," Althea mumbled against my arm, and I pressed her face deeper into me.

A chair scraped across the floor again, and I heard someone get up. I was so anxious not knowing what was happening out there.

"Did she tell you what she took from us?" the woman asked.

Momma muttered, "Uh... no... I mean, I can assume but no. She didn't." There was a pause that seemed to last forever. Finally, Momma broke the silence with a gasp. "Oh! Oh, dear. Yes. It makes even more sense now. Florida. Aquarium. She stole some money from ya, didn't she?"

"Not quite," Paul answered.

"More than money," the woman finished for him.

"And the child," Paul blurted. "The Great Beast wishes his daughter's return and…"

The woman slapped Paul across the arm. It was loud enough to hear across the room. "Paul!" she exclaimed. "Enough!"

"She didn't take any money from you?" Momma echoed. "Then what's all the fuss about? Besides Althea, I mean."

"A deck of cards," the woman replied.

"Pardon me? Did you say a *deck of cards*?"

"They're not just any cards. They're priceless. The Master wants them back," the woman said, her voice sharp.

"Valuable cards?" Momma muttered under her breath.

"When Lady Frieda releases the Thoth Tarot Deck—"

"Paul!" the woman cut in, smacking his arm again, harder this time.

"And Althea," Momma added coolly. "He wants the cards *and* Althea."

"That's right. His rightful daughter."

"Well, sorry to say, I can't help you," Momma said, and I heard her start to shuffle around the kitchen.

"Ya know, Ms. Baker, I'm not so sure I'm buying what you're selling," the woman said, her voice turning cold. That's when I realized who it was— Christina Combs. She ran one of the top factions in England. We'd crossed paths a few times back at the compound, and truth be told, I never cared

Chapter Two

much for her. From what I could tell, the feeling was mutual.

In a flash, the bedroom door opened, and Momma yelled, "Wait! Don't go in…"

My heart pounded against my chest in perfect rhythm with Althea's. Her little rabbit heart flutter flutter fluttered against my arm, and I squeezed her tighter.

Please stay quiet. Please stay quiet. Please stay quiet.

Lady and Moose were on their feet in an instant, guarding the bedside and giving the most threatening growls. A screech escaped Paul's throat, and he took a step to the side and backed up right against Bear who had begun growling as well. "There's two more of 'em in here, Christina," he said in a quavering voice.

"I can hear," Christina answered calmly.

"Those aren't the friendly ones," Momma said. "That's why I keep them in the room."

Christina mumbled something to Paul, and he took off out the front door. "Ms. Baker, if you hear anything about your daughter and granddaughter's whereabouts, you have an obligation to let us know."

"Oh? I do?"

"Kidnapping charges are about to be filed. Tildy will be prosecuted to the full extent of the law."

Bear snarled at her, and a low, rhythmic rumble barreled out of Lady and Moose's chests.

"I think it's time you left," Momma said confidently.

"Ms. Bay…" Christina began, but the pack started barking in unison. I'd bet money on the fact that Christina's insides jumped, and I heard her turn on her heel and walk quickly out the door.

The dogs settled down a little while after they left, and when they felt the threat was gone, Lady and Moose went into kitchen to their bowls and lapped at their water. Momma soon came into the bedroom with Bear. She plopped herself onto the bed as Bear jumped up next to her. She stroked his fur and spoke in a sweet and calm voice. To the outside ear, it sounded like she was praising the dog, calling him a good boy and showering him with affirmations. But she was really talking to *me* in code as I continued to huddle under the bed and under the blanket practically smothering my girl.

"It's all right now, Baby Bear," Momma cooed in that playful tone she used for the pup. "Everything's just fine. I'm gonna take good care of you, like I always do, Baby Bear. Isn't that so? Isn't it? No more of that nonsense, no sir! Nobody's gonna upset my Baby Bear, not ever again. You can rest easy now. Just breathe, honey, just breathe. I've got it all figured out. Don't you fret. Little Chickadee's gonna be the answer. I know just how to keep you safe."

Chapter Three

Saturday, May 13th 1944
Alice Baker's House
1100 Pelton Avenue
Staten Island, New York
Night of the Waning Gibbous Moon

Althea and I stayed huddled under the bed for what felt like an eternity. When Momma finally said the coast was clear, she let us out but ordered us to stay put in the bedroom all day. Saying she was cross would be putting it mildly — anyone could see the storm of emotions swirling inside her. She ranted and raved again about me getting mixed up with Aleister's crowd to begin with, but I could see the sadness in her eyes. She knew, same as I did, that we had to leave, for all our sakes. And deep down, we both knew this wouldn't be the last time his people would come harassing Momma.

Just like I figured, Momma had a plan in no time flat. If there was one thing I could count on, it was that Momma knew her stuff — and she knew people. Information had always been her currency, her ace in the hole. She kept tabs on the whole neighborhood, knew every whisper and secret in town. Folks called her the "Secret Mayor" because she always had her finger on the pulse. Lucky for Althea and me, Momma had just the ticket to get us out of the state and back into hiding. I heard her on the phone all day, speaking in that low, secretive tone. Every time she popped in to check on us, bring some food, or walk one of us to the bathroom, I'd ask what was happening, but she'd just say, "Sit tight. I'm working on it."

Althea was perfectly happy playing with Lady and Moose all day, but me? I was a bundle of nerves. Every time the dogs in the backyard so much as rustled, I'd tense up and dart my eyes to the window. We both tried to nap a bit, but it was the same restless sleep, no real rest to be had.

By nightfall, Momma came back into the room and jumped on the bed next to me.

"What? What's the matter?" I asked, startled.

"Okay, Tildy," she said with a serious tone, "it's happening tonight."

"What? What's happening?"

Momma's green eyes sparkled with that familiar look of triumph. I could tell she'd hatched a plan for me and the baby because she only got that gleam when she knew she'd come out on top. "Listen close," she said, her voice low and steady. "There's a car coming for you in fifteen minutes."

I sat up at attention. "A car? To where?"

"Grand Central Station. You're going to catch the Mercury train to Cleveland."

Chapter Three

"Ohio!" I exclaimed in disbelief. "Why are you sending me to Ohio?"

Momma jumped up from the bed and scooped Althea from the floor and into a tight embrace. She vigorously patted her back like she was burping a baby.

"Momma, please," I commanded and raised my eyebrows at her to stop pounding on Althea's back.

Momma looked down, realized what she was doing, and stopped. "Oh dear, I'm so sorry," she apologized and began rocking back and forth in place. "There's no time for explaining, Til! Just do what I say so we can get you two out of here s-a-f-e-l-y."

"Can you at least give me the abbreviated version?"

"Sure, sure," she said in a huff as she made her way into the kitchen.

Quickly, I got up from the bed and followed her.

"Here," she said and handed me a paper with scribbles all over.

I took the paper from her hand and inspected it while she opened the fridge, started pulling items out, and filled a bag. "*Chickadee?*" I asked in confusion.

Never once did she look up. "Chickie. She's Margaret Gainer's niece. Chickie's been staying with Madge for a few months now." She paused and looked up at the ceiling like she was searching her brain for a memory. "Come to think of it,

Chickie arrived right about the time I heard from you last."

"Oh," I responded flatly, the sound of a guilty conscience oozed with the word.

"Yeah, *oh*."

"So, what does Chickie have to do with me? Or Ohio, for that matter?"

"Chickie's an odd bird," Momma said as the upper half of her body seemed to get swallowed by the fridge again.

"That's ironic," I said sarcastically.

"Don't get cutesy with me," she scolded.

I rolled my eyes.

"Anyway," she continued. "Chickie has a friend who's in a traveling carnival."

"A carnival?"

"Chickie's friend told her that there's work out there. They need people."

"A carnival, Momma?" I repeated.

"The Gentry Brothers' Wonders of the World or something like that. They travel from state to state every few months or so. They're currently in... um... don't quote me on this, but I think she said the town was Glenmoor..."

"A *carnival*, Momma!" I exclaimed, my anger and confusion so clear in my voice that poor Althea's little body tensed up in Momma's arms. "You're sending us off to a *carnival*?"

Momma stood fully erect in front of the fridge and tightened her grip around Althea's back. Her eyes narrowed, and she blew strands of her dirty blonde hair away from her eyes.

Chapter Three

"Beggars can't be choosers, *Jane*," she scolded again. "It's the best I got. You'll be well hidden with all the freaks and sideshow attractions. Plus, they move around all the time. Crowley's goons will never be able to find you."

I marched over to her and reached my hands out to take Althea back into my own arms. "You don't know them. They'll find us. They have their ways."

She relented to give the girl over to me at first but ultimately obliged. "It's those damn cards, isn't it?"

I hung my head down and nodded. "And *h-e-r*."

"Why in God's green earth did you take something from them?"

"Momma, I told you what their intentions were for her!"

"No, Tildy! The cards! Why'd you take their cards? And what in heaven's name is all this about? What kind of hocus-pocus are you *really* wrapped up in?"

I sighed and shifted my weight from one leg to the other. "Oh, Momma. You wouldn't understand. You couldn't understand." If even I couldn't fully explain why I swiped the Thoth deck from Lady Frieda, there was no way Momma would get it. It was like a force inside me, pushing me forward. From the moment Aleister had shown me those first sketches of the deck, something in me stirred, like a song pulling me from a dreamless sleep. Back in England, I'd taken to cartomancy like a fish to water, could read anyone's fortune with a plain old deck of cards. But the Thoth cards—they sang to me, like music from another world, calling me to some far-off place that felt more like home than anywhere I'd ever known. If I couldn't sort it out for myself, how could I ever expect Momma to understand?

"Well, you've definitely gotten yourself into a world of trouble, Til. I don't see anywhere *but* that carnival for you to be safe in."

"There's no place that's s-a-f-e," I whispered.

"Well, do you have a better suggestion?"

I paused and looked at my sweet girl, her perfect angel face and her perfect green eyes. She was such a vision of loveliness and purity that I was overwhelmed with a sense of joy and pride. The thought of Aleister bringing harm to her sickened me, and I vowed to protect her until my dying breath. I shook my head at my mother's question, knowing there were no other options.

"Besides," Momma continued, "I'm sure it would be an upgrade from the madness you've lived with in that compound!"

"Mother!" I screeched.

"I'm sorry, I'm sorry," she said, throwing her hands up defensively. "I'm still a little sour."

"Ya think?"

"Don't be a smart aleck, Matilda." She paused and corrected herself. "Don't be a smart aleck, *Jane*. You're going to need your guard up and your wits about you if you're going to protect *Nancy* from them."

Chapter Three

I nodded and smiled, thankful that she had finally acknowledged our aliases.

"Alright," she said with a clap of her hands, "get your bag, and let's wait in the parlor. The car will be here any minute."

"Right now?" I squawked.

"Well, of course, my dear. No time like the present." She sighed. It was deep and rattled in her upper chest. I knew she was fighting back a sob or even a wail. Her mother's heart was aching—aching at the thought of us leaving again.

She led us into the foyer at the front of the house. The three dogs followed right behind us and sniffed at Althea's dangling feet. I knew they could sense we were leaving, and I thanked them for protecting us. "Say bye-bye to Lady and Moose and Bear," I instructed Nancy.

"Bye-bye, doggies!" she sang.

"Tell them 'I hope to see you soon.'"

"Hope see soon," she parroted.

I pressed a kiss to the side of Althea's forehead, my eyes drifting over to Momma. Then, like a freight train, it hit me—hard and fast. The heartache I'd caused her, the pain I'd selfishly ignored. How I'd just up and left without a thought for her. How I'd brought Althea into this world without her by my side. And those six long months when she had no idea whether I was dead or alive. The guilt twisted inside me, and I pulled Althea tight, as if I could squeeze that old life right out of us. We'd never go back. We'd never be those people again. As Momma looked at me, tears glistening in her eyes, I knew we'd probably never see her again, either. "I'm sorry, Momma."

Her tears slipped quietly down her cheeks, and she brushed them away with quick, nervous hands, as if swatting at pesky flies dancing around her face. "Oh, stop it," she said, her voice steady. "Life's strange, sure. Maybe even a little comical. But there's nothing to be sorry for."

"Thank you," I managed to croak.

She came over and wrapped her arms tightly around us, almost swallowing me and the baby up within her arms. She inhaled deeply as if trying to suck in the scent of my hair and preserve it to her final memory. "Anything for you. Anything."

"It's going to rain," I said quietly under my breath.

"Whatever do you mean!? It's a clear night out, and…"

Suddenly, a black car pulled up in front of the house, and within seconds, the sky opened up with giant tears as if it were crying for Momma and me both.

Momma's face dropped, and she pulled back from our embrace. "How did you…" she muttered in shock.

"I just know things sometimes."

Her face twisted in confusion, and for a split second, there was terror in her eyes. Fear. Like she was genuinely afraid of me. She shifted uncomfortably and ran her hands down the front of her

Chapter Three

floral housedress. "Okay now, ladies. You best be on your way."

"Momma, I…"

"Nope! You stop right there! This isn't goodbye." She moved forward again and pinched the baby's cheek. "This is just see-ya-later. Take good care of sweet Nancy."

"I'll write as soon as I can," I said, the words getting strangled in my throat.

"Oh no you will not!" Momma exclaimed. "That's too much of a risk. If they raid my mailbox before I get to it, they can see the postmark."

"Then I'll call."

"And risk them tracing it! God knows what they're capable of, girl!"

"Collect. I'll call collect. If you get a collect call from someone with a name you don't recognize, it's me. And I'm okay."

Momma smiled, and my heart slowly broke.

"Bye G-Ma," Nancy said quietly, almost mournfully.

"Bye, my love," Momma replied. "I'll see you again soon enough."

I nodded tersely as Momma planted a loud smackaroo on Nancy's face. Nancy squirmed and giggled and kissed her back as the dogs begged for Nancy's attention. Nancy reached down and grazed their heads with quick pets.

Momma smoothed my hair away from my temples and down my shoulders before squeezing my arm. "Go now," she said sternly, and the green in her eyes flickered and flashed. I kissed her check, hoisted the bag over my shoulder, adjusted Nancy on my hip, and walked out the front door. I didn't look back because I wanted the image of my mother's green eyes to be the last thing I saw of her face and form. I wanted her green eyes to stay with me for the rest of my days.

Nancy bounced against me as I hopped down the front stoop. The rain pelted against us, and I remained steadfast, not once turning my head toward the house, but I could feel Momma's green eyes burning through me, filling me with her love and concern.

I turned my head quickly from side to side, surveying the street and making sure we weren't being watched or followed. I felt calm and at ease, like there was no real threat imposed upon us at that moment. I breathed a sigh of relief as I opened the back door of the car and slid in.

The bright, beaming smile of the young woman in the car threw me for a loop at first. Her teeth, perfectly straight, practically gleamed against the shadows inside the vehicle, set off by the dark red lipstick outlining her mouth. She slipped off a white glove and offered her hand, and suddenly I felt rumpled and out of place in her immaculate presence.

"Jane?" she sang.

I shook her hand and nodded.

"And Nancy?" she asked, turning her voice up an octave as she touched Nancy's fingers.

I nodded again.

"Chickie," she announced.

Chapter Three

"N... nice to meet you," I stammered, trying to find something appropriate to say.

"My Auntie Madge is good friends with your momma, so it's a pleasure. Glad I could help."

"We appreciate it. Truly, we do," I answered, taking in the bubbliness that exuded from her aura. Every word, every movement was like a long, hard sip of ginger ale— sweetly effervescent but scratchy on the throat at the same time. I knew it would take me a little while to assess whether I enjoyed being in her company or not.

The long ride to Grand Central Station was filled with Chickie's nonstop chatter. Getting a word in was nearly impossible, but that suited me just fine. I wasn't in the mood for small talk, anyway—especially with my eyes glued to the window every few minutes, making sure we weren't being tailed. Chickie didn't seem to notice a thing. She was head over heels for Nancy from the jump, rambling on about some boy who'd broken her heart in New York and how she couldn't wait to start her new life with the carnival. "Isn't it thrilling?" she chirped. I just nodded, keeping quiet, taking in the smell of her—sweet, like cinnamon-covered pecans. It made the endless prattle a little easier to bear.

Chickie got real quiet and focused when we got to the station. She purchased our tickets and marched the three of us right to our seats on the train like a pro. She'd done this before, it was obvious, and I was comforted by that fact.

I sat Nancy next to me in the booth and wedged my bag in between us. Chickie sat across from us and rested her elbows on the table top. "Not long now," she huffed. "You hungry? Tired?"

"No, no. We're fine. Once the train gets moving, I know Al..." My mouth closed with a pop, and my eyes went wide. I paused, collected, then corrected myself. "I know *Nancy* will conk out straight away."

Chickie smirked. "Where we're going, you can't make mistakes like that, ya know," she said in a low voice.

My eyes cast down. "I know," I replied.

"I mean, *no one* uses their real name out there anyway."

I hummed as the engine of the train revved up.

"Chickadee is the nickname my Daddy gave me when I was born, and it just kinda stuck! But you bet your bottom dollar, I'll never tell *anyone* what it *really* is."

I wrung my sweaty hands together and pushed my hair away from my eyes. "Understood."

"So, tell me, Jane," she began with an excited smile. "What business do you seek at The Gentry Brothers' Wonders of the World?"

"Pardon?"

"The world's a stage, Jane! What role are you going to play?"

"Hmmm... well, I haven't really thought about it. I mean, this all kinda fell in my lap rather suddenly, and..."

Chapter Three

Chickie took her white gloves off and placed them on the table. She rolled her shoulders around a few times and ran a hand through her short, sandy brown hair. When her hand made its way to the back of her head, the top of her hair fluffed out and I could see tiny strands of gold and white on the undersides. Her hair was fine and feathery and reminded me of the down of a baby chick. And the nickname clicked in my head—*Chickadee*. "Madame," she blurted with finality.

"Excuse me?" I nearly choked on my own saliva when I heard her declaration.

"I want to be the Madame. The Fortune Teller. Mommy Fortuna!" She wiggled her fingers in front of her face, and for a second, the air around her shimmered, like heat waves rising off the hot pavement. I thought my eyes were playing tricks on me, so I blinked a couple of times until it disappeared.

As expected, Nancy curled her body up in the booth—she brought her little knees to her chest and rested her head on the bag between us. I reached my hand over and petted her hair, letting her know it was safe to rest.

"But do you have any experi…" I began in subtle protest.

"The girl who's the fortune teller now is not feeling very fortune teller-y. I hear the Carny Boss wants her to take her clothes off," she said, cutting me off. "Sis says I have a real good shot of gettin' the job." She paused and tilted her head side to side as if she was examining me. "Besides, I have a fella I've been writing to who thinks I'd be a perfect fit for the job!" She paused and exhaled. "Ya know, I think you would be a good snake charmer! We could call you Lady Python! Oh no, wait... how about Mistress Viper? But with a 'y' instead of an 'i' 'cause that would be oh-so-carnival!"

"Oh, no. I don't think..."

"Well, do you have any acrobatic abilities? Can you contort your body?"

"No. I..."

She hummed and pressed her forefinger against her lips in deep thought. "I don't think you'd be a good fit for the Cooch."

"The Cooch?" I asked.

"The Nudie Revue. The Tittie Show. The Strip Tease." She paused and sighed like I was the stupidest person alive. "I mean, on account of you having a kid and all. I'm sure you've got a fine figure under that baggy dress, but Sis said the Carny Boss is very particular on who he chooses for *that* show."

A gulp rose up to my throat at her rapid-fire dialog and her backhanded compliment. "I... um..." I stammered.

"They'll probably make you costume designer or makeup artist at best. Just pray they don't put you on food vending." Chickie's red lips pursed together in mock sadness, and my head swam as the train started its journey. There was something condescending in her tone that made me uneasy.

Chapter Three

I gently pressed Nancy's head a little tighter into my lap in a protective way and gazed out the window at the endless blackness whizzing by.

Chickie folded her hands together on the table and stared at me. She leaned in closer, and her pecan scent wafted up my nostrils. "This must be so exciting for you!" she exclaimed in a low voice.

I narrowed my eyes.

"You're like an... an *outlaw* or something!"

The excitement in her voice rattled me. There was nothing exciting about being on the run, and certainly nothing thrilling about the fear of your own child being sacrificed. But I couldn't let Chickie in on that. She couldn't know the whole truth. "Please, Chickie..." I began, letting the desperation creep into my voice. I didn't know exactly how much my mother had relayed to her aunt, but Chickie apparently was informed enough to know I was in a dire predicament. My shoulders tensed and I clenched my jaw.

"No, no, no. You're right. Your secret is safe with me!" She put one finger up to her lips and made a key-locking gesture, as if to assure me that she wouldn't reveal anything.

I sighed. I didn't quite believe her, but a part of me had to convince myself to. If I was going to be with her on this thirteen-hour journey to Ohio, and quite possibly for the foreseeable future, I had to trust her at the bare minimum.

"So!" she proclaimed, clapping her hands together. "Audition me!"

"Pardon?" I asked, confused.

"Let's pretend you're the Carny Boss, and I'm auditioning for the part. Sis says I'll have to audition once I get there, so I guess we should practice some."

"Mommy Fortuna?"

Chickie huffed and a puff of air blew up strands of her feathery hair from her forehead. "Of course, silly! Let me show you my skills." She reached out for my hands, and I stretched my arms across the table. Slowly, she unraveled my clenched fingers and turned my palms upward. "I am Mommy Fortuna," she said, changing her voice to an odd, quasi-Eastern European accent (not a very good one, by the way). "I am from the foothills of Latvia. My ancestors were the Gypsies of the Southern Mountains."

"Wait. What are you talking about?" I interrupted.

"Shhh! Just go with the story!"

Even if the whole thing's a load of baloney? I wondered to myself.

"Sorry, sorry," I apologized.

"Let me have a look at you," she continued, her silly accent wavering in and out. "I will examine your palms and tell you everything you wish to know." She traced the lines of my left hand with her fingertip and quietly chanted some kind of nonsense. Then she closed my hand up, closed her eyes, and cocked her head as if she was listening for something. It was all very theatrical, all very *carnival-esque*. "Mommy Fortuna sees great things for you," she said after a dramatic

Chapter Three

pause. "You have a strong love line which will present itself to you in good time. Your soulmate is still out there, searching for you. You will meet very soon."

I giggled at the ridiculousness of it all. Chickie's eyes furrowed in displeasure.

"You have a strong wealth line," she continued. "Mommy Fortuna sees you coming into great riches beyond your wildest dreams."

"Hmmm..." I hummed in protest.

"What?" she barked angrily, and Nancy jolted a little next to me.

"Well, don't you think that's a little too much?"

Her face darkened with indignant frustration. "Too much! What do you mean too much? I need to tell people what they want to hear!"

"I don't know," I replied. "I just think you should make it more ... *believable*."

"Okay, smart aleck," she huffed. "Let's see you do any better."

She dropped my hand onto the table and extended her own. With a lift of her perfectly arched eyebrow, her brown eyes implored me to pick them up and demonstrate to her how *I* would read *her* palm. I hesitated and my hands quavered slightly. She was a stranger—a girl I had known for all of three hours, maybe less. She had no way of knowing the things I had seen, the things I had done, and I wasn't about to open up to her at that moment and spill all my tales of magic and wonder, for she wouldn't believe half of what I said. But her condescension and derision tore my guard down, made me weak and vulnerable for a brief moment, so I laid her left hand in mine, and hovered my right hand directly over her upturned palm.

The roar from the engine filled my head, and subtly, in the background of it all, I thought I heard music playing. The rhythmic crunching of gears and hissing of pistons combined together to form a mechanical song that instantly lulled me. It was beautiful! Whistles and motors and rumbles from underneath the seat made my body sway to and fro. And soon all the metallic sounds transformed—blended, meshed, became voices. Voices I had never heard before, yet they sounded so familiar. They sounded like the comforts of home. Home with Momma. Home with Aleister before Nancy arrived. Home in my head when I was alone. Home in the darkness and in the sky and in the stars and in another time and space. And the voices all sang to me—sang *for* me in words that I couldn't understand but only knew in my heart. Gurgles of words. Grinding words. Words that grated on my eardrums and scraped the back of my throat but covered me in cold honey.

Before I could make sense of my jumbled thoughts, a magnetic sensation stirred in the space between our hands, and I gently moved mine up and down to heighten the feeling. Chickie's eyes went wide with surprise, and she opened her mouth to say something, but my bottom hand gave her a little squeeze and she

Chapter Three

quickly refrained. I closed my eyes and inhaled as a wave of white light began to swirl in the void. Images began to rapidly flash in my mind—indiscernible pictures that flickered like a film reel out of control. Suddenly, it stopped, and an image finally stayed still long enough for me to make something out—a girl's lifeless body wrapped in two green blankets and a torn pink slip around her shoulders, laying on the side of a street, hidden in weeds.

My eyes snapped open in an instant, and Chickie stared at me, puzzled. I let go of her hands and quickly put mine down at my sides.

"And?" she inquired.

"And *what*?" I asked, my voice shaky as I fought to steady my breath, not wanting to tip her off.

"If you're gonna be a fortune teller, Jane, you're gonna have to tell me a fortune. Love line, health line, wealth line, all the palm reading stuff."

My body shivered on the inside. "Oh, yeah, um... I guess I'm not good at that," I lied.

Chickie huffed. "Well, jeez! Ya think?" She chuckled and ran her hand through her fine hair again. "I may have been a little dramatic, but at least I put on a show. And Sis said the Carny Boss is looking for *extraordinary* performers."

"Sis?" I asked, desperately trying to change the subject—to let Chickie run out the conversation so I could collect myself proper.

"My friend, who's been out there for a spell. She's the one who got me into this whole thing. She's been filling me in on the ins and outs of carnival life. So don't you fret; I'll bring you up to speed on everything before we get there. This way, there won't be any surprises."

I took one more deep breath to settle myself down. "Oh."

"And we have a long ways to go, so we'll figure out what's your best niche. Because if there's one thing you don't ever wanna be, it's a Carnival Girl."

"Why? What's a Carnival Girl?"

Chickie puffed out her lips in sneer. "Oh Jane! It's terrible. A Carnival Girl is a girl who kinda does a little bit of everything, yet no one knows who she is. She has no real identity, no shtick. It's a lonely, miserable existence. When you're in the carnival, you want to be remembered! Revered! You want the people to come back for more because of *you!*" She gave a long, lingering sigh. "Don't you worry. We'll come up with some way to present you to Tophat Trent!"

"Tophat *who*?"

"Tophat Trent, the Carny Boss. Sis says Tophat's the real deal, the genuine article. He's got real magic in his veins, and that's what keeps all his workers safe. He does something called a shimmering? A clamoring? A glimmering? A…"

"A glamouring?" I offered.

"Yeah. Something like that. It's supposedly a strong spell to keep the carnies protected or something spooky and crazy like that."

I knew what a glamouring was. I'd done many while under Aleister's tutelage, but hearing the word spoken so nonchalantly by Chickie made

Chapter Three

me a little uneasy. I knew I would have to keep my guard way up when we reached our destination. Especially around this Tophat guy.

Chapter Four

Monday, May 15th 1944
The Gentry Brothers' Wonders of the World Carnival
Glenmoor, Ohio
Late Afternoon of the Last Quarter Moon

What was supposed to be a thirteen-hour trip turned into a much longer journey. The train let us off in Cleveland right on schedule, but the second leg of our adventure took far more effort than we had anticipated. Getting from Cleveland to Glenmoor required crafty maneuvering, a couple of nights in sketchy motels, stops at a few greasy diners, and some dicey hitchhiking.

Meanwhile, Chickie wouldn't stop chattering about the boy who broke her heart. It was relentless! She also rattled on about her secret "feller," and how she was thinking about meeting up with him when we got to Ohio, "but that's neither here nor there," she said, waving her hand around dramatically. There were moments when I thought she'd finally wrap up her tale and flash-forward

Chapter Four

to the present, only for her to burst out with, "And you know what happened next?" in that high-pitched voice of hers.

But come to think of it, Chickie's self-centered dialogue wasn't all that bad. I was able to tune her out when I had to, and her chitter-chatter prevented me from having to talk about my past and why I was *really* on the run. The mindless conversations also afforded me the opportunity to keep a close eye on our surroundings—without having to be fully engaged in Chickie's tales, my heightened senses were always on full alert watching out for Aleister's goons. I knew Momma had thrown them off the trail, for now at least. In my mind's eye I played out *their* sequence of events that took Paul Kendrick and a small group south to Florida (just to be sure), and Christina Combs on the line with Aleister himself getting further instructions on how to find me. They didn't call Aleister Crowley the Beast for nothing, and I knew it would only be a matter of time before he would use his mojo to pinpoint our location.

Every now and then Chickie would go off on a tangent and would tell me bits and pieces about the place we were going to. Tophat Trent, the Carny Boss, was a man who garnered much respect in the business, and according to Chickie's source, we would have to do a lot to impress him. But again, like the stories of her failed lovelife, I conditioned my ears to tune out most of what she said.

Through it all, I was truly grateful that Nancy was as well-behaved as she was. Chickie remarked on Nancy's calm demeanor numerous times, noting how unusual it was for three-year-olds to show such restraint, especially in high-stress situations. She might not have had any magical properties in her soul, but hot dog, she was every mother's dream of a child!

"She's such a good girl!" Chickie exclaimed, her eyes wide with admiration. "Why, my nephews are around the same age, and they're Grade-A Hellions!" With that statement, the stream of consciousness about her ex-boyfriend faded, giving way to an hour-long monologue about her young nephews, Timmy and Johnny.

To say I was pooped by the time we made it to the gates of the carnival would be an understatement. Poor Nancy dangled almost lifelessly in my arms, and to an outside observer, it certainly would have looked like I was carrying the corpse of a child. Chickie huffed and puffed when she made her way out of the car and even tried to stiff the driver on our agreed upon fare. She slammed the door, and as the car peeled away, she screamed "Jerk!" and flounced over to me at the entrance.

I stood there, speechless, with babe in arms and my bag flung over my shoulder. The entrance was a wooden structure that resembled an archway. It was held down by stakes in the ground, and the sign above read "CARNIVALE" in red block letters. Each letter was displayed on

Chapter Four

its own plank of wood, and I could tell right away it was old.

"*Carnivale?*" I asked, reading the word out loud.

"It's ancient or something. Never mind that, Jane. We're finally *here!*"

Yes. We were finally there. And yet, there was something ominous about the entrance that was needling at the back of my head. Carnivals were magic and illusion—a place where you could be anyone and give yourself over to reckless abandon. It was said the sights and sounds of the Midway could temporarily transform someone into their primal self and make even a priestly man forget his sacred vows. Lights and music and all modes of entertainment filled the space for a fraction of time with a sense of wonder and awe. Beyond the rickety wooden entrance, tents were set up for the evening's festivities. The smell of the sugary fairy floss being whipped up into form had made its way to my nostrils, and the lights of the Ferris wheel were starting to blink to life. Suddenly, I had the feeling that if I crossed the threshold to the other side—to what was deep within the parameters of the faire—I would never walk out the entrance and into the real world again.

"Excuse me, ladies?" A small voice rose up from the ground.

I looked down and at thigh-height was a little man dressed in a tuxedo and a top hat. His body and features were in proportion to his size and stature, and his voice was high-pitched with a tinny sound to it as if his vocal cords were small as well. I'd never seen a midget before in real life, and it took some clearing of his throat for me to realize I was staring at him with round eyes. He furiously tapped the edge of his cane into the dirt as he stood in the center of the entranceway.

"Ahem..." he repeated.

"Oh, yes. Hi. I'm sorry. My name is Jane. This is my daughter, Nancy." I extended my hand and bent over a little, trying not to drop the child.

The little man stared up at me, his eyes disappearing into his dark, bushy eyebrows.

Chickie's silence made me so very uncomfortable, so I blurted, "Oh! You must be Tophat Trent! It's a pleasure to meet you."

He narrowed his eyes at me, his round face darkening with malice. An audible gasp escaped my lips, and I dug my fingers into Nancy's back. Chickie looked at me wild-eyed with a frantic expression of desperation and embarrassment. Then suddenly, the sound of laughter rattled from his throat, and he nearly doubled over in hysterics.

"Keep it moving, ladies. Gates open at eight," he snarled between his hiccups of hilarity.

"No!" Chickie said in protest. "You're Buster Blue, aren't ya?"

He wiped a tear from his eye and stood upright—all two and a half feet of him—and again he lowered his chin so his eyes peered up at us under a mess of wild brows. "Yeah? And who wants to know about it?" His voice deepened as much as it could.

Chapter Four

"I'm Chickadee Sassafras," she announced, extending her hand. "My best friend Sis told me all about you."

Buster tilted his head, and his caramel-colored eyes seemed to glow in the fading sunlight. His questioning glare started to melt from his face. "Sis? *Our* Sis?"

Chickie smiled brightly at him and puckered her lips. "You betcha! The Magnificent Sis Savoy! Bearded Lady extraordinaire. Why, she's been writing me the last six months and told me all about The Gentry Brothers' Wonders of the World."

"And Sis told you all about me, eh?" he crooned.

"But of course!" she sang back, her voice shifting slightly, taking on a sultrier tone. Chickie bent down, shaking her shoulders just enough to make her bosom jiggle, the pearls around her neck bouncing against the fabric of her dress. Buster's eyes gleamed with sudden hunger as his gaze followed every movement. His tiny tongue darted across his thin lips, a clear sign that he was mentally undressing her, his desire unmistakable.

"What did good ole Sis tell you about Little Buster?" He laughed again, only this time there was a flirtatious tone to it that was far from subtle.

She giggled back. "Well, she told me that if I ever made my way out here, the first person I needed to be on the lookout for was Buster Blue!"

"Awww, go on," he said as he waved his tiny hand in the air. "Lies! What else did she say?"

"She told me that Buster likes peaches... a lot! Sis said Buster likes to look at peaches, likes to pick peaches, likes to eat the peaches, and likes to rub his face in the fuzzy peaches. Now..." she added coyly, her voice dripping with faux innocence, "I don't have the foggiest as to what she meant by that."

A sniggering little laugh rose from his tiny chest, and a coughing fit soon rocked him. He doubled over then spit into the dirt. "Well, she wasn't wrong about that! What else did she say about me?"

"Come on now, Buster!" she teased. "Us girls gotta have our secrets, ya know! But Sis did say yous was looking to bring on some new people to work the World. *Fresh blood*, she said."

A smile expanded over what seemed like the entire width of Buster's face, revealing a mouth of gnarled and yellowed teeth. It was a sinister smile—like a bad elf. He gripped her hand and shook it as heartily as he could. "Whad'ja say your name was again?"

"Chickadee Sassafras," she said, and he kissed the top of her hand. "My friends call me Chickie."

"A pleasure and a delight, Miss Chickie. Any friend of Sis is a friend of mine."

"Pleased to finally make your acquaintance," she beamed.

Nancy stirred in my arms and called out, "Mommy," interrupting the light-hearted and flirtatious exchange.

Chapter Four

Buster eyed me coolly. "This ain't no daycare, ya know. We got more kids here than we can stomach!"

"Oh! No! Absolutely not," I said quickly. "I wasn't expecting..."

"Nancy's a *really* good baby," Chickie said, jumping in to my defense.

"I not a baby," Nancy mumbled against my neck.

Buster narrowed his eyes again.

"Look, Jane is a great cook," Chickie continued, stepping closer to him with a deliberate grace. She bent down, her brown hair brushing softly against his cheek as she leaned in. I watched as his eyes rolled with excitement, his breath catching as he inhaled the sweet perfume from her perfectly styled coif. "And she's in kind of a bind right now," she whispered, though loud enough for me to catch every word. "Bad breakup. Needs a place to cool her jets. And we promise, the kid won't be a problem at all. Besides, Sis said you needed someone for the grab joint." She straightened up and flashed her dazzling smile, her voice dripping with that signature charm she used to get her way.

I shot her an angry look, and Buster eyed me up and down as he rubbed his chin. "Well... I guess we could..."

Chickie leaned in and planted one on his cheek, leaving behind the imprint of her dark red lipstick. She clapped her hands together in triumph and squeaked. I sighed in relief, thankful for her alluring performance.

"Let me run this by the Big Cheese. Not sure how he's gonna feel about bringing on another broad with a rugrat, but..." He lingered on the word, but his lusty attention was focused on Chickie.

"Pretty please, with a cherry on top!" she begged playfully.

Buster smiled again. He stepped to the side and extended his arm in a welcoming way, beckoning us to step foot into the dusty domain.

"Where we now?" Nancy chirped innocently.

"A fun place," I answered. "With really fun people," and I glared down at Buster.

"Well, Hon," he said to Chickie, "let me find the Boss. In the meantime, you go see your pally. Sis is in a trailer on the south side of the Lot. You can't miss it—she's got it all decked out with pink and sparkly shit."

"Thanks, Buster!" she gushed dramatically. "You're a saint."

"Yeah, yeah," he grumbled. "Don't cha go spreading that around!" He gave her a wink and picked up speed ahead of us, as much as he could on his stinted legs.

I tugged on Chickie's dress sleeve, almost dragging her down to the ground.

"What the hell, Jane?" she squawked.

"We never finalized what job I was going in for!" I growled. "*Cook*? I'm a shitty cook!"

"Mommy!" Nancy yelled. "No bad words!"

"Hush, Baby. I'm sorry," I said to her.

Chapter Four

"Oh, stop it, Jane!" she whispered. "I had no other choice but to improvise. The little guy was about to turn us away!"

Buster looked over his shoulder at us, but I'm pretty sure he didn't hear what she said. Chickie straightened up, smiled, and wiggled her fingers in a little wave at him. He smirked and continued walking.

"Just. Keep. Smiling," she emphasized from the corner of her mouth. So, I did and plastered a big ole phony smile on my face. The weight of Nancy's body over my shoulder felt like she was gonna drag me down to the ground, and I desperately wished I could find a spot to set her down and rest my head.

Soon, we approached a food stand, and Buster started veering off to the left. He pointed his arm straight ahead to guide us to Sis. "She's down that way," he called out before he disappeared amid the tents and booths.

We followed in the direction he said as the humming of lights turning on simultaneously filled the air. A calliope revved up in the distance, and Nancy *oohed* and *aahhed* as the game stalls and food stands popped to life. I can't deny that I too was a little awestruck as everything in the carnival felt like it was waking up. The sun had fully set, yet the brilliant lights of the World illuminated the area as if the day had never ceased.

"There she is!" Chickie exclaimed as we passed the Midway and reached the Lot on the south side. She pointed toward a rickety old trailer. A pink scarf was tied to the wooden railing, fluttering in the night breeze like outstretched arms, as if beckoning us in. My heart quickened, and without thinking, I picked up my pace, trotting to catch up with her.

Chickie raced up the little staircase and furiously knocked on the door while Nancy and I hung back, our nerves wound tight with anticipation. Suddenly, the door swung open with a creak, revealing the silhouette of a burly woman framed by the dim lamplight behind her. Her features were impossible to make out in the shadows, but I could tell one thing for sure—she was tall, round, and imposing.

"Chickadee?" she said, and I was taken aback at how deep her voice sounded.

"Sister?" Chickie yelled and the two of them squealed and stamped their feet like crazy pitter patters against the wood. Chickie's arms extended, and it looked as if she was swallowed up in the darkness of Sis's being—as if the dark shadows gobbled her whole and their bodies meshed together. It was unsettling, and I looked away for a second to get the image out of my mind.

"You made it!" Sis bellowed, and again, I was startled by the sound of her voice.

"Yes!" Chickie huffed. "It felt like it took for-*ever*! And what's with that Buster guy?"

"He's such a little lecher! I warned you about him. Pay him no mind." Sis paused and her body tilted to one side. Although I couldn't see them, I

Chapter Four

could feel her eyes glaring through me. "Chickie? You've got company?"

Chickie pulled away from Sis, and I could see her body shifting in the shadows so that she was looking over in my direction. "Jane!" she called to me. "Come and meet Sis!"

Hesitantly, I moved forward and met her at the footsteps of the trailer. As I drew closer, the shadows began to fade, and her full figure emerged from the darkness. Sis's black, curly hair framed her round face in tiny wet ringlets, contrasting against her round, jet-black eyes. And she was large—massive, in fact. A blue cotton muumuu draped over her body like a carnival tent, and I had to stifle a chuckle at the irony of the image. She was more woman than woman with a neatly trimmed black mustache that blended into the long, thick beard cascading down her chin.

"Sis, this is Jane and her daughter Nancy," Chickie sang the introduction. "Jane, Sis."

A grumbling sound stirred in Sis's barrel chest.

"You know us girls gotta stick together, right?" Chickie began, and it sounded like the introduction to a really long explanation.

Sis crossed her arms over her chest and sighed.

"Jane here..." Chickie continued, "well, she got in with some unsavory individuals, and she just needs a place to lay low with sweet little Nancy."

Sis sighed again in apparent displeasure.

"I promise she's good people. And I know *you* of all people know what it's like to..."

Sis raised her right hand, palm out, instantly quieting Chickie. Then, with a slow, deliberate motion, she extended it toward me for a handshake, though it felt more like a test than a friendly gesture. "Pleasure," she muttered through her nose.

I moved Nancy on my hip and cautiously replied, "Pleasure," as I reached for her hand. The moment our hands connected; my eyes widened in surprise. Sis's hand was enormous—thick, with meaty fingers and a solid, powerful palm. Her grip was strong, almost painfully so, and I had to stifle a wince as she shook with a force that felt anything but feminine.

A knowing smile spread across her face as she let me go. "Come, ladies! Come in my humble abode," she said, and we followed her inside her trailer.

The pungent smell of incense assaulted my nostrils as Nancy gave a little cough. I eased her off me, and she slithered down the length of my body and scampered over to the oversized plush couch.

"Had you told me you'd be traveling with companions..." Sis began.

"It was last minute," Chickie jumped in. "If I could have gotten a message to you, I would have."

Sis waved her hand around. "I don't care. I'm just so glad you made it safe and sound. We'll figure it all out. Once Tophat officially brings you on, he'll probably put you up in the old

Chapter Four

psychic trailer so Jane and little scamp here will be better settled."

"I'm looking for work, too," I blurted, and my words sounded so small to my own ears.

Sis regarded me with a curious eye. "Oh honey," she said with a pouty face.

Quickly, I looked to Chickie, and she ushered me over to the couch. "It's fine, Jane. Sis said we'll figure it all out. We have to trust her."

I sat down, and Nancy pulled herself up into my lap. She curled up, laid her head down, and closed her eyes. I felt her body immediately sink into mine, and I petted the top of her head.

The petting motion helped to relax me as well, and for the first time in what felt like a million years, I let my body go limp. The trailer was decorated very eclectically with colorful scarves hanging from the ceiling. Patchwork tapestries covered the small trailer windows so as to block out the light during the day. I assumed since the carnival ran during the night, Sis and the other performers would need to sleep during the day and would want to keep out as much sunlight as possible.

Chickie sat next to me as Sis took a seat on the rocking chair across from us. "Are you performing tonight?" Chickie asked.

Sis turned her head to the full-sized wooden mannequin in the corner of the room. It wore a low cut flowing red dress with lace at the ends of the sleeves. A black shawl wrapped around at the shoulders, and strings of long pearls draped around the neck. "Yes. It's the opening week, so Tophat's got us all lined up to do our thing."

"How long have you been with the show?" I asked.

Sis took a long, contemplative breath and exhaled. "A long, long time," she said and spread open her legs to push herself back in the rocking chair and stretched her arms high above her head.

As she did that, I noticed something in her lap that gave me pause—a lump, a bulge, a *something* that shouldn't be there. I nudged Chickie on the leg, hoping to get her attention so she too could see the evident growth between Sis's legs.

"What?" she snapped.

I opened my eyes wide and glanced at Sis's crotch.

Chickie smiled. "Oh? That?" she crowed.

"What?" Sis asked, returning from her full body stretch.

"N... n... nothing..." I stammered, trying to regain my shocked composure.

Chickie laughed—this time more heartily.

"What? What did I miss?" Sis asked.

"Sister! I think Jane just figured out you aren't a..." Chickie lowered her eyes, and Sis followed them to the center of her lap, at the rod-like entity that stood out from underneath her muumuu.

Sis laughed, too, and tugged at what I realized to be her massive hard-on. "You didn't tell her, Chickadee?"

"Tell me what?" I asked.

Chapter Four

Chickie composed herself from her laughing fit. "No! And break the illusion of the World?"

"What? Tell me what?" I insisted.

"The only proper way for a bearded lady to be a bearded lady is to have a bearded man do the job!" Sis said through a round of snorts.

I cocked my head to the side, still in a fog of confusion.

"Sister is really a brother, Jane," Chickie giggled. "But these things don't ever get spoken of, you understand? It's important to maintain the illusion."

"We carnies call it *kayfabe*. The more time you spend here, the more you'll understand," Sis said as she scratched at her crotch.

"Okay," I said, and that really was all I could come up with because the weight of Nancy's sleeping body in my lap was starting to make me sleepy as well.

"Oh no!" Sis roared when I rested my head back against the couch. "There's no time for that! We got a show to do, and you two are coming with *me*!"

Chapter Five

Monday, May 15th 1944
The Gentry Brothers' Wonders of the World Carnival
Glenmoor, Ohio
Night of the Last Quarter Moon

"Each night the carnival kicks off with a bang in the Big Tent," Sis told us as we walked to the main tent where the opening festivities took place. "The main acts huddle behind the scenes, getting ready while Tophat Trent, the Carny Boss himself, takes center stage to give his grand opening spiel. That man can talk the horns off a Billy goat, and he sets the night in motion with just a few well-placed words. Now, not everyone comes straight to the Big Tent. Some folks make a beeline for the grab joint to get their mitts on the cotton candy and hot dogs. Others head straight for the flat joint, ready to part with their dimes on the rigged games. Then you have your thrill-seekers, the ones who can't wait to hop on the Ferris wheel or, if they have the guts, brave the Tilt-A-Whirl. Of course, you always

Chapter Five

have that secretive bunch—the ones who sneak down to Sideshow Alley for a peek at the freaks. The Conjoined Twins, the Bearded Lady..." She paused and rubbed her long, black beard. "But for most of the crowd, it's all about the Big Tent. Packed in like sardines, shoulder to shoulder, they come for the whole shebang—the razzle-dazzle, the magic, and the spectacle of the night. And they won't leave until the World has given them every last bit of its wonder."

The hum and pulse of the crowd sparked life within the tent—an energy I had never felt even in the most magickal of places. I stood in the far back with Chickie and Sis at my sides and my hands placed firmly on Nancy's shoulders. She had whined a few times about not being able to see the stage, but Sis had silenced her with an, "Oh sugar, you don't need to see. You just need to *hear*." I gave Chickie a questioning look, but she shrugged.

"The Boss does this every night," Sis explained. "It's his way of opening the show and welcoming the crowd. When he's almost finished, we'll head backstage, and you can see first-hand how this all goes down!" She clapped her meaty hands excitedly, and Chickie smiled in wonder at her. I, too, felt myself starting to get swept away in that same awe. It was like that feeling when you start to get a little tipsy from too much wine. It started to overwhelm me—the lights, the sounds, the smells—everything was happening so fast, and I was being swept up in a tidal wave of smoke and illusion. But deep inside, I kept reminding myself that I needed to keep my head on straight if I was going to protect my kiddo.

When the lights in the tent dimmed, a murmured hush fell over the crowd. Sis grabbed the top of my shoulder and whispered, "Here we go!" A smoky haze blanketed the space like a shadowy fog descending upon the patrons. It stung my eyes, and I had to squint a little in order to see the main stage clearly.

Nancy turned her little head upward and asked, "What's happening, Mommy?"

"The show's about to start," I answered.

"But I can't *see*!" she whined again.

"It's okay," I reassured. "Auntie Sis said we'll go backstage and get to see everything up close. Just be a good listener for now."

"Yes, Mommy," she said dejectedly and turned her head face forward.

Soon, the lights went completely out, and the crowd gave a collective gasp. A spotlight exploded into life, illuminating an empty space on the stage. The crowd fell silent with anticipation as they waited with bated breath for the Ringmaster to appear. My hand squeezed harder on Nancy's shoulder, and I heard her give a little squeal in her throat. With my other hand, I smoothed her hair back from her face, petting her in a comforting way.

And just like that, as if he'd stepped out of a dream, the Carny Boss appeared from the misty shadows, greeted by a roar of applause. He

Chapter Five

flashed a knowing grin and tipped his black top hat with a dignified nod to the crowd. There was something uncanny about the way he moved — gliding smooth as silk, flicking the front of his black tailcoat with practiced ease, his steel-gray eyes cutting through the noise until every soul in the tent sat silent and spellbound. Something about him felt familiar, like I'd seen him somewhere before but couldn't quite place it.

He has gray eyes, I thought. But that was impossible for me to know! I was so far away from the main stage that there was no plausible way for me to know that! But yet, I *knew*. I *saw*. His body seemed to dance in the smoke, and a light shone all around him — not the light from the spotlight, but a light that came from within him. And his eyes... his blazing gray eyes stormed and laughed and looked right through me. Quickly, I looked away and blinked rapidly, but his smiling eyes whispered to me, and soon, I was locked in — staring at the magnanimous figure on the stage, hypnotized by his otherworldly presence.

With a wave of his hand, the crowd fell silent again, waiting for him to speak. He paused dramatically, putting the audience in a state of proverbial pins and needles, longing for his words. "Ladies and gentlemen, boys and girls of all ages, gather 'round, gather 'round! The hour has come for a night of thrills, chills, and unforgettable sights! I am your humble guide through this evening of awe and astonishment. My name is Gideon T. Solwood, but as my closest and dearest friends, you can call me..." He paused, waiting for a collective response.

The crowd screamed back at him with fervent enthusiasm, "Tophat Trent!" They cheered and applauded as he soaked it in, breathing their response deep into his lungs. It put a wide smile of pride onto his face, and he bowed reverently to them.

Another wave of his head quieted them down and he continued. "Now, you're about to step into a world where the curious, the mysterious, and the downright unbelievable are brought to life before your very eyes. That's right, folks, you've found yourself at the doorstep of the incredible..." He swept one of his arms in an arch over his head. "Gentry Brothers' Wonders of the World!"

Another thunderous round of applause shook the tent, an electric wave sweeping through the crowd. "Now, now..." his voice rang out, deep and commanding, "when my great uncle, Galen Gentry, and his brother, my grandfather—my namesake—Gideon Gentry, set off on this wild ride back in the late 1800s, they had no notion of what their little traveling fair would become." He paused, letting the gravity of his words sink in. "Starting with two tents and a handful of magic tricks, Grandpa Gideon and Uncle Galen changed the carnival game forever. And now, folks, I'm honored to lead you into the next chapter of their legacy." He placed a hand on his chest, bowed his head, and for a moment, the flash and spectacle gave way to something deeper—sincere gratitude.

Chapter Five

To say I was mesmerized would be putting it mildly. I was utterly captivated by his performance, ensnared by every word that spilled from his lips. The tent felt as if it were closing in, shrinking around us until it was just the two of us—Tophat and me. He spoke as if I were his sole audience, and in that moment, it seemed there was no one else present. His gray eyes locked onto mine, piercing through the haze as if I were the only soul in the entire arena. My vision adjusted to the swirling smoke that danced in the beam of the spotlight, and all else faded into a blur.

"And what wonders do we have for you tonight? Oh, you'll see, alright! You'll witness the mighty feats of a man who could toss a train off its tracks! Duke Steele! But you know him as The Iron Giant. Duke may be the silent type, but he's a mountain of muscle that's sure to leave you breathless! Duke is not only going to show off his rippling muscles, but he will exhibit his unmatched strength in ways never thought possible.

"Or maybe your curiosity will take you down to our Odditorium to meet our Tattooed Lady, Zora Heart. The Living Canvas. The Walking Masterpiece. Each tattoo on her body tells a story. Sit with her for a while, and she might regale you with her exciting adventures of how and why she got her ink—like being captured by pirates or belonging to a secret society! She'll even sign your entrance ticket as a souvenir.

"Perhaps you're more inclined to witness nature's unimaginable! Now, keep those eyes peeled and ready because tonight we will present to you a spectacle so rare it defies belief! Jack and Jill, the Conjoined Twins—one male, one female, two souls sharing one incredible existence. A medical marvel, if you will, right here on this stage, to whet your curious appetite!"

"Lobster Girl!" a man from the crowd shouted. "We want Lobster Girl!"

Tophat froze in his tracks and tipped his head as if he were scanning the arena for the voice who spoke. When he found him, he pointed to the crowd. "Ahhh, my good man, seems you are familiar with our show!"

"We followed you all the way down from Ravenna," the man called enthusiastically.

"From Ravenna?" Tophat responded, but the tone of his voice gave me reason to pause. It sounded questioning, almost accusatory. I got the feeling that Tophat was not pleased that there was a repeat customer from out of town. "That's quite a way, sir," Tophat said.

"Well," the man beamed, "we're your number one fans!"

A sinister smile crept across the Ringmaster's face as he tipped his hat to the crowd, oozing reverence. "You see! You see, ladies and gentlemen! Folks travel from all corners of this great nation just to witness *this* show. That speaks volumes about the power of the World! From Ravenna to East Liverpool. From the peaks of New Hampshire to the bustling streets of Staten Island, New York…" He paused, turning his head

Chapter Five

sharply in my direction. My heart skipped a beat, and for a fleeting moment, time stood still. Was he looking at *me*? His piercing glare landed on me, holding for a split second that felt like a lifetime, before he went back to his speech. I gasped softly, struggling to catch my breath.

"We want to see Lobster Girl, Tophat!" the man from the audience repeated.

"Well, well, my dear friend from Ravenna, I'm afraid that Lobster Girl had to return to the sea." A collective groan permeated the crowd. "I know, I know," Tophat said regretfully, "it's just one of the unfortunate downsides to this life. But I promise you will delight in all the other attractions we have to offer. For those of you with a taste for something truly extraordinary, you will see the most enchanting woman you've ever laid eyes on—Sis Savoy, the most stunning Bearded Lady this side of the Mississippi! As strong as she is striking, she is a true marvel of grace and grit!"

At the sound of Sis's name, my head instinctively jerked to the left to look at her. But she was gone. I looked to my right where Chickie had been standing, and she was gone too. My body tensed up, and I went to squeeze Nancy's shoulder again, but it soon dawned on me that she was also gone. Gone. *Gone.*

My heart slowed with a deep thumping rhythm as I swung my body around from side to side. I knew my movements were swift and jerky, but everything suddenly felt slowed down, like my body was trapped in a dream. "Nancy?"

I called out, but my voice was nothing more than a whisper against the raucous noise of the crowd. "Nancy?" I said again, but this time it was caught in my throat, and I don't think I actually said anything. Immediately, the tears swelled in my eyes, turning the arena and all the people within into a giant, watery blur. Faces blended and bled together in monstrous shapes as I took flight within the area around me, searching like a bloodhound. "Nancy!" I screamed, and this time the sound pierced a small section of the crowd.

A woman in my vicinity looked at me quizzically, and I rushed over to her. I had no way of discerning her countenance through the wall of tears at the base of my eyelids. "Have you seen a little girl? Dirty blonde hair, green eyes, three years old. She's wearing a pink dress, and…"

She frantically shook her head no. Through my blurred vision, I could see the woman had blonde hair and dark red lips, and her eyes looked at me painfully like she knew what it was like to lose a child. I grabbed onto her shoulders and pushed off her, springing back into the crowd and to the far end of the tent by the side exit. My feet felt like they were stuck in molasses as the entire tent seemed to spin round and round and round. And all the while I called out, "Nancy! Nancy! Nancy!"

They got her, I thought. *Christina Combs and Crowley's goons found us and snatched her right from under my hands.*

It took every fiber in my body to remain standing and searching when all my insides

Chapter Five

wanted to do was curl up onto the floor and cry the rest of my heart out—the rest of my eyes out.

Chickie and Sis were by the side door getting ready to leave the tent when they saw me scampering around.

"Jane! Jane!" Chickie yelled. "What's the matter?"

"Nancy!" I screamed. "I can't find Nancy!"

"Oh, good heavens!" she yelled as she, too, sprang into action, screaming for Nancy through the crowd.

The people around us started to take notice, and like a collective manhunt, heads began turning toward the floor in search of the missing child. Through it all, I had to remind myself to breathe, or I would have surely passed out, maybe passed away. My head darted in every direction until I could no longer take the dizziness. I stopped in my tracks, closed my eyes, and breathed deep, centering and grounding myself. I let the smoky air fill my lungs in an inhale that expanded my lungs as far as they could, and I exhaled slowly and gently, letting the release help to end my vertigo.

Althea, I said in my mind. *Althea Aisling Circe Crowley. Althea, baby. Where are you? Mommy needs to find you.*

"Janey, girl! Look!"

It was Sis's voice that made my eyes flash open. I looked over at her as she pointed to the stage. "There she is!" Sis bellowed again.

Witch of the Midnight Shadow

I turned my head to the main stage. My tears finally escaped my bottom lids and spilled down my cheeks. My vision cleared and there, plain as day, my little girl stood on the stage, with one hand clutching the upper part of her dress and a look of fear on her face. Tophat knelt beside her, holding her other hand gently in his as the spotlight shone brightly on them.

The air in the room got dense—so dense that it slowed down the very fabric of time, and I gasped at the sight of her. "Althea," I whispered in relief and pushed my way through the sea of sardined bodies like a salmon fighting its way upstream. Among the people and in the thick air of the tent, it took me nearly a million years to make it to the stage! Tophat spoke softly to Nancy, yet the words that came from his mouth didn't match the words I heard him speak, but I chalked that up to my heightened anxiety and immediate relief. I also heard music as if far off in the distance. A low, throbbing drum beat coming from backstage. It fell in rhythm with my own heartbeat. I flung my body against the stage and exclaimed, "Nancy!" as loudly as I could, and I was surprised to hear the sound of my voice lift above the thrum of the crowd.

Tophat glanced at me from the side then looked back to Nancy. "So, that's your name? Nancy." But the tone of his voice made it seem like it was more of a question than it was a statement. Like he didn't believe us. Like he knew that we were lying.

Chapter Five

Nancy nodded at him, and he smiled. His perfect white teeth glinted off the rays of the spotlight.

"And do you know who that woman is?" He pointed over at me.

Nancy nodded again. "That's my mommy," she said with her soft voice.

"Oh, I see," he said, and he pushed himself off his knee and stood up. He held Nancy's hand, then extended his free one to me, beckoning me to join them on the stage.

I hesitantly obliged, and when I put my hand in his, an electric shock raced up my arm. Instinctively, I tried to pull away, but he held on tightly, forcing me to feel the energy pulsate in my wrist and up to my shoulder. I think he winked at me as he helped hoist me up on stage.

I straightened up, standing hand-in-hand with Tophat, who lifted both our arms high in the air—mine and Nancy's—like we'd just won the grandest prize of all. The crowd erupted, roaring with thunderous applause, their cheers shaking the very walls of the Big Tent. The energy crackled, almost as electric as Tophat's firm grip. The men chanted his name like he was some kind of hero while the women wiped away tears of relief. I glanced down at Nancy, and for the first time in what felt like forever, a smile began to bloom on her face. The whole scene washed over me, surreal and overwhelming, like I'd stepped into a dream.

In one swift movement, Tophat placed Nancy and my hands together and took a step forward to address the audience. He lifted his hat to them, and the crowd took that as a cue to quiet down.

"Ladies and gentlemen, I assure you what we just witnessed here was nothing short of a miracle. Reuniting little Nancy with her mother is a privilege that so many families do not get to experience. So often we hear of tragedy befalling the most undeserving homes where a child goes inexplicably missing or is met with some unexplainable misfortune. The heartbreak and ruin that is left behind is simply unthinkable. But The Gentry Brothers' Wonders of the World extravaganza aims to ensure the safety of all our guests, both young and old. A promise we make to all parents at our events: we pledge to protect your little ones and guard them like our own. If you have any issues whatsoever, please do not hesitate to let one of our esteemed members know about it."

The crowd cheered again, and Nancy moved closer to me, clutching me at the thighs. Tophat motioned an arm out as if to usher us off stage. I nodded and mumbled, "Thank you."

"Keep sight of her," he said to me from the side of his mouth. "Don't want the little crow flying away again." His gray eyes twinkled, and for a second, for a split second as the beams of the spotlight raced across his face, I thought I saw a violent storm raging in his pupils. A powerful twister made its way from one eye to the other

Chapter Five

in a frenzy of whites and grays and fog and rain. Then, with another little wink, it was gone, and I stepped off the stage with Nancy right behind.

My breath hitched, and I hurried to the back of the tent where Chickie and Sis met us with open arms and "Oh-my-gods!"

Tophat outstretched his arms. "Now, my dear friends, here in this tent, under this great canopy of stars, we've suspended the rules of the everyday. You'll laugh, you'll gasp, and perhaps, you'll even catch your breath as the impossible unfolds right before your eyes. But remember, you're not just spectators tonight—you're a part of the magic! Enjoy the wonders of our world, my friends. But remember this—you may gaze upon them, but they may also gaze back at you. There is something … peculiar about tonight, something in the air. Perhaps it's curiosity. Or perhaps… it's something else. Just remember as you engage in the wonderous sights and sounds and activities—keep your good thoughts flowing and your actions to match!"

We hustled offstage, and I threw a quick look over my shoulder, hoping to catch one last peek of Tophat. His final words lingered in my head, hitting a note that felt strangely familiar, but I couldn't pin down why. As I scanned for him, the curtains seemed to swallow him whole, and just like that, he'd vanished. In his place stood little Buster Blue, decked out sharp as a tack in a pint-sized tux and top hat—a spitting image of Tophat himself. Every gesture, every little move, he was the Carny Boss in miniature. After the crowd settled down from their applause, Buster announced the next act: Bendy Bella, the contortionist wonder. But before I could catch a glimpse of her entrance, Chickie and Sis whisked me out of the tent and backstage.

Chapter Six

Monday, May 15th 1944
The Gentry Brothers' Wonders of the World Carnival
Glenmoor, Ohio
Night of the Last Quarter Moon

The backstage area of the Big Tent was hustling and bustling with all kinds of action. My head was still so fuzzy from my close brush with losing Nancy and the strange feelings I had gotten from the Carny Boss that I scarcely noticed the half-naked women scrambling to get into their costumes or the frantic rush to put the final touches on the performers' makeup. But as long as Nancy was okay and with me, that was all I cared about.

Everyone "ooh-ed" and "aah-ed" at her when we sat down by Sis's station, and Nancy really enjoyed the attention. Some of the performers patted me on the back and gave me words of encouragement like, "Good job, Mom!" or "So glad she's safe." The feeling of family and camaraderie was palpable, and I started to understand the allure of such a place. It reminded me a lot of England and Aleister's group and the feeling of being part of something larger than myself.

Chickie and I settled into the fold-up chairs at Sis's makeup desk, and to my surprise, Nancy scurried right into Chickie's lap. I'll admit, it stung a bit to see her seek out a near stranger for comfort, but it also brought me a little relief. Knowing Nancy felt safe enough with Chickie to accept that comfort was more than I could've hoped for. A few of the other performers swooped in and hovered within our little circle, curious to meet the new players in town.

Sis looked into a lighted, oval mirror and fussed with her eyelashes. They were a set of long, black falsies that curved so high they touched the tops of her eyelids. As a matter of fact, the more I looked at Sis, the more she reminded me of the actress Mary Astor who played Brigid O'Shaughnessy in the film *The Maltese Falcon* (except Sis was a little heavier and a little hairier). I remembered seeing that movie right before Nancy was born. Aleister's group had decided to go to the cinema and enjoy a night out, but I wasn't feeling well that night. Nancy was squirming something awful, and it made me nauseated! But as soon as the movie began, she had quieted down immediately, as if she was invested in it as well.

"Everyone okay?" Sis asked us in the mirror.

I nodded sharply.

"Peachy keen," Chickie sang.

Chapter Six

"Peachy," Nancy echoed.

The other performers gave a little laugh at Nancy's adorableness. She smiled brightly, basking in the attention.

"Why'd you walk away from your Mommy, Little Crow?" Chickie asked her.

Nancy went quiet and picked at her fingernails. She shrugged her shoulders after a few moments.

Sis swiveled around and looked at Nancy. "You know you really need to stay with a grown-up at all times," she said sweetly.

"Yes, Nancy," Chickie continued. "Your mommy, me, Auntie Sis…"

"And me, too!" a voice interjected.

We all turned our heads, and standing between my chair and Chickie's was a beautiful giantess of a woman in a gold belly dancer's costume with a thick white python draped across her shoulders. She seemed to sparkle, and the serpent she carried only added to her exotic glow. Chickie gasped when she noticed the reptile flicking its curious tongue in her direction, and Nancy's mouth dropped at the sight of the snake.

"Tina," Sis said in a ho-hum tone. "Chickie. Jane. And Little Nancy."

"Lady Serpentina, The Gentry Brothers' resident snake charmer," Tina interrupted. "But you can call me Auntie Tina, sweetheart." She put a hand out and rubbed Nancy's chin lovingly as I stared with a cautious eye.

"You're up next," Sis said and turned back to the mirror.

Tina giggled and stroked her hand down the bottom half of the snake. Nancy couldn't take her eyes off the creature, and Tina, taking notice of this, bent forward toward her. "You can pet her if you want to," she said.

Nancy shook her head and curled up against Chickie's chest in fear.

"Oh, no, sweetie! Winnie is a good girl. She loves to be handled. She won't hurt you."

Chickie crinkled up her nose. "Why is her name Winnie?"

Tina crouched in closer, putting her face and the head of the snake within close range of Nancy and Chickie. Nancy squirmed and Chickie turned her head away in disgust. "Well, that's what she told me it was," Tina said with an ominous tone.

"Ease up, Tina!" Sis scolded from her vanity.

A wide smile spread across Tina's face, and she gave a small snort. "Just joshin'. How would I know? She was Tophat's snake before I got here. He named her." She turned her attention back to Nancy. "So, sweetie, you wanna pet her?"

"That's okay," I said firmly, defensively. "Maybe once she gets more … acquainted…"

Tina paused and stood upright again, the ornaments on her belt jingling a happy little tune. She stood at least six feet tall, and her long black hair fell past her waist. She was slender but toned—the muscles of her flat stomach looked as if her flesh had been hand-chiseled and slathered with bronzing oil like a statuesque goddess. "Understood," she said with a coy smile.

Chapter Six

"You two are the new recruits Buster was blabbering about to us before," another voice from the group rang out. "Don't worry. It's overwhelming at first, but we all eventually become one giant family."

"You're Vesper St. Clair!" Chickie squealed, her eyes lighting up like she'd just bumped into Rita Hayworth or Ginger Rogers themselves. The way she got all starry-eyed was almost enough to make me roll my own. But there was no denying Vesper had the looks to turn heads with her perfectly coiffed blonde curls and that movie-star glow. "Sis filled me in on all the details—you're the fortune teller!" Chickie added, her voice dripping with admiration.

Vesper straightened her back like a soldier called to attention and smoothed her hands down the front of her pink polka-dot dress. Her figure was all hourglass—a nip at the waist with curves spilling over at the top and bottom. She didn't have the mystic aura of a fortune teller; in fact, it was easy to see why Tophat wanted to shift her to the Cooch. "Soon-to-be ex-fortune teller," she quipped with a tilt of her head and a knowing smirk.

"Well, I'm the-hoping-to-be-new fortune teller," Chickie said, using Vesper's same singsong cadence.

Vesper lifted her hand high, like she was raising a glass of bubbly. "Well, here's to good fortune for us all!" she announced with a wink.

"Hear, hear!" Sis echoed, mirroring the gesture.

The others joined in, and a round of laughter spread through the group. Each note of their laughter felt like it rang through me, easing my nerves and wrapping me in a rare, peaceful calm.

"And you, honey?" Vesper asked, nodding her head in my direction, stifling my moment of peace.

"Me? Me, what?" I asked protectively.

"The World? Are you the hoping-to-be-new-snake-charmer?"

"Over my dead body!" Tina joked and everyone giggled again.

"Or are you the hoping-to-be-new-bearded-lady?" Vesper pushed.

"She couldn't pull it off," Sis sneered. "She'd need a beard first, wouldn't she?"

Again, more laughter.

"No, really, hon, what's your angle? What brings you to our little fam?" Vesper pressed, her eyes narrowing with a curious gleam.

My tongue twisted, and the words scrambled before I could say a thing. Chickie jumped in, leaning close to the group, like she was letting everyone in on some juicy gossip. I shot her a look, silently begging her to keep it buttoned, but before I could get a word in, she blurted out, "Janey's on the lam! She's like an international outlaw. Wanted in two countries!"

"Chickie!" I admonished as a collective quiet gasp echoed in our group.

"Wanted by the fuzz?" Tina asked.

"No. Even better!" Chickie continued.

Chapter Six

"Chickie, don't..." I don't know why I said it because I hadn't divulged any of that info to her previously; I guess it was just a knee-jerk reaction.

Chickie waved her hands in the air like she was shooing off a stray cat. "Oh, quit it, Jane! They're square. They're not gonna dime you out or anything!" She turned to the group with a knowing smirk. "Besides," she added with a little flair, "Jane's been tighter-lipped than a bank vault about her backstory, so let's just call her a lady of mystery."

"Madame Mistinos!" Sis cried.

"That doesn't even make sense, Sis!" Tina chided.

"Well, it does in my head," she replied.

They laughed again, but I breathed in heavily, angrily. My face flushed hot with rage, and a searing pain throbbed over my left eye. I rang my hands and pursed my lips together, certain there was steam coming out of my ears. I couldn't believe she outed me like that! It felt as if my heart had dropped down into the pit of my stomach.

"Hey Chickadee? Is there a reward for the Madame Mistinos!" Vesper joked.

"Not funny, V," Sis scolded.

"Sorry, sorry," she responded.

Instinctively, I stood up. I wanted to run. Take Nancy off Chickie's lap and leave the carnival and find another place to hide. Tina must have seen how uncomfortable and irritated I had become because she put a hand on my shoulder as Winnie slithered closer to my face. "Hey, hey. No worries.

No one here is going to give you away. Trust me — we're all here for one reason or another. We all have our secrets. We all have something we're running from."

I looked over at Vesper and Sis. Their faces, once lively and laughing, had gone stone-serious, and they both nodded in agreement.

"We'd be hypocrites to turn you over to whoever you're running from. The World's a safe haven, Jane. Safe for all of us who don't quite fit," Tina said with a warm smile. Her words did ease the knot in my stomach a bit, though I was still burning up inside over Chickie for letting the cat out of the bag in the first place.

Suddenly, the dour mood changed when the roar of the crowd made its way to us behind the red fabric curtains. It was the signal that Bendy Bella's performance was done, and the next artist was about to make their way to the stage.

"Shit! I'm up!" Tina said as she adjusted Winnie at her shoulders.

Vesper quickly scuttled over to her and patted Tina's face with a paper makeup blotter. Then she kissed her on both cheeks and told her to break a leg. Tina moved closer to the slit in the drapes, waiting for her cue while we all sat in silence and listened intently.

Buster's voice was smooth and lilting as he addressed the eager crowd. "Ladies and gentlemen, boys and girls, gather 'round for a sight that's as mesmerizing as it is mysterious! Step closer now, for you're about to witness the

Chapter Six

hypnotic enchantment of the one, the only... Lady Serpentina!"

Our little backstage group gave a quiet applause of encouragement, and Tina smiled as she looked over at us. She inhaled deeply and adjusted Winnie again. I couldn't tell if she was anxious or nervous or scared. I hadn't suspected that she was any of those things by the way she spoke and presented herself earlier, but at that moment, there was a look in her eye—like a dead glimmer. When I said that in my head, it didn't make sense, but it was the only way to describe it. Something was off. Something appeared off. I know the others couldn't tell because they were too wrapped up in their silent cheering to notice. But I did. The air shifted around her, like there was a wavy, hazy outline around her body, and when she glanced over at us again, I could have sworn there was a red X flashing on her forehead just underneath the lip of her golden headpiece. I blinked my eyes, and it flashed away as quickly as it had appeared.

"Yes, dear friends," Buster continued, "prepare yourselves for a vision of beauty and danger entwined. Lady Serpentina is not just a performer—she's a master of creatures both wild and wicked. And tonight, she is accompanied by a creature as rare as she is remarkable. Meet Winnie, a ghostly albino Burmese python, her scales as white as moonlight. Do not be fooled! Winnie is a powerful carnivore, known to devour a whole deer! But you will soon see that the dangerous beast is

Witch of the Midnight Shadow

no match for Lady Serpentina. Lady Serpentina's beauty is as mesmerizing as her movements, her charm as powerful as the serpent she commands."

"He's good," Chickie remarked under her breath, and Tina inhaled one last time in anticipation.

"So, if you dare… watch her move, watch her sway… but beware, for once her spell is cast, you may never escape it. Now, without further ado, I present to you the bewitching beauty, the snake charmer of your wildest dreams and darkest fears… Lady Serpentina!"

At the last call of her name, and the wave of applause, Tina made her way out onto the stage. The music cranked up on the victrola—an exotic song that had an Indian flair to it. It reminded me of the music that Aleister often played at the compound as he regaled me with tales of his adventures in Sri Lanka and India and Burma at the turn of the 20th century.

"Do you want to watch?" Vesper asked us.

Chickie and I fervently nodded, and she waved us over to the thin slit in the curtain. We stood on opposite sides of each other with Nancy in between so the three of us could get an up close and personal (albeit, semi-obstructed) view of the performance.

The crowd was as still as statues as Tina gyrated with Winnie wrapped around her body. She moved in time with the music and swayed her hips with a seductive rhythm. Every now and then, the audience would gasp and "ooohh" and

Chapter Six

"aaahh" and how the snake seemed to obey every command Tina's body gave. And occasionally a loud hissing sound came through the record player, giving the illusion to the crowd that Winnie was as dangerous as Buster had said she was. They were so transfixed by the performance; they had no idea it was simply a recording.

I had to admit, I was mesmerized by Tina's act as well. The way the muscles of her tight body rippled with her every movement, the way the snake draped itself over and under and around her—it was all too perfect and so surreal. The body of the white serpent contrasted boldly against Tina's bronzed flesh, giving them both a glowing appearance. Their dance truly was hypnotic, and I couldn't take my eyes off them.

"There's a man coming up through the crowd," Chickie whispered after a few minutes.

"A man?" Sis asked.

"Yeah. A big fella with a cowboy hat. He's really tall. Walking close to the stage. Is he supposed to do that?" Chickie paused for a second before gushing, "Oh, he's hunky!"

Vesper huffed. "No!" she replied in a weird kind of shouty whisper.

Sis stood up from her chair and peered through the opening over Chickie's head. "It's *him* again," she whispered with disgust.

"Him?" I asked.

Sis stepped back, blending into the shadows as we watched the whole show go down. The big guy in the cowboy hat pushed through the crowd, all elbows and shoulders, just to claim a spot at the front. His face was round and clean-shaven, but a slick shine of sweat glistened on his forehead just under the brim of his hat. Something in his eyes had a shifty gleam that made my stomach turn. And then he licked his lips, dragging his thick, meaty tongue across them as Tina approached him. That tongue looked like a fat, wriggling snake coiled right in his mouth, and I felt bile creep up into my throat at the sight of it. Tina knelt down in front of him and spread her legs apart. Then she guided Winnie down to the front of her body and wrapped the serpent around one of her thighs. The man took his giant hands and placed them on Tina's knees, trying to spread her even farther apart. And he gazed at her, stared at her, his eyes brimming with lust so strong that I knew the rod between his legs was at full attention like a G.I. Joe reporting for duty. Quickly, I understood the look of apprehension Tina wore earlier. She must have anticipated this.

"*That*," Sis said, "is Sheriff Tannehill McCrory. *Hill* to his close friends and constituents."

"The sheriff?" Chickie asked. "What is the sheriff doing around here?"

"Trying to get us shut down, I reckon," Vesper complained.

"Why's he trying to do that?" I asked, but my eyes were still trained on the stage.

"Well, rumor has it Hill McCrory don't like the carnival. Hill McCrory is a God-fearing man. Hill McCrory is a rat bastard who has a bone to pick

Chapter Six

with anything or anyone who doesn't conform to his Christian values," Sis rattled.

"And don't forget that Hill McCrory is working on a murder case that he ain't been able to solve for a few months now," Vesper said.

"*Cases,*" Sis emphasized. "Plural."

"All those stories about the Shadow Man of the Carnival are making him stick his nose in our business!" Vesper finished.

Chickie clenched hard onto the side of the curtain. "Shadow Man? What's the Shadow Man? What are you talking about *murder investigation*?" she asked frantically.

"*Investigations,*" Vesper corrected. "Plural."

Sis pried Chickie's fingers from the curtain and started to guide her over to her makeup station. Chickie put out her hand and Nancy took it and walked away with them. "Relax. There's nothing to get worked up about. Just a silly little legend," Sis reassured her.

"You never told me about no murder investigations, Sis! What have you drug me into?"

"Oh, stop it!" Vesper howled. "Sis said to calm down. It's no big deal, really."

I scarcely listened to their conversation because my attention was focused on the stage. Tina continued to dance seductively with the snake wrapped around her. Her belt jingled and jangled with every hip thrust, and Hill McCrory stood mesmerized, fawning over her (as the rest of the crowd did for that matter). Near the end of her performance, Tina hovered at the edge of the stage holding Winnie's face in one hand. She brought the snake's head dangerously close to Hill's—the serpent's tongue flicked in and out, and McCrory closed his eyes and smiled a smile that let me know he was completely turned on by both Tina and her companion. Tina moved back to do another move in her dance routine, but McCrory's eyes popped open and he grabbed her wrist and dragged her back down closer to him. I gasped, and I think I heard someone on the side of the stage echo my sentiment.

I clenched the opening of the curtain even tighter as a shock of electricity shot up through my forearms. A seething rage pulsated in every fiber of my being, anger that boiled up and over and into the depths of my chest. The air around me grew dense—heavy. Filled with an oppressive weight that bore down on my shoulders and shifted my vision. I stared at McCrory's face while the energy bubbled up to my throat and filled my ears with a clogged sensation. His face started to change. It warped and transformed as if I was looking at it through a kaleidoscope or a Fun House mirror. It was monstrous and evil-looking, and it drove the rage all the way up to my temples and behind my eyes. I envisioned myself tearing at his face! Digging into his eye socket with my thumb while I jabbed my forearm up under his nose causing it to break and smashing the bone all the way up into his brain! Just when I thought I'd reached the pinnacle of my energy, I let go of the curtain, and the record suddenly

Chapter Six

scratched to a halt. Buster came bustling out onto the stage, and when McCrory saw him, he let go of Tina like a hot coal.

I startled myself something awful, for it had been quite some time since I had felt an energy surge as powerful as that one. I got to thinking that maybe there was something more to this place than I had originally thought.

Buster bid the audience give Lady Serpentina a final round of applause. She did a curtsy for herself and one for Winnie and quickly turned on her heel and made a beeline for the opening in the curtain. When I saw her marching, I separated the opening just enough for her to slip right in and followed behind her. I didn't even pay attention to who Buster announced next.

Tina was fuming! She practically flung the serpent into its glass enclosure at her station and muttered and cursed as she sat down in front of her mirror. "That god damn rat bastard McCrory!" she shrieked.

"See," Sis chimed in, "didn't I say he was a rat bastard!"

Tina took a handkerchief and frantically wiped the heavy makeup from her face. "He's so... so..."

"Disgusting?" I said jumping in.

Nancy, who was sitting back in Chickie's lap, gave a giggle. "Di-guh-ting," she repeated and laughed.

"Disgusting!" Tina agreed. "I can't believe I let him put his hands on me like that!" She made a retching noise in her throat, and I thought she was going to vomit.

"Now, now," Vesper admonished, "Tophat said we have to be extra nice to the sheriff."

"Extra nice, my ass!" Tina protested and Nancy's eyes went wide when she heard the swear word. "Sorry, sweetie. Auntie Tina's just a little angry right now," she said apologetically to the kid. "Extra nice, my *foot*! My stupid, bare, bottom-blackened foot that I'd like to ram so far up Hill McCrory's…"

"Language!" Chickie exclaimed just in time for Tina to correct herself.

Tina took a deep breath and composed herself. "Throat. I'd like to put my dirty foot down his throat. And if Tophat thinks I'm about to get any *friendlier* with dear old Johnny Law, he's got another thing coming."

"That's a different type of show, Tina," Sis teased.

"Har, har," she said sarcastically.

"So, no one's gonna tell us about the Shadow Man?" I blurted out.

The area got quiet and still, and Sis, Vesper, and Tina eyed each other cautiously, beckoning one of them to come forward with the dirt. Finally, after some hemming and hawing, Sis spoke up. "Look, sugar, every carnival has their version of the Shadow Man. It's an old carny legend. Anything to spook the showfolk."

"But what is it?" Chickie pressed.

Chapter Six

"Well," Vesper took over, "the Shadow Man is a ghost, a ghoul, an apparition. Like Sis said, every carnival has their own version." She looked at Tina as if she were desperate for words.

Tina stood up from her table and turned to face us. "The Shadow Man is the carnival necromancer."

"Necromancer?" Chickie squeaked.

"Yes," Tina continued. "Someone who can commune with the dead."

"A psychic?" Chickie asked, still not understanding.

"No," Vesper intervened, "it's deeper than that. A true necromancer can call up spirits and make them do their bidding."

"I don't see how that's any different," Chickie huffed.

"It is," I uttered and then quickly clamped my hand over my mouth. Chickie shot me a nasty look. But I was correct, and I knew it. Aleister had taught me all things having to do with sorcery and his version of black magick. In such ways, I was no stranger.

"Necromancers try to raise the dead, Chickie," Sis explained.

"But they need dead people for their rituals," Vesper added.

Nancy winced in horror in Chickie's lap.

"Sorry, honey," Vesper said in a sweet voice. "The grown-ups are just telling spooky jokes. We don't mean it. It's all just made-up stories. There is no Shadow Man. It isn't real."

"Hence, the investigation McCrory's working," I declared matter-of-factly.

"So they say," Tina answered. "He's got two 'unsolveds' in a six-month period. And they started right around the time the brand-new carnival rolled into town. So, McCrory goes snooping around, digging something deep. Hears the stories of the infamous Shadow Man. Tries to make some ungodly connection and hasn't been off our tail since."

"But don't you travel around? Won't Tophat be taking the show to a new city soon?" Chickie asked.

"Not if McCrory has anything to say about it!" Vesper exclaimed. "He's hellbent on taking us down… taking Tophat down. He's desperate to prove his connection between us and the…"

"M-u-r-d-e-r-s," I spelled out, reminding them of the tiny pitcher in the room.

Vesper nodded her head feverishly, and Chickie sank back into her chair and crossed her arms indignantly. "Ya know, Sis, I really wish you would have mentioned all this *before* I came all this way!"

Chapter Seven

Monday, May 22nd 1944
The Gentry Brothers' Wonders of the World Carnival
Glenmoor, Ohio
Night of the New Moon

Chickie, Nancy, and I stayed with Sis in her trailer as her esteemed guests. The couch was fine enough for me and Nancy to cuddle up on while Chickie took one of the plush chairs. The living situation was less than ideal considering the demanding needs of a three-year-old and the tight space to which we were confined. To make matters worse, we had no idea when Tophat was going to speak to us about our potential positions at the Carnival. The not-knowing aspect made my anxiety go through the roof, and I know Chickie was a ball of nerves herself, but I tried to keep my cool for Nancy's sake.

Nancy was none-the-wiser and was enjoying every moment of our stay at the World. She never met a stranger as everyone was immediately drawn to her. Of course, a three-year-old running around in stocking feet and an oversized tee shirt was more than a sight to behold; the carny folk weren't used to youngins running around on *their* side of the business. Regardless, I indulged her, and whatever attraction she wanted to explore each night, I couldn't tell her no. Believe it or not, there was something comforting and safe about the Carnival—a real feeling of family and camaraderie. Which is not to say I let my guard down in any way, but there was something in the vibe of everything that put me, I don't know, at peace?

A few hours before opening, Sis had already hightailed it to the Big Tent, eager to doll herself up for her act. She was set to kick things off and wanted to look her best when the lights came up. We'd promised her we'd be in the audience as soon as Nancy finished her bite to eat. But it wasn't long before Buster was pounding on the trailer door with word that Tophat wanted to meet with us. Chickie panicked, glancing in the mirror and fretting she wasn't quite done up enough to pull off her full "Mommy Fortuna" routine. She pleaded with Buster for a few more minutes, but he just shook his head and shrugged. "Nope. When the Man calls, you don't keep him waiting."

"But I'm not saying no!" she whined. "I'm just saying I need a half an hour. Twenty minutes, tops."

"Sweet little chicken head," he sang, "I'm sorry, but that's not how Tophat does things. When he says now, he means *now*."

Chapter Seven

Chickie sulked and was all sourpuss face. I thought I saw an actual tear escape her eye.

Buster narrowed his eyes at me. "And you?"

I pointed a finger at my chest. "Me? What about me?"

"Are you gonna bellyache, too?"

"No. I have no issue," I said, shrugging my shoulders.

Buster was put off by my nonchalant reaction and raised his hand in the air as if to silence me. Only I was finished speaking, so his act of authority was for naught. "The rugrat stays. Leave the kid with someone."

"Um... no. Absolutely not," I protested. "Nancy doesn't leave my sight."

Buster pursed his thin lips together and made a huffing noise in his throat that sounded like an agitated puppy. He stared at me for a few seconds, lowering his head in as much of a condescending manner as he could muster, but when he realized I was not budging, he exhaled noisily and grumbled, "Fine! Your asses better follow me close!"

I ushered Nancy out of the trailer and looked back at Chickie. She was exasperated and threw her hands up wildly in the air. "I... I don't... I don't see how I can..."

"Hush!" I warned. "You've been practicing for days. You're gonna be fine. Let's just do this and get it over with."

She groaned again and slumped her shoulders forward. "Fine. Fine," she relented. "But I'm not happy."

"I don't think the Carny Boss cares much for your happiness when he has a show to run."

Chickie rolled her eyes, and I made my way out of the trailer, spotting Nancy already trotting ahead of me, sticking right to Buster's heels. She quickened her step, slipping to his side opposite the cane, and reached her little hand out to hold his. For a moment, he seemed reluctant, but then he took it, and she started swinging their hands back and forth with a playful sway. "Alright, alright, take it easy, kiddo," he scolded, though she just let out a carefree giggle, filling the air with her laughter.

Buster opened Tophat's trailer door with an ominous creaking sound. All was quiet and still. Candles of all different shapes and sizes flickered in the darkness, and Nancy innocently gasped, "Oh, so spooky," when she tip-toed up the steps.

Buster knitted his bushy eyebrows and mumbled, "Good luck." It sounded more like a warning than encouragement.

Before I could question him, a voice boomed from within, and Chickie nearly jumped out of her skin. "Have a seat!" Tophat said, his arms outstretched, and beckoned us to approach his table in the corner of the trailer. We took a collective, albeit tentative, step forward as the door slammed shut behind us, and as it did, I inhaled so deeply it was as if the very air had been sucked out of my chest, and I was fighting to find it. I nearly choked as my hand instinctively shot up to my throat to make sure I was, in fact, still breathing.

Chapter Seven

I knew that feeling—the heaviness, the artificial atmosphere. I felt it before. I lived it before. It was the feeling of a glamour—a very powerful spell that masks reality and the perception of the human eye. Nancy and Chickie gave no indication that they felt it, and that was probably for the best, 'cause I could feel that the entire carnival was under some kind of spell, some kind of glamour, even Winnie the snake.

The trailer glowed with candle light, but for some reason I couldn't tell if there were actual flames dancing on the wicks. The light looked unnatural, like it had a flameless, otherworldly origin. Rays from the full moon tried poking their way through the curtains, and the scent of cedar and lavender permeated the air around us, giving a sweet but smoky aroma. It reminded me of being in the woods on an autumn night, and the farmer who lives in a cottage deep within the forest is burning a brilliant fire to keep warm in the cold. And yet, I saw no censer, no incense burner.

The walls were adorned with oil paintings mounted in ornate frames. A playful image of a lion at a circus hung behind where Tophat sat, and next to it was a large wooden bookcase filled to the brim with books, but every time I tried to see what the titles were, the candle light seemed to flash in another direction, and it was too dark to read anything on the spines.

And there, in the center of the trailer, sat the man himself—Gideon T. Solwood—Tophat Trent! Tophat had the look of a fella who'd seen the world and could play it like a fiddle—the devil's favorite instrument. He was dressed to the nines in a sharp black-and-gray suit with silver pinstripes, and his black, slicked-back dark hair peeked out from under his black satin top hat. It cast just enough shadow over his gray eyes to give them that extra flash of mystery. Goosebumps bloomed on the flesh of my arms when I thought about his eyes—how they raged with a storm when I first saw them on stage. Those eyes of his had a way of making you feel like he was onto your deepest secrets—and maybe willing to use 'em to his advantage. Quickly, I mentally cemented myself and realized I had to keep my guard up. That still didn't save me from being distracted by his handsome movie star looks! Oh, boy! Was Tophat a looker! He was all sharp lines and strong angles with broad shoulders that filled out that suit like it was stitched right onto him.

"Ladies!" Tophat gushed with a smile as his white teeth shone in the darkness. His voice was low and powerful, rolling over us like the rumble of a train. "I'm so glad we can finally sit down together and get the formalities out of the way. I take it you've been enjoying your stay with us?"

Chickie and I both nodded, and Tophat gestured for us to take our seats across from him. We obliged and Nancy clambered into my lap. The circular table in front of us was draped with a delicate black lace doily, and at its center sat a large crystal ball nestled in a golden base with intricate arms that curled around it like something

Chapter Seven

alive. My eyes were immediately drawn to the crystal—it seemed to glow from within, casting a strange light across the room. As Tophat leaned in to speak to Nancy, the crystal's shadows fell across his face, making it look like he was cloaked in shifting clouds. "Are you enjoying my carnival too, Little Crow?" he asked her.

Her green eyes sparkled when he spoke to her, and she nodded emphatically. Her head bounced up and down, making her hair dance all around her face. Her reaction pleased him, and he smiled wider (which I didn't think was possible but apparently was).

"So," he began clapping his hands together, "I hear the rumors and rumblings of from whence you two came, but I'm going to be honest—none of that matters to me." He picked up a small stack of papers in front of him and tapped it against the tabletop. "Here at the World, we're all misfits and outlaws of our own design. I don't care. I want good workers who can get the job done and keep the crowds coming back for more. Do you think you have what it takes to fill my tents?"

Chickie nodded just as emphatically as Nancy had, but I gave a curt bow of my head. Nancy mimicked Chickie's dramatics, and Tophat chuckled. "Well, I can say this for sure, the Little Crow *definitely* has the job."

Chickie laughed harder, but it was a nervous laugh—a forced laugh. One that I knew Tophat had picked up on.

He looked down at his papers and flipped through a couple of the pages as he hummed. "That's a very interesting name."

Chickie wrung her hands anxiously. The tension coming off her was palpable. Poor thing looked like she was going to either faint or bust out into tears. "It was from my…"

"No, no," he said interrupting her. "No explanation needed, my dear."

"Oh," she said with a pop of her mouth.

"I hear you're looking to replace Vesper St. Clair as the new psychic?"

"Yes. Yes, sir," she said, shifting uncomfortably in the chair.

He snickered under his breath at her formality, but his eyes remained focused on his papers. "I've reassigned Vesper to the Cooch."

"Cooch?" Nancy squeaked. "Wuss that, Mommy?"

"It's a silly show. You wouldn't like it," I coaxed. "Girls play tricks on boys with stinky flowers."

Nancy crinkled her nose. "Eww, gross."

"Yes, it can be rather vile sometimes," Tophat said with a sly smile. He tapped the papers on the table again and looked at Chickie. "So, I'd like to see what you got. Consider this your formal audition." He reached underneath the table and pulled out a deck of Tarot cards.

Chickie straightened up in the chair and took a deep breath. "I don't do the cards," she said flatly, and the lilt in her voice at the word "cards" gave her nervousness away.

Chapter Seven

Tophat tipped his head down curiously. "Oh? A fortune teller who doesn't read? Will you be scrying?"

Chickie's face twisted.

"Using the crystal ball," I whispered, and I noticed Tophat glance in my direction for a split second.

Chickie smiled brightly. Her perfectly straight teeth were almost as white as Tophat's, and the way her red lips curled up on top of her pink gums looked freakish against the gloomy flames and the subtle illumination of the crystal ball. "Well, kind sir," she began in that Eastern European accent she put on when we were on the train, "I am Mommy Fortuna, and I do not require cards to see what's in your heart."

Tophat leaned forward a little in his chair, and his eyebrows raised with curiosity. "Do tell, Mommy," he said smoothly, almost seductively.

"Your hands. Let me see. Let me see the lines of your past, and present, and future."

Tophat stretched his arms across the table, and Chickie took one of his hands in hers. "Ah..." she sang. "The lines on your palms hold a story, one that stretches far beyond today and back to the day you were born. The hand is like a road map—each crease, each curve, a signpost in the journey of your life." She traced a finger up and down the lines of his palm.

"And what do you see, Mommy?"

"Why is he calling Auntie Chickie 'Mommy,' Mommy? She not his mommy!" Nancy said.

"Shhh," I hushed her.

Chickie glanced angrily in my direction, and I mouthed a "sorry." She continued, "Here, we have the life line, wrapping its way down the side. This tells me not just about the length of life but its quality, the trials you may face, and the vitality within."

"Trials?" he asked, playing along. "What do you mean by that?"

"Life is not without its hardships, kind sir. You've traveled long and hard to be where you are, and I see some bumps in the road ahead, but I have a sense that you will prevail."

"Prevail?" he asked, and he sounded skeptical, unsure.

Chickie ignored his question and changed the subject. "You see this?" She pointed to another line in his hand. "This is your head line. Intelligence, curiosity, dreams, and decision-making rest here. Strong and steady, or faint and meandering—it all speaks volumes about how you approach life."

"And how will I do that?"

Chickie paused and closed her eyes like she was getting a message from another realm. "You approach the world very carefully. Very, very ... cautiously. Your head line is strong, but there is something in your life right now that makes you second guess yourself—makes you self-conscious and unsure." She stopped again, looked at the ceiling and hummed for a moment. "But I feel... I see that you will eventually make the

Chapter Seven

right decision. Even though some of the people in your life will hate it, it will be right for *you*."

"Hmmm..." Tophat hummed like he was not convinced. Like he was not impressed.

Chickie felt it too, and I could sense the panic rising in her chest. She was blowing it, and she knew it. So, she shifted gears and gently caressed Tophat's hand with feather light touches. She propped her upper body on the table, moved forward, and pressed her elbows into the sides of her chest so that the cleavage of her bosom was more pronounced. "Your heart line pulses with tales of love, loss, passion, and companionship," she resumed. "There's much it can say about the relationships you've cherished — or the ones still waiting in your future."

"Tell me about that," he said. "Tell me about my future love."

She tilted her head closer to him. "You run hot with desire. Very hot. And soon you will find a woman who will match the fires of your loins."

He smirked. "The fires of my loins, you say?" Then he released his hand from her grip and sat back in his chair. His sudden movement made Chickie sit back as well. She folded her hands in her lap and swallowed hard.

"Too much?" she whimpered. "I... I could change it up if you..."

"No, no," he interrupted. "That won't be necessary." He turned to me. "And what about you, Jane? Jane Crowe and Little Crowe."

"I Nancy!" Nancy bellowed in childish offense.

Tophat laughed. "That's right. I forgot!" he teased. "Jane and *Nancy* Crowe. So, I hear that you haven't quite landed on your role here at the World."

I shook my head.

"You have no preference either which way?"

"Um... not really. I guess," I muttered.

"Well," he scoffed, "if you want to stay, you know you're going to have to pull your weight around here. Especially with the Little Crow in tow."

"Hey! I not a..." Nancy began.

"Crow. I know. *Nancy*," he mock corrected.

"I understand, Mr. Solwood. It's just that I'm not sure if I have any skills that would be appropriate for the carnival."

Tophat tilted his head, giving me a smile that was equal parts patience and mischief. "Oh, don't you worry, kid," he replied, "We all start out thinkin' that way. But there's a place for everyone here, whether you got a knack for a crowd, a talent for makin' folks laugh, or just a bit of *fire* in your spirit." He thought for a moment. "I have an idea. Let's make this an even steven square-off. Audition for me now. For Vesper's spot."

Chickie's face went frantic, and she nudged my calf with her foot as if begging me to say no. "I... I... I don't know. I don't think I..." I stammered.

"Don't think you could what? Put on a good performance? Convince me you can see my future? Read the cards?" he questioned.

Chapter Seven

Not those cards, I said in my head, and immediately Tophat looked down at the Tarot deck on the table then back up like he had heard me, like he had read my mind. A knowing look swept across his face, and his eyes stormed under the brim of his hat.

"What kind of deck *do* you have?" he asked out loud, and Chickie's face contorted with confusion.

"You wouldn't know it," I answered flatly. "It's not a popular one."

"Mommy likes to play with cards. They're funny looking," Nancy chimed.

"You never told me you read the Tarot cards!" Chickie said with surprise.

"It... it... it's not a big deal or anything. Jeez," I said, feigning annoyance and trying desperately to sweep the topic under the carpet. "And I don't do no palm reading either."

"But you *know*, don't you?" he said, and his voice felt like cold fingers wiggling inside the back of my skull. I couldn't be sure if he said that out loud or in my head, but either way, my eyes cast down in acknowledgment.

Tophat glanced at the hazy crystal ball then back at me. "The ball," he said jutting his chin out in its direction.

"I never..."

"Just look at it. Tell me what you see."

Chickie forced a puff of air out of her mouth, making her lips vibrate. "She's not gonna see nothing!"

Tophat ignored her. "And if you don't see anything, then just tell me what I want to hear. I'm the paying customer. You're the madame. Give it a shot," he urged.

He reached out his hands across the table, so I handed Nancy over to Chickie and accepted his grasp. Touching his hands was like sending a bolt of lightning up my arms and throughout my body. There was an instant surge of something electric, something unnatural, yet something familiar. Instinctively, I pulled back, but he gripped my hands tighter and secured them on the table. I couldn't move them away even if I tried with all my might.

Take a look, I heard him say, but his mouth never moved, and no words escaped his lips, yet it was his voice—distinct and clear, echoing in my head with the low hum of music faintly playing somewhere in the distance. At first, I chalked it up to the calliope of the Midway greeting the early customers of the night, but the more I strained my ears to make out the melody, the more I realized the music was coming from somewhere in the trailer but not. It was beyond the trailer. Beyond the Midway. Beyond the time and space of human flesh and bone. Beyond the oceans of blood and bile. I closed my eyes and shook my head rapidly, afraid of my own thoughts. Why did I think that? Why was I hearing this sweet tune that both haunted and thrilled me at the same time?

Look, Tophat said again directly into my head.

Chapter Seven

I opened my eyes, and my gaze was held hostage in the depths of the orb. A gray storm churned like the one in Tophat's eyes, and I stared, mystified at the sights I saw. Smoke swirled from within like fog gloom over a somber cemetery, and in its misty hands, images began to appear—began to reveal themselves to me. I sank into the pictures. Sank into the feeling of being stretched across time and space. Stretched across the boundaries of flesh and bone. Drowned within the oceans of blood and bile. And it was all so glorious and serene. The way the sky felt as I stood in the center of the cosmos surrounded by millions of stars. Yet they weren't stars. They were the names of beings I had never heard of before, and their ancient breath sang to me a discordant song that filled my ears and filled my heart.

Their mournful cries were so heavy, and I ached when I realized they were speaking to me. They told me they were lost and alone and wanted to come home. And I wept with the stars. I felt their pain and anguish when they begged me to help bring them home.

And suddenly in the cosmos, they began to gather together until all the stars connected into one long line that stretched across the past and the present and the future. I stared at the line until it started to shift and move and spread apart like it was opening up. When I looked longer and harder, I realized the stars were no longer stars, but they were women holding hands—a woman with long white hair and black tattoo markings all over her body, a woman with red hair and green eyes reading from an ancient book, a woman with black hair and gray eyes just like Tophat's. So many of them. So many I didn't know (but knew). So many I couldn't see (but felt).

And like the shifting of a dream, giant dead tree limbs clawed through the bodies of the women from the other side of our known dimension, tearing through them. The sky wept with their blood as something tried anxiously to emerge. Like being born. Like coming home. And in the stormy, bloody horror of it all, I watched. I stared. And there on the other side of the tear in the sky that had ripped open the cosmos, I saw a light. It was dim, but I could make out a scene. There on the other side was a child. A little boy with scruffy white hair tinged with blood it almost looked pink. He was a baby, younger than Nancy, but the words of the women's song told me he was much, much older. Ancient.

Every time I blinked my eyes to clear my vision, the boy aged—grew up right in front of me as each second blipped away. His years were mere seconds, instantaneously warping him to adulthood. Beyond adulthood. Beyond the time and space of human flesh and bone. Beyond the oceans of blood and bile. Beyond that which is forever cast and forever set. Ancient. Eternal. Trapped in a mortal shell.

Tophat.

"Well, Jane!" Chickie cried, and the shrill sound of her voice pulled me back out of the

Chapter Seven

center of the crystal ball. "Tell us! We're waiting to hear what you see."

I pulled my hands from Tophat's and sat back in the chair. The music stopped like how the record scratched off my first night here, and everything went quiet in my head. Slowly, the sounds of the carnival in full swing hung heavy in the air of the spring night, and I knew I was back—back in the trailer, back on this earth. My heart raced and danced so hard, I could feel it tight against my chest. My breaths came fast and heavy.

"Well?" Chickie pressed.

I wasn't sure how to say it all or even if I should. There were no human words that I could have used to describe the images I had seen. I glanced up at Tophat, who had a small grin at the corner of his mouth. He bent his head forward, and as he did, I glanced behind him and caught the title of one of the books on his shelf.

Blodheksa? I read in my mind.

Blood Witch, Tophat responded, but his mouth actually said, "Still with us, Jane?"

I nodded. "I... I saw *you*," I said to him.

"Of course. You're supposed to say that. You're reading *his* fortune!" Chickie blabbered.

I paid her no mind. My eyes were locked with Tophat's. "You," I repeated. "But it wasn't. But it was. You're not who you say you are, are you?"

Chickie stiffened and made a croaking noise in her throat. "Jane!" she admonished.

"Go on," Tophat said, ignoring her, urging me to continue.

"You're... you're..." I struggled for the words.

"Janey, come on now, this is our prospective boss. You don't want to come off as rude," Chickie said through one side of her mouth.

But Tophat continued to hold my gaze, and in his eyes, the scene from the crystal ball seemed to be repeating. Like it was echoing over and over again.

"You're *them*, aren't you? You're one of the stars. But that can't be. You're *all* of them. All of the stars. All at once."

With that, Chickie sighed an exaggerated sigh and quickly stood up with Nancy astride her hip. "That's it!" she yelled and grabbed my shoulder. "Mr. Solwood, I am so sorry about this. I think Jane just has a little stage fright is all. We apologize for wasting your time in any way. I promise we'll figure something out for her to do as soon as possible."

I stood up and Chickie pushed and pulled me toward the door of the trailer, but Tophat never once took his eyes off me.

Chapter Eight

Thursday, May 25th 1944
The Gentry Brothers' Wonders of the World Carnival
Glenmoor, Ohio
Morning of the Waxing Crescent Moon

The carny folk gathered in the cookhouse every morning, filing into that battered, brown canvas tent like clockwork. It looked as if it had seen a few wars itself, patched in places and downright threadbare in others. Dust clung to my ankles, making 'em itch something fierce, and I'd catch myself scratching like a mutt with fleas. Nancy had it just as rough, coughing on smoke from the sizzling pans. Breakfast was a steady stream of bacon, eggs, and pitch-black coffee. Now and again, we'd get toast or potatoes on the side, but if the performers had managed a quick trip into town the night before, sometimes they'd bring back a jar of honey or jam. That little taste of sweetness would make the rounds, giving everyone a reason to smile. Most ate inside, but I took my plate out to one of the picnic tables in the open air, where the morning sun was gentle, and I could catch a decent breath.

Discomfort gnawed at me that morning, and it wasn't just the smoke and dust swirling in the air. Nearly a week had passed since Chickie and I had tried our hand at impressing Tophat, and yet, we hadn't heard so much as a whisper about our fate. The carny folks' stares felt sharper by the day, piercing through me and, I sensed, Nancy too. Every glance seemed filled with disdain, like they thought of us as nothing more than dead weight—freeloaders taking up space and reaping the benefits without lifting a finger. Every snigger in our direction was fueled with disgust, and I was starting to fear the worst. What if they lashed out at us? What if they found out why I was there and contacted someone from Aleister's group? My head went to all kinds of dark places, and I wished Tophat would make some kind of decision soon.

Sis and Chickie trailed right on our heels as we stepped out of the tent, Nancy clinging close to me. Vesper sat at one of the old picnic tables with Zora Heart, the Tattooed Lady. Zora was a vision that seemed plucked straight from a storybook and painted with a sailor's dreams. Her skin was a living tapestry, every inch covered in intricate artwork that told tales of love, loss, and adventure. A pair of black birds fluttered across her collarbones, their wings seemingly in midflight. The image immediately caught my attention, drawing me into the story of her flesh. I

Chapter Eight

wanted to read more. Roses bloomed on her arms, their thorny vines winding down to her wrists, where delicate anchors were etched as if to keep her grounded. A gold head scarf was tied securely at the base of her skull, and a squiggly ink spot peeked out at the side of her temple, making me wonder if she even had hair at all.

Both Zora and Vesper looked troubled as all get-out, their faces drawn tight with worry. Catching sight of us, Sis gave Chickie a sharp nudge with her elbow, her chin tilting subtly toward Vesper. Chickie followed the gesture, locking eyes with the blonde bombshell. Vesper's face lit up like the midway at dusk, her lips parting into a nervous but relieved smile. She waved us over, her hand fluttering in frantic little arcs, her whole frame practically vibrating with urgency. Whatever was on her mind, it wasn't good news.

"What's cookin'?" Sis asked when we all set our plates down at the table. She reached into her plate and brought a thick piece of crispy bacon to her lips. "How's the Cooch treatin' ya, V?"

Vesper drummed her fingers on the wooden tabletop. Her big blue eyes looked upward, glazed with a fine layer sheen of almost-tears. I could tell she was holding them in.

Sensing something was off, Chickie asked, "What's wrong, Vesper?"

Vesper drummed harder, more agitatedly until Zora finally reached over and grabbed Vesper's hand in hers, arresting the sound. "It's

Tina," Zora whispered, and she looked over her shoulder. "She hasn't come back."

Sis took a hearty gulp of her coffee and nearly choked on it mid-way down. "Wait! What? What do you mean Tina hasn't *come back*?"

"She went up into town a few nights ago after one of the shows, and … nothing," Vesper answered in a faraway voice, like she wasn't really there with us.

"Are you sure she didn't just leave?" I interjected. "Was there someone that could have come to pick her up, or was she unhappy? Did she meet somebody? Was someone sweet on her and maybe swept her off her feet?"

"I've never known Serpentina to have any love interest, come to think of it," Zora pondered.

"Yeah, no," Vesper agreed. "Tina is pretty much destined to be a spinster. Reserved. Disinterested in romance."

The crunch of bacon in my ears was a good distraction, muffling the thoughts tumbling through my mind. Tina? Disinterested in love? No itch for affection, no longing for companionship, no hunger for… well, anything like that? The idea felt completely foreign. I couldn't wrap my head around the thought of a life spent without someone by my side, whoever he might be, wherever he might be hiding out there. I had thought I found a partner in Aleister, but that charm wore off quickly. Still, I knew love was in the cards for me, just maybe not now. But to think of never? It was strange, to say the least.

Chapter Eight

"The only person sweet on Tina is Hill McCrory," Zora said, her voice even lower than before.

"The sheriff?" Chickie blurted at full volume, to which we all "shushed" her instantly.

Hot tears tumbled from Vesper's eyes. "Tina had no reason to just leave like that. She wouldn't do that to me. We've been bunkies for the last two years—she'da told me *something*... anything! She loves this place, and she'd never just pick up and go. Not without me and especially not without Winnie! Hell, I think she loves that snake more than anyone or anything."

"I don't like snakes," Nancy grumbled in between bites of toast.

I stroked her dirty blonde hair back from her face. "I know, baby. That's okay."

"Why she crying, Mommy?" she innocently asked.

"She's not, baby. She just got some dust in her eye."

Nancy furrowed her brow. "I don't like the dust," she groaned again and went back to munching on her breakfast.

"Why'd she go off into town in the first place anyways?" Chickie asked.

Zora huffed and rolled her eyes. "It's something we do from time to time. Ya know, to get away from it all. Change of scenery. Cut loose. It's not out of the ordinary for someone to..."

"How long?" Sis interrupted.

"Since Sunday," Vesper said.

"Did you tell Tophat?" I asked, glancing over my shoulder.

Vesper shook her head. "Buster," she said, her voice low.

"And?" Sis pressed, leaning in with a glint of urgency in her eye.

Vesper huffed. "Well, what's he gonna say, Sister? He gave me the usual 'she must be gone' sob story. Then he went on his whole spiel, griping about how 'you can't have a snake without a charmer.' He was steamed, like she'd just up and disappeared to make his life harder. Not a lick of concern, mind you! Just ticked he'd have to hustle for a new act." She paused, her face troubled. "But I swear, I know Tina. She wouldn't pull a stunt like that. It's not her style."

Chickie leaned close to my ear. "Maybe this is your shot, Janey. Fill the snake charmer's shoes!"

I pulled away from her, disgusted by her remark, and kept my focus on the conversation about Tina.

"Does Tophat know?" I asked.

Vesper shrugged. "Heck if I know."

Zora reached her arm out and brought Vesper's head to her shoulder in a comforting way. "I know for a fact that Tina told Tophat to fuck off when it came to McCrory," she said. "She told him 'that's what the Cooch is for.' But apparently the good sheriff has a thing for snakes."

"Wait! Do you think that's why Tophat put you on the Cooch, Vesper?" I exclaimed.

Chapter Eight

Nancy scrunched her button-nose up into a little ball in the center of her face like she had smelled something awful. "Stinky flowers!" she bellowed to no one in particular, and we all laughed at her remark.

Vesper shrugged again. "Heck if I know. Since I've been on the Cooch, McCrory hasn't set one foot inside the tent, so I doubt it."

"Tina was adamant that McCrory stay away from her," Zora continued.

"And Tophat wasn't hearing it," Sis added to the round-table deduction.

"Apparently not," Zora confirmed.

"But was it enough to make her split town? I mean, how far did it actually get with the sheriff and Tina?" Sis asked.

"Not as far as he would have liked it," Vesper said.

"What's his deal, anyway?" I asked. "If he's such a pious and godly man, why on earth is he sniffing around the World? Would a pious and godly man be so open in his overtures to the serpent queen?"

"Overtures?" Sis sneered. "Oh, I see you're one of them educated broads, aren't you?"

"Get bent!" I retorted. "I'm being serious. If he's making his intentions known out in the open, in front of crowds of people... there's gotta be something else going on."

Zora shifted nervously. She looked over her shoulder and then crouched in close. "Look, I hear McCrory is getting heat from the mayor on those unsolveds. I hear McCrory has an inside man who's leaving him breadcrumbs like little ole Hansel."

"Or Gretel," Vesper interjected.

"Exactly. Now, whether those breadcrumbs lead back to Tina, I ain't the one to say. But he's convinced that the story of the Shadow Man isn't a story at all."

"Or Shadow *Lady*," Vesper added.

"Yep. And that Shadow Man or Lady is here. Right in the World. Doing their dastardly deeds of necromancy and making shit real hard for him to solve."

"Oooohhh, she say a bad woooord," Nancy sang through bites of egg.

"Sorry, sugar," Zora apologized.

"So, you're saying Tina's a rat?" Chickie asked.

Zora shook her head. "No. But McCrory didn't have his sights set on her for no reason."

"'Cause he's a pious and godly man," I said.

"Uh huh," Zora said, and she took a swig of her coffee.

We all sat back in silence and continued eating our food. Vesper was clearly worried about Tina's whereabouts as the tears seemed to hold steady at the base of her eyelids. Every now and then she would swat at them, and the gentle flicking of her hand reminded me so much of Momma and the last day I had seen her. It made me uneasy to think that she was being surveilled by Crowley's group, and for a second, I feared she might even crack under the pressure and give up my location.

Chapter Eight

Where would I go then? What would I do? I knew that as long as I had Nancy and the Thoth Deck, I was always going to be hunted. They would most likely kill me, take back the cards, kidnap Nancy and...

"Do you think the sheriff kidnapped Tina?" Chickie wailed. The loud shrill of her voice snapped everyone out of their individual daydream, even Nancy.

Sis kicked Chickie from under the table and shushed her again. "Keep your voice down, Chickadee. You never know who's lurking."

"Oh, and a-lurking I will be," a voice called from behind me. Buster steadied himself on his cane as his wobbly gait brought him closer to the table. Vesper and Zora eyed each other, and Sis turned her head up to the sky, pretending she didn't notice him there. "Ya know, you kids best watch what you're talking about out in the open like this and in such a free manner."

"Oh! Hello, Buster!" Sis feigned surprise. "I didn't see you there!"

"Yeah, yeah. Go on with your plots and schemes. Just remember to *try* to keep your traps shut. Especially about things you know nothing of."

"And *you* do? You know about Shadow Men and Ladies?" Chickie chirped.

Everyone froze as Buster fixed Chickie with a hard stare. It was the kind of glare that sent a chill through the air, letting her know she was treading on thin ice and had better watch her tongue. He opened his suit jacket, reached into the interior pocket, and pulled out two envelopes. He handed one to me first, then to Chickie. "From the Boss Man. He finally made up his damn mind on what he wants you to do."

Chickie clutched the envelope tightly and looked at me with a wild expression of excitement. She squealed and stamped her feet into the dirt, causing small plumes of dust to rise up under the picnic table.

"Hold your horses there, Sassafras," Buster said flatly, "or you're gonna charge right out the gates."

I held the envelope up, feeling its weight and tracing the letters etched on the front. *Jane*. But it didn't feel like my name. I read the letters, clear as day, but something in me recoiled, as if another voice murmured the name back to me, speaking to a part of myself I didn't even know. Somewhere, a low rumble echoed in the distance. My fingers smoothed over the thick calligraphy, each letter sharp, deliberate, the ink a deep crimson, almost wet to the touch. It looked as if Tophat himself had pricked his thumb and let the blood flow, swirling in wide, ornate loops. The *J* and *A* danced in bold curves, the *N* sliced with a keen edge, and the final *E* curled like blood-red lips daring me to draw closer. I couldn't look away. My head swam with a feeling of fullness—of near intoxication.

Chapter Eight

"Beggars can't be choosers, ladies," Buster crooned. He bid farewell to everyone at the table and sauntered down the dirt field.

Chickie could barely contain her enthusiasm as she elbowed me in the side. "C'mon, Janey! Let's do it together!"

"Oh, girls! The moment of truth!" Sis sang.

My hands twitched a little—not a full-on anxiety shake, but I certainly couldn't deny there were nerves jolting through my fingers. Carefully, I tore the top edge across and fished for the paper within. Chickie, so juiced up with excitement, ripped the envelope open like a savage and shrieked as she pulled out Tophat's letter.

"Now, now," Zora admonished, "don't get too excited. Ole Tophat might be giving you your walking papers."

Chickie pressed the letter to her chest and sighed. "I highly doubt that, Zora. I'm pretty confident I got *something*." She looked at me. "Ready?"

I nodded and opened the paper up. The words washed over my eyes, but the actual meaning didn't register in my head because Chickie began reading hers aloud. "'Dear Miss Sassafras.'" She sighed and pressed the letter to her chest again in a dramatic way. "Oh, so formal!"

"He tends to be like that sometimes!" Vesper exclaimed.

"'Welcome to the Big Show, kid,'" Chickie continued. "'Consider this your official invite to the inner circle of the strange and the spectacular. After careful consideration, we think you've got just the right stuff to bring a little extra shine to our cooch show."

Chickie stopped abruptly. Her face darkened, and her smile turned sour with confusion.

"Cooch?" Vesper asked. "I thought you auditioned for the Fortune Teller."

"I did," Chickie spat as I froze, caught red-handed. The second Vesper said "Fortune Teller," the words seemed to leap right off the page in front of me, glaring like they'd been there in bold red ink all along. I didn't need to read much more. Tophat had made me the new Fortune Teller, and I knew that wasn't gonna sit right with Chickie. At the bottom, there was a P.S. addendum. It was written in funny shapes like some kind of familiar symbols. Runes. I stared hard at them, squinting my eyes, trying to remember where I had seen their likes before. The harder I squinted, the shapes began to transform before my eyes so that they were discernable. I heard them say to meet him in his trailer at midnight to discuss the details. *Alone.*

Heard them? How could I have possibly heard written words?

But I did. And they sounded like the title of the book in Tophat's trailer. They sounded like it said "Blodheksa." Like a kid with their hand in the cookie jar, I quickly folded up the letter and shoved it under my thigh, hoping no one else had noticed. My heart jumped in my chest, and my mind raced in all different directions.

Why did he want to see me at that time by myself?

Chapter Eight

"Well, go on..." Zora urged.

Chickie took a deep breath and continued reading, "'The Cooch is no ordinary number—it's a fine art, a showstopper for those who can draw a crowd and keep 'em coming back for more. You'll need to be a mix of savvy and sass, my little Sassafras, with enough mystery to make 'em sweat a little. The role calls for charm, boldness, and a healthy dose of guts. But I think you'll do just fine. Report to Vesper immediately; not only will she be your new bunkie, but she'll get you started on the ropes. I suggest you pack a good smile and leave your jitters at the door—this gig's not for the faint-hearted, but if you play your cards right, you might just find yourself at home among us carny folk. So, here's to making a splash. The lights are hot, the stakes are high, and there's nothing quite like the thrill of the carnival. Yours in the Big Tent,

Tophat Trent.'"

Vesper lowered her head at the news of being paired up with Chickie. "Tina was my bunkie, though," she said forlornly. *I guess Tophat doesn't think she's coming back*, I heard her voice say. It was her troubled inside thought, and it came to me loud and clear. I gave her a puzzled look, but she kept her focus on the plate of food in front of her.

Violently, Chickie crunched the letter up in her fist. "The Cooch? The *Cooch*?" she repeated in disbelief. "I... I... I don't understand. What impression did I give to Tophat that I was suited for the Cooch?"

Sis wrapped her arm around Chickie's shoulder lovingly. "Aw honey, take it as a compliment. He musta saw somethin' in ya. He musta had one of his visions or something and…"

Zora angrily kicked Sis under the table and gave her a stern look. Chickie was too distraught to notice, but I sure wasn't.

"But I can't do it!" she wailed. "I don't want to!"

"Sweetie, if that's what Tophat says," Zora tried to coax. "It's either that or…"

"Hit the bricks," Sis finished.

"Besides, it's not all that bad," Zora continued. "There are rules, ya know."

Chickie let out a loud huff, sending a stray tuft of her feather-light hair fluttering around her face. "Oh, Jane," she sneered with a slight edge, "nearly slipped my mind. What about you? What job did Tophat hand *you* on a silver platter?"

I shifted my leg subtly, just enough to cover the letter, tucking it tight beneath me. The last thing I needed was her snatching it up, reading it right here, and kicking up a colossal fuss. "Oh… I… it's… um…" I stuttered.

"Well… spit it out, girl!" Sis complained.

"Spit out, Mommy," Nancy said putting in her two cents.

"Excuse me, ma'am!" I scolded. "Mouth closed tight."

"Really, Jane? Are you going to make us beg or what?" Zora added.

Sweat pooled in my palms, making them clammy and uncomfortable. I forced a smile,

Chapter Eight

trying to play it off. "It's no big deal, really," I muttered, hoping my voice didn't sound as shaky as I felt.

"Sure it is! Tell us!" Sis bellowed, dropping her voice down to her normal manly octave.

The sound startled me, and I looked at Chickie with a pained expression. "Fortune Teller," I mumbled, and Chickie gasped with doubt.

"You're joking, right?"

"No," I answered solemnly. "He said he wanted me to be the new Fortune Teller." I paused, trying to gauge her reaction. "And Nancy and I are going to move into Zora's trailer." I paused again, but she was a blank canvas, a block of stone, a wall of ice. "As soon as possible."

Sis propped her head in her hands. "Really? I thought for sure you'd be going into the old psychic trailer."

"No one's lived in that old thing for years, Sister," Vesper said.

"But it's a trailer!" Sis retorted. "Why keep it abandoned? I mean, we've been traveling for so long, it's practically dead weight now. Now that we have a new psychic, doesn't it make sense to put the psychic in there?"

"I heard Buster say that they're using it for extra storage or something," Zora added.

Chickie's eyes flared, a mix of envy and pure indignation sparking like fireworks. "You?" she practically howled. "The Fortune Teller? Oh, that's rich! I can't believe this—this is downright ridiculous!"

Zora's sudden movement startled me, but I was grateful for the distraction. She extended her arm like a queen granting a favor, her smile as warm as the morning sun. "Well, then," she declared, her voice carrying just enough cheer to cut through the tension. "Seems to me we ought to get my new bunkie and Baby Crow all set up!"

Her words had a finality that silenced Chickie mid-rant, though the sour look on Chickie's face said she wasn't done with her gripes. Zora's wide-eyed glance in my direction, quick as a flash, told me all I needed to know — it was time to make tracks. I pushed myself up slowly, careful not to draw more attention, and slid the letter from Tophat down the front of my dress. The paper felt hot against the flesh of my soft bosom, like it was searing itself into me, marking me as its own.

"I not a baby!" Nancy huffed.

"No, sugar, you certainly are not! Now, you and Mommy come follow me to your new trailer. Oh, isn't this so exciting!"

I adjusted my shoulders, trying to act natural, and flashed a tight-lipped smile. "Lead the way," I said, eager to escape the boiling pot of Chickie's jealousy.

Nancy snaked her way around the picnic table, and I made a move to gather our plates up to be taken to the dishwasher. Vesper put up a hand and shook her head to say, "I got it." It was obvious that everyone just wanted me removed from the situation before Chickie got any more heated. I nodded a thanks to Vesper, and as I

Chapter Eight

walked passed Chickie, I could practically feel her glare of contempt burning holes right into the back of my head.

When I reached her, Zora grabbed my hand and swung it back and forth excitedly. "There's so much to do! We'll go pick you out a costume in the Big Tent and get you and the little one nice and settled. And of course you're going to want to get acquainted with our neighbors."

I picked Nancy up and swung her on my hip. "Neighbors? What about Nancy?"

"Don't you worry. I'll explain everything. There's a reason Tophat made y'all bunk with me!"

We turned to walk away, and Zora blew kisses over her shoulder to our friends at the table. "*Au revoir, mes amours.*"

"You're not French, Zora. You're from Texas for Christsake!" Sis joked.

"Yeah, yeah," she shot back. "Have fun with Vesper, Chickie. Don't let her get too fresh with you! Fare thee well, friends."

They grumbled their goodbyes, but in the din, it was obvious Chickie's voice was absent from the words of parting. I wasn't quite sure if she still considered me a friend.

Chapter Nine

Thursday, May 25th 1944
The Gentry Brothers' Wonders of the World Carnival
Glenmoor, Ohio
Evening of the Waxing Crescent Moon

Zora took me "shopping" in the backstage area of the Big Tent. That's where the costumes and props were stored for the performers, and when someone left a position (or in Tina's case—disappeared), their belongings that were left behind became community property for the next person. Some of the time, the carnies would go up into town and, with whatever working money they had, would buy their own supplies. Most of the time, they raided the reserves backstage. Vesper had returned all of her Fortune Teller attire, so there was much for me to choose from. Zora pointed out all the scarves and dresses and head pieces and costume jewelry that Vesper had used. There were even some pieces from a girl named Rocket who came before Vesper and a girl named Persimmon who came before Rocket.

Chapter Nine

I came to find out that Zora had been with the World for quite some time—ten years to be exact. At fifteen, she'd run away to the carnival when they were out in Kansas, and she never looked back. She'd been with Tophat since the management had changed hands from his grandfather and great-uncle to him. And she'd seen many acts come and go. As the senior performer, she'd witnessed and had been a part of the all the carnival drama. Heck! Zora had been with the show even before the days of Tophat's right hand man, Buster Blue.

Even so, I wasn't exactly bowled over by the costume selection. That's all they felt like—costumes. They didn't suit my style, didn't speak to me in any real way. As for the prop pieces? Forget it. They felt as lifeless as stage decorations, and I swore to myself that if I was going to do this, I'd do it right. It had to feel genuine, not like some cheap gimmick.

Zora, bless her, understood completely. That didn't surprise me, coming from the woman who was probably the most authentic soul in the whole World. If anyone knew the importance of staying true to yourself, it was her.

She took us back to her trailer. It was a living canvas, much like Zora herself—a dazzling spectacle of artistry and eccentricity. The exterior was painted a rich, glossy black, edged with swirling gold designs that mirrored the intricate patterns on her skin. Bold red lettering above the door read: *Zora Heart, Tattooed Lady*.

Inside smelled of lavender and clove cigarettes. The walls were papered with framed sketches of tattoo designs, some faded with age but lovingly preserved. A small dresser against one wall was crowded with bottles of ink and an assortment of antique hand mirrors with floral engravings. Tucked among the clutter was a black-and-white photo of Zora with Razor Heart, the rugged-looking sword-swallower, and three little boys.

"You and Razor? Are these your...?"

"We're not married if that's what you were thinking. I mean, don't cha think he'd live with me if we were?"

"But your names? 'Heart?'"

"Um... *Jane Crowe*?" she emphasized, reminding me of our stage monikers.

I put Nancy down, and she scrambled over to the couch. "Those kids? Are they yours?"

"Oh, heavens no!" she roared. "No offense, Nancy," but Nancy was clueless as to what she meant. "No, no... those are the Creed boys. My sister's kids. Their trailer is a few over from us."

"Oh yeah! I've seen those kids hanging around."

"Oh yeah. Tophat uses them as plants. They help get the crowd jazzed up at the flat joints. Like, they'll purposefully let the boys win so the people see just how 'easy' it is, and then they get jammed! It's actually a brilliant strategy." She paused and looked at Nancy. "It makes sense that Tophat made you my bunkie. Nancy will have the

Chapter Nine

boys to be around, and my sister Elaine is awesome for sitting."

I shifted. "Oh, I'm not so sure I feel comfortable leaving Nancy with a stranger."

"I no talk to strangers, Mommy," Nancy chirped.

"I know, baby. And I'm so proud of you for that," I assured her.

"Well, you're gonna have to sooner or later. More sooner than later 'cause you can't have a kid running around your psychic tent!" Zora pointed out.

I huffed and changed the subject. "So, you and Razor... you're a *thing*?"

"Oh yeah! I love that big lug like crazy. Even though he is a pain in my ass most of the time."

I gave a knowing chuckle.

"Oh, Jane Crowe? You got a pain-in-the-ass-man, too?" she sang playfully.

I took in her words. Drank them down. Let them touch my memory in places I had avoided for so long. And the thought washed over me—did I ever really *have* Aleister? I mean, yes, I was a mildly obsessed and enthralled teenager living out her dream. In my mind, I was his and he was mine, and our union brought us together—brought us this perfect little person. But I never really *had* Aleister. He was just a fantasy. And when the smoke cleared, and the veil lifted, and my eyes opened up to the reality of my baby girl, I saw light. Truth. So, no. I had never really had a man, not even a pain-in-the-ass one. I had a wish and a spark and a flash of a moment.

"No," I answered thoughtfully. "Nothing like that."

Just then, as if hearing my words, there was a knock on the trailer door, and Zora answered. A smile a mile wide spread across her face, and she leapt into the caller's arms. Razor gave her a giant smackaroo on her lips and weaved his way into the trailer. "Oh, hey Duke!" she said when she saw the person standing behind him.

"Hello lady," he replied in a deep and soothing voice.

My flesh tingled at the sound of it, and it felt like all thoughts and memories of Aleister at that very moment had vaporized into the ether. I could scarcely remember what I been thinking about just seconds before I heard Duke's voice.

I had seen Duke "The Iron Giant" Steele when he performed in his Strong Man act. He was your typical carnival strong man with broad shoulders and a barrel chest. At 6'5", he was attractive enough where I could understand the appeal he had with the ladies—smoldering dark eyes, impeccable physique, clean-cut chestnut hair, a strong square chin with chiseled cheekbones that made him look like an ancient Greek statue come to life. I mean, sure... if you liked that sort of thing.

But then he opened his mouth to speak.

I heard his voice just then for the very first time. *And I stirred...*

Zora stepped aside, letting him in and cutting off my budding daydream. He had to duck in order to clear the doorway, and as he came into

Chapter Nine

the trailer, in full-bodied view, my cheeks got hot all the way up to the tips of my ears, and I quickly untucked my hair so I could hide it.

"We came to welcome your new bunkies and to congratulate our new Fortune Teller," Razor said with a devilish grin.

Zora's face screwed up. "How did you... oh, let me guess..."

"Sis," she and Razor said at the same time.

Everyone chuckled, and when Duke made eye contact with me for a split second from across the trailer, my head immediately focused on the floor with my eyes cast down.

"Nice to finally meet you, Jane," he said to me.

I was paralyzed. Every muscle in my body locked tight, and my mind churned blank, like a record skipping over the same empty groove. What was wrong with me? Embarrassment burned hot in my cheeks, crawling up my neck like a slow fuse. I wanted to shake myself loose, slap some sense into my frozen limbs, anything to jolt free from the thick tar of my own silence.

The words I needed hovered just out of reach, teasing me, mocking me, as the moment stretched unbearably long. I could feel the eyes around me, their weight pressing heavier and heavier. Why couldn't I just move? Speak? Do something to break this awful stillness?

"Nice to meet you, too," I mumbled. Or at least I think I said that. I can't be sure. I know my brain said it, but whether or not the words actually came out will forever remain a mystery.

Duke took a step forward in my direction, and I sheepishly looked up and smiled. He reached out his hand and gave me a small bouquet of fresh dandelions. "The kids picked them," he said. "For you... and your girl. They're excited to have a new friend in the World."

I heard his words, but I heard *through* them as well. And as his gaze lingered, I knew right away he wasn't really talking about Zora's nephews.

"Th...ank you," I managed to respond. "They're lovely. And I'm sure Nancy is looking forward to getting to know her new playmates, too."

He smiled a closed mouth smile and bit his lower lip. Again, I had to look away from him to break from his stare.

"Well, ladies," Razor said heartily, "we shall see you later tonight. Duke and I have some prepping to do for the show later."

Zora kissed Razor on the cheek, and Duke raised his hand and waved goodbye. When they were gone, I brought the flowers to my nose and inhaled their floral aroma. Zora closed the door and sighed.

"They'll be time enough for all of that," she said.

"Huh? What do you mean? All of what?"

She eyed the flowers at my face. "Ya know, Jane, Duke's been here for a while. He and Razor are the best of friends. I've seen women come and go, and that man never gave anyone a second look. But what I have never seen is Duke Steele coming to call on a newbie with flowers."

"Get bent!" I exclaimed with a huff.

Chapter Nine

Zora went to one of the cabinets above the couch and pulled out a glass vase. She set it on the table and motioned for me to deposit the flowers. "You don't have to play dumb with me, Blondie. I have a sixth sense for these types of things. Don't lie; you can't stand there and tell me you didn't have at least a little bit of a butterfly belly roll."

I smirked. "Maybe."

"The flowers are berry boo-full, Mommy," Nancy remarked.

"Yes. They are, aren't they, honey. Mr. Duke was so kind to give them to us, wasn't he?"

She nodded. "He a nice man. He not a stranger now, right?"

"No, baby, I guess he's not now."

Zora wagged her forefinger in the air and *tsked*. "Too much to do, Jane. We'll have to go up into town tomorrow to get your threads. There's a place I know off the beaten path. I think she'll have just what you're looking for."

"You know a lot of places, don't you?" I said slyly.

"Well, when you've been around the block a few times like I have, you pick up a thing or two."

"Stories, too?"

Zora cocked her head to the side knowingly. Like she knew what I was getting at. The look on her face begged me not to take my line of questioning further.

"Sure," she nodded, "ten years' worth."

"Stories of the Shadow Man?"

Her shoulders slumped forward, and she took a step toward me. "Listen, Janey, I know you're all spooked about Tina going missing. But I promise you, I've seen it happen a hundred times. The carnival life sometimes just does *stuff* to people and makes them do things that might seem out of the ordinary or out of character. It's a strange life we've chosen, and it can sometimes grip its invisible claws into a person's brain."

She wasn't kidding. I knew what she meant. Even in my short time here, I'd felt that tingle rush up my spine. In the archway of the entrance, in the Big Tent with Winnie wrapped around Serpentina's shoulder, in Tophat's trailer. I felt a sort of pulse throbbing in the atmosphere and heard music that I knew wasn't really there.

"And I get it that Vesper is rattled. Tina was her bunkie, her best friend. They were like Frick and Frack," Zora continued.

"You didn't answer my question, though."

"About the Shadow Man?" she huffed, trying to brush me off. "Every carnival on the circuit has their own…"

"Version of the legend," I finished. "Yeah, yeah. I got *that* much. So, why did you kick Sis under the table during breakfast when she was talking about Tophat?"

Zora blew out air from her pursed lips, making them rattle and hum. "Oh, stop Janey! I just didn't want Sis giving y'all the wrong impression of the Boss."

"And what impression would that be?"

Chapter Nine

Zora took a step backward, so she was at arm's length distance from me. I could tell she was trying to guard herself or hide something. She fidgeted with the ends of her head scarf that sat at her shoulder.

Nancy looked wide-eyed at me, startled by the sudden raising of our voices. I knew she was still so young, but she was also very perceptive. I wondered how much of the conversation she actually understood. To what degree was she able to comprehend the reality of her world around her? "Level with me, Zora. I can handle it. I've come a long way to be here, and I've seen a thing or two on the journey. I just want to know if this is a dangerous place. Is Tophat on the up and up? I hear stories of unsolveds and Shadow Men, and it makes me wonder if what I'm running from..." I stopped mid-sentence and closed my mouth with a *pop*. I'd said too much.

Zora paused and her face relaxed a bit. "We all ran from something, Jane. Hell, I'm *still* running. But I will tell you this: there isn't anywhere else I'd rather be. There isn't anywhere on this planet safer than the World. And Trent? I trust that man with my life. I'd lay down my life for his if he needed me to. He saved me. So don't you go thinking no bad thoughts about him."

I reached into the front of my dress, pulled out the letter from Tophat, and handed it to her. "So, I shouldn't be worried that he told me to meet him in his trailer at midnight?"

Zora took the paper, and her eyes flashed as she read what it said. Quickly, she folded it up and gave it back to me. She stepped forward again, looking over her shoulder and around me, to ensure we were alone. "Listen," she said slowly in a hushed tone, "you're right. Tophat isn't like the rest of us. The others think it's just an act—that it's all for show. Even Buster. But I know the score. Whatever he does is what keeps us all safe here. Every illusion is a mask of reality. And he has a kind of ... *power* that holds everything together."

"Why are you telling me this? What do you mean?"

"How did you know he wanted to see you at midnight?"

"It's in the letter. It's in the note he wrote."

"No," she urged. "It's actually not stated anywhere in the actual letter."

"You're confusing me, Zora."

"The symbols at the bottom. The only way you could have known what it said is if you knew how to read them. Do you?"

I pressed my lips together and hummed.

Zora raised her eyebrows. "Now it's my turn—what does *that* mean?"

"No. But yes. But not really. But kind of."

Zora looked at Nancy. "Hey Sugar! Can you do me a big favor?"

Nancy perked up and nodded.

"I have a beautiful necklace in my bedroom dresser that I think would be perfect for your

Chapter Nine

Mommy to wear. Can you go find it for me? It has a long chain and big black feather on it."

"A bird feather?" she squeaked.

"Yes! A big bird feather!"

Excited to be given a "big girl" job, Nancy clambered off the couch and trotted into the back room. Zora swiftly took a step closer to me so that her mouth was practically on my ear.

"That's Trent's calling card, Jane. He has plans for you. If you can read the runes, then you're where you're supposed to be."

"You call him Trent?" I mumbled but wasn't sure if she heard me or not. Either way, she didn't acknowledge my comment.

I leaned back so I could see her eyes. Curious they were—a brilliant shade of swirling yellow that I was noticing for the first time. The color was unnatural, inhuman. An overwhelming feeling came over me: *No other living being on the planet has eyes that color!* My hand trembled, and I sucked down a gasp.

"The others—there's only so much they can understand," she continued. "There's only so much they can see or *allow* themselves to see. But Trent is the light and the truth and the way, Jane." Upon saying my name, her yellow eyes flickered like candle lights dancing in a gentle breeze. "But you see. I know you can see."

I stared again into her pupils, and there in the flames was the shape of a girl. A goddess. A bronzed belly giant of a woman with a snake around her shoulders. "Tina?" I whispered.

Zora nodded tersely.

"She's not coming back, is she?"

She shook her head.

"The Shadow Man? Tophat?"

She put a finger on my lips to silence me, then unraveled her head scarf. As I had suspected, Zora was bald, but adorning her head were hundreds of tattoos. Ancient runes lined up in row after row from the back of her neck to the top of her forehead. She was marked with ancient words. I squinted my eyes like I did with Tophat's letter, and words began to appear on Zora's flesh. I saw *necromancer*, and *heksa*, and *old ones*, and *New Eden*, but Nancy came out from the beaded doorway with a scowl plastered on her face, and I turned my attention to her.

"I can't find it!" she whined with hands on her hips.

"Oh! Silly me!" Zora exclaimed, reaching down her shirt. "It was on me all along." She fished out a long silver chain with an enormous black feather dangling from it. "It's a crow feather. I think it suits you," she said as she looped it over my head.

Nancy began to giggle. "Why you no have no hair? Mommy! Zora is *bald*!"

Zora smiled, and I too couldn't help but laugh. "I know, baby. I know."

Chapter Ten

Friday, May 26th 1944
The Gentry Brothers' Wonders of the World Carnival
Tophat's Trailer
Glenmoor, Ohio
Early Morning of the Waxing Crescent Moon

By 11:30 pm, the carnival was wrapping up. The vibrant energy had ebbed into a sleepy hum. A few stragglers loitered, clutching their half-eaten popcorn or cotton candy as they shuffled toward the exits. The Midway had mostly cleared, save for the odd souls trying their luck at one last rigged game. Around the Big Tent, lingering fans clung to the hope of catching a performer off-duty, their eyes scanning the shadows for a hint of magic beyond the stage. The rides had stilled—the Ferris Wheel stood tall and lifeless, its lights dimming one bulb at a time. The Bumper Cars had stopped bumping, and the horseys of the Merry-Go-Round had neighed their final neigh of the night with their glossy eyes frozen mid-prance.

I had tucked Nancy into the bed she and I were now sharing in our new trailer and was waiting for Zora to return so I could rendezvous with Tophat like he had instructed. Of course, I was hesitant at first about leaving Nancy alone with anyone at the carnival. I mean, with her father's people hot on our tails, all the horror stories I'd heard about missing girls in the town, and the incident the other night with Nancy going almost-missin', well, it was nerve wracking to even consider leaving her in anyone else's care. But Zora was different. She *felt* different. I couldn't describe it, but she felt almost like kin. She gave off a sisterly vibe, and I knew pretty quickly that she and I had aligned interests.

When Zora came bustling into the trailer, she gave me a deep and knowing nod to leave. "The girl asleep?" she asked.

"Out cold."

"Good. You get going. It's almost the Moon Hour, and you really shouldn't keep Trent waiting."

"Got it," I said and trotted out the door.

The night had a strange weight to it, as if the cool spring breeze carried something unseen. The air wasn't unpleasant, but it was thick enough to make my chest tighten. It hit me the moment I stepped outside, like an invisible shroud wrapping itself around my shoulders. My footing faltered, and I had to stop for a deep breath to steady myself.

The performers' trailer lot lay still under the dimming lights of the World. One by one, the

Chapter Ten

carnival's glow flickered out as the workers methodically pulled the switches, their sparks of life fading into silence. In the distance, Buster's gruff voice carried through the quiet, "Hey! Quit neckin' and beat it home!" he barked at two teenagers tangled in the shadows, sending them scurrying with a laugh and a grumble.

Soon, the lot would come alive again. Music from victrolas would hum through the air, joined by the shuffle of cards and the low murmur of voices from trailer porches. The carnies would gather to shake off the chaos of the night, a brief moment of camaraderie before another day began. But for now, it was quiet—eerily so—as I walked alone toward the edge of the World.

Tophat's trailer was set apart from the rest, sitting just beyond the reach of the carnival and the bustling trailer lot. It wasn't so far away as to seem removed from us all, but it was far enough to make a statement: close enough to observe, distant enough to remain untouchable. It was a fitting choice for him, really—a man who was always present yet never fully within anyone's grasp.

I followed the faint glow in the distance, and as I approached, the door to his trailer creaked wide open, yet there was no one behind it who could have done so. "Hello?" I called into the dark abyss within, and I swear, my voice echoed back. "Eh-lo?"

"Precisely on time," Tophat responded. "Door's open."

Witch of the Midnight Shadow

I knew that it was my signal to go inside, so I stepped cautiously up the rigid stairs and pushed the door open wider. The trailer greeted me with a sight so jarring, it stopped me cold in my tracks. It was almost unrecognizable from the last time I'd seen it. Gone was the dim, brooding atmosphere, the deep reds and shadowy corners that had made the place feel like a magician's lair. Instead, it was as though the trailer had been drenched in sunlight itself. Bright, warm hues radiated from every surface, as if the very walls had absorbed and now emanated the golden glow of the morning sun. The wood gleamed like polished honey, and curtains in a pale, buttery yellow swayed gently at the windows, letting in soft streams of light. Even the air smelled lighter, carrying a faint hint of citrus and fresh linen instead of the musky scent I had come to associate with Tophat's space. It was impossible—utterly impossible. No light could have pierced through the cracks and corners of this trailer in the dead of night. And yet, here it was, as if some unseen force had transformed the space entirely.

My eyes darted around, taking in every unfamiliar detail from the glistening brass fixtures to the delicate patterns of sunlight playing on the floor. One thing that hadn't changed was his peculiar little bookshelf behind him. Each shelf was stacked with various books, and this time, in the brightness of the trailer, I could make out the titles on their spines: *Malleus Maleficarum, An Encyclopedia of Witches, Demoniality, Letters*

Chapter Ten

of *Demonology and Witchcraft,* and *Blodheksa, Blodbrødre, og Blodsøster.* Next to the bookcase was a glass enclosure where Winnie the python lounged lazily on a thick piece of bark. I clenched the invitation in my hands and stepped farther inside, my unease growing with every step. This wasn't just a change of décor—it felt like the trailer itself had shifted, as if it were alive and adapting to something I couldn't quite understand.

I ran my hair behind my ear and tried to contain my nerves. "I like what you've done with the place," I said jokingly.

Tophat sat at the round table in the middle of the room. He made a short huffing sound in his throat, and I couldn't tell if he was annoyed or amused at my silly comment. Without a word, he extended his arm, bidding me to sit across from him.

I obliged, placed the invitation on the table, then folded my hands in my lap. I tried so hard to structure my face in a way that wasn't so awkward. I imagined my flesh a hunk of clay and a sculptor residing inside of me working the material into something that looked remotely happy, remotely unfazed, and remotely human. "You wanted to see me?" I asked like a timid child being reprimanded in the principal's office.

Tophat gave me a sly smile. "Do I frighten you?" he asked after a long uncomfortable silence.

I paused, letting his words hang in the air like cigarette smoke. Something about him held me there—commanding, magnetic, larger than life.

The light inside the trailer wasn't just light; it wrapped him up like he'd stepped straight out of some golden dream. For the first time, I saw him clearly. Not cloaked in shadows, not hiding behind the glow of the Big Tent spotlight or the flicker of candlelight. Every pore on his skin caught the light, every fine line at the corners of his mouth danced when he moved, every sharp plane of his cheekbones carved like something out of a masterpiece. And those lips—smooth, curved, smug—they curled in that way of his, a grin like the devil's himself. But it was his eyes that got me, and once I caught their gaze, I couldn't look away. Those gray eyes weren't just gray—they shimmered, catching glints of gold and silver like they had secrets tucked away in their depths. And just for a second, I swore I saw something else there. A flash of yellow, sharp and unnatural, like the spark in Zora's eyes. Like they were one and the same. Cut from the same cloth.

"No," I finally mumbled after what felt like an eternity trapped in Tophat's stare. "I wouldn't say 'frightened.'"

"No. You wouldn't be," he reassured. "Frightened isn't the right word. You've seen too much in your life to be frightened by anything. Born of violence, weren't you?"

Shocked by his words, I gulped hard. "How did you…"

"There are shadows that surround you, Jane. Shadows that you run from. Shadows that bubble and boil within you. Shadows that you work so

Chapter Ten

hard to keep from coming to the surface. But the shadows speak to me. *Sing* to me. Their voices are so loud every time you enter the room; they practically give me a headache!"

I bit my lip and lowered my head. "Chickie is angry that you gave me the Fortune Teller role," I blurted, unsure of what to add to the conversation.

"She shouldn't be. It's rightfully yours. She has no real power. Hell, she doesn't even have the pizzaz to fake real power."

"Well, neither do..."

"Uh," he said, silencing me with a *tsk* and a wag of his forefinger. "What do you see right now?" he continued.

"Pardon?"

"Look around you. Tell me what you see."

I swallowed hard again. "Everything is so bright in here. Like it's daylight."

He hummed, and I knew my answer pleased him.

"I don't know." I shrugged. "I feel like I can see everything. The books, Winnie... *you*."

A smile slowly plastered itself on Tophat's face. "You can *see*. The light you see is from your inner eyes. The ones that guide you on the inside. The ones that brought you overseas until they opened up even wider and brought you back home. The ones that drew you here. To me."

"Oh no," I protested. "My ex's people are..."

"Yes. The cards. The child."

Stunned, my mouth opened wide, ready to fire off a barrage of questions that were equal parts shock and fury. But before I could get a single word out, he raised a hand—calm, steady, commanding. The kind of gesture that didn't just ask for silence; it *demanded* it. My voice died in my throat like a match snuffed out before it could catch.

"Jane, everything happens for a reason. And when the moon aligns with the stars in a very particular way, the shadows are the loudest. I *heard* you coming six months ago."

"I don't understand. Why did you tell me to come see you tonight? Are you gonna turn us over to the people who are after us?" My voice rose with a high-pitched, frantic tone.

He sighed heavily and relaxed in his chair. "Nothing like that," he assured me. "There's an old Bible story I'm very fond of. Are you familiar with the Bible, Jane?"

I paused. I was and I wasn't. Momma knew the Bible inside and out and passed that knowledge on to me as I grew up, but there was a clear difference in knowing the Bible and *knowing* the Bible. Momma thought she *knew* the Bible until that moment my daddy came and robbed it from her. Then she just knew the Bible. The words, the verses, the stories, and she eventually taught them to me. But her *belief* and *faith* in the words, the verses, the stories had disappeared—become empty.

Tophat scanned my face and hummed. "Yes. Yes, I can see that," he mused. "Well, when *I* was a child, a very long time ago, a group of Christian

Chapter Ten

missionaries came into my village preaching the word of God. They had hoped to convert my people to their religion. A man named Michael used to give his boisterous sermons on a weekly basis, and in his passion for his cause, he was quite convincing—he managed to convert many of the townspeople. People who had worshipped the old gods and the old ways their entire lives. While I didn't believe in what he was saying, I was smart enough to understand that most of his appeal wasn't exactly what he said but how he said it. He had charisma, and I admired that—used it as a basis for how I modeled my own life."

"Pardon, but what does this have to do with me?"

"The first book of Samuel, chapters twenty-five and twenty-eight. The story goes like this: King Saul, the king of Israel, was in a war against the Philistines. He prayed to his god for help in how to defeat his enemies, but he got no reply. God was silent. So, he goes out on a search for a necromancer, only Saul had banished all heksas from the land."

"Heksa?"

"Witch."

"Like the title of that book over there?" I pointed to the shelf behind him, and he swiveled his head over his shoulder. "Blodheksa?"

"Blood Witch," he confirmed but quickly went back to his story. "Anyway, someone got word back to Saul that there was a necromancer living in the small town of Endor, so he traveled to see her. Crossing dangerous enemy lines, Saul disguised himself and begged the heksa to call forth the spirit of the dead prophet Samuel to aid in his decision making. The heksa was hesitant at first because she knew that magic had been outlawed, and if she was caught practicing, she would have been killed for her crimes. But Saul assured her that no harm would come to her, so she proceeded with the ritual.

"During the spell, the heksa realized who Saul was and was angry for his deception. But again, he promised her she wouldn't be punished for the ritual."

"So, did the spell work?"

"Well, Saul asked the heksa what she saw, and she told him she saw 'gods rising.' *Multiple.* But Saul asked what it looked like, and the heksa described it as an old man wrapped in robes. Saul immediately knelt down because he believed he was in the presence of the powerful prophet, Samuel."

"So, it worked."

"And therein lies the mystery. It depends on who you ask. Apparently the spirit was agitated. Said it was being disturbed. Told Saul he was an abomination for seeking the aid of the heksa."

"She was a necromancer. Calling forth the dead," I say matter-of-factly.

"Uh huh. One with the power to channel the spirits from the other realm."

"The witch said she saw gods, though. How could it have been the prophet if there were plural beings in her sight?"

Chapter Ten

"Excellent question. What the heksa actually saw has been hotly debated in spiritual circles for centuries now. Was it God? Was it the Devil? Was it something else that lurks beyond our realm?"

"What became of Saul?" I asked.

Tophat sat back in his chair and adjusted his black top hat. "That's not the point. Whatever the heksa saw, it was angry. It told Saul things he really didn't want to hear—about how his army would be defeated and his sons would end up dead. Saul committed suicide the next day."

"Fascinating story, but again, I ask you, *what does this have to do with me?*"

"Well, my lady, this is who you are now. Madame Jane Crowe from the Shadowlands of Endor."

I pulled back and my face screwed up in half terror and half confusion. "Shadowlands? Shadow *Man*? I... I don't know if that sits quite right."

"Oh? Pray, tell."

"Shadowlands. Shadow Man. All those rumors surrounding the World. The missing girls? *Tina!* And that sheriff who's been sniffing around here... I don't know. It doesn't feel right. The last thing I need is for him to connect me to some ancient carny legend and start digging and poking, and someone from somewhere far away gets a word of who and where I am. It puts me in too much danger. It puts *Nancy* in too much danger."

"Oh, but on the contrary, my dear," he crooned, his voice sliding over me like silk dipped in honey. It wasn't just his voice that stopped me cold. It was a symphony, a thousand angels harmonizing with a thousand devils, a chorus rising from somewhere deep, somewhere dark, somewhere inside *me*. Shadows he'd claimed were mine joined in, their melody weaving through the air with a sweetness that was intoxicating. The sound wrapped around me, a warm embrace that tingled at the edges of my fingers, trickled down my spine, and spread like a slow flame through my whole body. Even my toes curled in response, though I could've sworn the real heat settled somewhere much closer to my center, sending a shiver of guilty delight rippling in my nether region.

"You're my Witch of Endor," he said, but those words never left his mouth. They went straight to my soul. "I have work to do, and I need you to help me."

"Work beyond the World?" I asked.

"Worlds beyond the World," he replied. "There is someone in the other realm that I need to commune with, and I believe you're the only one who can open that door."

"So, that makes you the Shadow Man, doesn't it?"

Tophat gave no response. He continued to stare at me with a knowing look.

"But Zora..."

Tophat caressed the feather necklace around my neck, like he was pleased, contented. "Zora is an acolyte," he crooned like a doting father

Chapter Ten

would boast about a child. "An associate. She has her role to play, but hers is different from yours."

"And the sheriff?"

"You'll be safe from him, I promise."

I mulled over this new twist, turning it over and over in my mind like a puzzle piece that didn't quite fit. Memories of Aleister and his lot crept in — their endless rituals, the painstaking month-long ceremonies meant to draw power from the spirits of the other realm. I thought of the failures, the forced possessions that went nowhere, the stolen scraps of knowledge that crumbled in their hands.

"You can't control them," I blurted out before I could stop myself. "The spirits, I mean."

Tophat's eyebrows arched, his curiosity sharpening like a blade. He tilted his head, the faintest flicker of a grin playing at the corner of his mouth, like he was waiting to see what else might spill from me.

"I've seen..."

"That's never the intention, Jane. The intention is to learn from them. To be blessed with their knowledge and to help them."

"*Help* them?" I squawked. "*Help* them with what?"

Tophat dipped his head closer to me. "Don't pretend that you don't know."

"But Aleister always tried to..." but I shut my mouth as quickly as it had opened. I didn't mean to reveal the name of the one I had tried so hard to be free from.

Tophat stared at me with his intense gray eyes. The flecks of yellow shot through me like miniature knives piercing into my brain and carving out pieces of information. Aleister's name out loud, in some strange way, seemed to fill Tophat with a surge of power. Soon, music crept up in the distance—that familiar song that played disharmoniously in the other world, the familiar song that made me feel comforted and safe and uneasy all at the same time. Tophat scanned my face for what felt like forever, and finally huffed an, "Oh."

"Yeah. *Oh*," I responded unenthusiastically.

"And Nancy? She's…"

"His," I said, cutting him off. "But she's empty. Of no use to him. They say she lacks a spark that doesn't align with them. One of his people called her *Bambina Vuota*."

"Italian. Empty baby."

"Yes. They called my child an empty baby."

A toothy smile spread wide on his face. His pearly whites shone even brighter in the faux daylight of the trailer. "The man I told you about… the man from my childhood… Michael. He told me another story. One about the Virgin Mary. Are you a Christian, Jane?"

I paused, taken off guard. Momma was a Christian, raised me Christian, but the whole *practicing* part was another story altogether. Besides, I think my Christian days ended when I ran off to England to practice dark magick. "Um… I was raised in the faith, but I…"

Chapter Ten

"Understood," he said cutting me off. "You see, the Christians believe that Mary was the mother of God—she herself born perfect and without sin so she could bring their lord into the world as a man. So yes, while Nancy is, as they say, *empty*, and void of magical abilities, she is free from the shadows that hover in *your* aura. Nancy is pure and clean. She will be a perfect vessel for something great and magnanimous. She will be a conduit for someone with great power. Someone who will be important to shape the new world. The New Eden. Just like Zora's daughter, Nancy will serve well."

Zora's daughter? Zora doesn't have a daughter, I thought.

"Yet," he said out loud, responding to my inner monologue.

"But they said..." I began, trying to reemphasize Aleister's determination in reacquiring Nancy.

"We'll keep her safe, Jane. And you."

"But why? You don't know me. You don't know us! You could turn us in to the sheriff and try to pin Tina's disappearance on me for all I know! Why would you go out of your way to keep us safe?"

He gave me his side smirk. "Let me show you." A wooden box on the table carved with an intricate design suddenly caught my eye. I couldn't remember if it had been there the whole time or if it had just suddenly materialized out of thin air. Tophat opened it, and when he did, the air around us turned cold—frosty. I exhaled and could see my breath in front of my face in little white puffs. The light that once illuminated the space slowly grew dimmer and dimmer—like the sun setting off the purple horizon. I shifted in my chair, uncomfortable at the change of scenery, but again, fascinated all the same.

Tophat slid a deck of six Tarot cards from the box, fanning them out on the table with practiced ease. These weren't like any deck I'd ever seen before—each card bore strange intricate drawings and runes. They were the same symbols from the book, his letter, and the tattoos on Zora's head. The cards had a certain heaviness to them, their thick, yellowed stock speaking of ancient origins, yet somehow they gleamed like they'd just been printed. I couldn't tear my eyes away. The images pulled me in, their allure irresistible. And then, as if the world tilted, the drawings began to shift. They moved—alive! Each card turned into a tiny nickelodeon show right before my eyes. The first card caught my breath in my throat. A child lay in a bed, small and fragile while a towering naked woman stood at the foot of it. But then the child sat up, her tiny hand stretching toward the woman. The woman's arms extended, impossibly long, until their fingers met. And then, like some unholy magic, the two figures began to merge, their forms melting into one. I blinked hard, but the image didn't stop. It was beautiful, terrifying, and mesmerizing all at once. My pulse pounded in my ears as I thought, *Well, Jane, they'll be*

Chapter Ten

carting you off to the funny farm now. You've cracked clean through.

"They're beautiful, aren't they?" Tophat said dreamily.

"W... what are they? Where did they come from? And how can they do *that*?" I tried in vain to hide the shock and wonder in my voice, but as the pictures continued to dance and move and blend into each other, I knew there was no use masking my utter astonishment.

"An old friend created these. She was a powerful heksa who was dedicated to the cause.

"The cause?" I squeaked.

Tophat sighed. "There is great work to be done, Jane. Work that has been in motion since the beginning of time."

The music in the distance crescendoed in my head, and my eyes fluttered as I tried to decipher the words in the song.

"She called it the Augen Deck. The eyes. The cards see things like little mirrors or windows. The cards can show you things, too. They are sacred tools. Much more powerful than those painted cards you have."

I gulped hard. "Is this old friend of yours the one you seek to commune with?"

"*Aisling*. It means dream or vision," he replied, ignoring my inquiry.

"Excuse me?"

"Nancy. You named her Althea Aisling. *Healer of the Vision*. It is a testament to her purity. You knew the moment she was conceived that she was everything good and pure in the world."

"What does Nancy have to do with this?"

"Everything. She is a part of you. You are a part of her. And her child will be a part of us. When Nancy conceives, she'll know. She'll know that she will be carrying greatness in her womb. And just like you, Nancy will protect her child at all costs."

My head swam, and I planted my hands on the tabletop and began to rise from my chair. "I'm sorry. I can't. I can't do this."

Tophat reached across the table and grabbed my wrists, cementing me in my place. "Look," he commanded. "Look at the deck, and you'll see what I mean."

My gaze drifted back to the cards, almost against my will, and I sank slowly into the chair. The more I stared, the images on the cards began to shift again, but this time, they didn't move—they vanished. They faded, like ink washing off in a storm, until all that remained were tiny black specks, scattered across the ancient paper. Then, those specks came alive. They shimmered, faintly at first, then brighter, like stars caught in some celestial dance. They moved closer together, clustering tightly until they formed a thin, straight line stretched across the six cards. The air shifted. It grew colder—bone-deep, breath-stealing cold. The strange music that had been swirling around the room swelled, louder and louder, until it was a roar in my head. My chest tightened, and I

Chapter Ten

wanted to look away, but I couldn't. The line on the cards began to tear. Slowly, impossibly, it split open, like a zipper being undone by invisible hands or a snag in pantyhose unraveling beyond repair. The tear widened, deeper and darker, and from its depths, I thought I saw something—no, I was *sure* I saw it. Claws. Jagged, gnarled, and straining, reaching from the other side. Every part of me screamed to run, but my body wouldn't move. My eyes were locked on that gaping chasm, waiting, curious about what might emerge.

Chapter Eleven

Sunday, September 5th 1965
The Napa Inn
Napa, California
Morning of the Waxing Gibbous Moon

The sunlight poked its way in through the cracks of the thick hotel curtains, casting a thin ray of light across Nancy's face. At the demands of her husband Brian, she had wrestled almost relentlessly with the curtains the previous night to ensure that no speck of morning light would come through and disturb their much-needed rest. Nancy briefly smiled in spite of herself; she didn't mind the sun's gentle wake-up call. What she would mind, though, was Brian's grumpy demeanor if the offensive light woke *him* up. He'd be a grouch all day, no doubt, and being their last day in Napa, Nancy wanted it to be as picture perfect as it could be. So, no grumps allowed! Slowly, she shifted her body closer to him on the bed so as to shield him from the encroaching day. But it was no use. As the sun slowly crept up the side of the world, the ray of

Chapter Eleven

light got thicker and brighter until it finally shone right on the tip of Brian's nose.

He stirred in the bed, threw his arm across his eyes, and grumbled. "Jesus Christ, Nance! I told you to make sure the curtains were all the way shut!"

Nancy propped herself up on her elbow so that she was fully in the path of the sun, shielding her now-grouch of a husband. "Sorry, sorry," she apologized as if it was her fault, as if she could control the light of day. She looked at him lovingly, her sweet husband of three years. Even though he was abrupt with his words most of the time and cussed too much for her liking, she was still crazy for him as much as she was the day they first met. And with his short brown hair, bright green eyes, and his husky physique, she was just as attracted to him as ever.

Brian was a good provider for their little family, and she appreciated all the hard work he did in order to make ends meet, but she knew the one thing he really wanted was a child. A son, to be exact. But after three years of marriage, Nancy still wasn't able to give him what he so desired, and that bothered her deeply because at the end of the day, her one goal was to be a dutiful wife.

Brian's resentment of her was becoming palpable, especially during the last year when there were more and more invitations to their friends' baby showers. He would often make comments about who had a bun in the oven and notably point out that "oh, not you, Nancy!" He joked, of course, but the words started to sting a little, like scratching a mosquito bite too hard. Nancy had started to panic that maybe she was incapable of having children. Where would that leave Brian and her? Divorced, probably. She shuddered to think.

Desperate for help, Nancy had turned to her mother Jane for advice on how to handle the childless situation. "Maybe *he's* the problem," Jane had stated, but Nancy quickly shushed her and told her to never speak of that again. Anything that would diminish the idea of Brian's position as an alpha male should never be brought up. "Well, I'm no expert in these things, Nancy, that's for sure," Jane had crowed, "but it seems to me like maybe you two need to relax. Take a vacation. Enjoy each other's company. Reconnect." And with that, she suggested spending a few days out in California. Actually, come to think of it, Nancy's mother had more like *insisted* they go, even offering to pay for part of the trip.

So now, there they were, in Napa Valley, taking in all the sights and sounds of the west coast—absorbing all the culture differences (California was much different than their native New York, that was for sure) and doing exactly what her mother had said to do—rest, relax, and enjoy each other in every sense of the word.

Brian remained with his eyes closed, but after a minute, one opened and his brow furrowed into deep cavernous lines at the top of his nose. "I can't sleep with you staring at me like that!" he barked.

Chapter Eleven

Nancy playfully ran her fingers across his bare chest. "Well, who said we had to sleep?"

Brian rubbed his eyes. "What the hell time is it anyway?"

Nancy ignored his foul mood and craned her neck to read the clock. "6:45."

He groaned. "That's ungodly, Nance. We're on vacation, ya know."

"Exactly," she cooed. "Vacation. We can do just about anything you want." She drummed her fingertips up to his chin and outlined his lips seductively with her thumb, hoping she could interest him in another round of sex before they started the day.

Brian turned his head. "What I *want* is to sleep."

"Well, I thought we could… ya know… before we go on the vineyard tour today."

He looked at her with one raised eye. "Fuck? If you wanna fuck, just say it, Nance. You're a big girl. We don't have to play cutesy games, ya know."

"Brian! Language!" she exclaimed.

"Seriously, Nancy. We're both adults. If you want me to fuck you, all you gotta do is ask." He grabbed her hand and placed it on his Johnson. It was raging with morning hunger, and she could feel it throb underneath the thin bedsheet. "I mean, come on," he said as he moved her hand up and down on his manhood with long strokes, "you act like we never did it before."

Disgusted, she quickly pulled herself free from his grasp. "Well, certainly not when you're so crude about it," she huffed and slid off the bed and over to the small table by the window. The ray of light from outside had grown larger. A thick rope of sunshine bounded into the room and shone directly onto Brian's face. He squinted and grumbled, his face scrunching up into a meaty ball, and Nancy silently snickered at his discomfort. *Serves you right*, she thought.

Brian sat up and sighed with displeasure. "So, what the hell do you have planned for us today?"

"Vineyard Voyages," she said. Her voice crackled as she tried to suppress her tears. "But the tour doesn't start until noon."

"Exactly. *Noon*," he emphasized.

"Oh, come on, Brian! It's our last day here. We take a tour of a vineyard, then have dinner and go dancing at an elite country club."

"Oh, gee, dancing at a country club. Just what I want to do," Brian mumbled and got up.

Nancy's heart sank at Brian's sarcasm. "But Brian!" she pleaded. "This is the tour my mother booked for us. She paid for us to go. We can't *not* do it!"

"Great. Just tack it on to our already unpayable debt to her," he growled and went into the bathroom. He slammed the door behind him, and immediately the water from the shower turned on.

A tear rolled down her cheek, and she quickly swatted it away with the back of her hand. He was always like this—ranting and raving at the slightest inconvenience. That was Brian, for ya, yet despite his unpredictable demeanor, Nancy was committed to her marriage vows no matter

Chapter Eleven

the cost. She sat at the table with her legs curled to her chest, trying hard to gulp down heavy heaps of sobs that swelled inside her while she pondered every angle of her current situation. She felt like she was always questioning her happiness or making skatey-eight excuses for her husband's brash ways, and sometimes it was exhausting to even try to pretend she was happy.

But she was happy.

He made her so very happy.

He gave her a life that was wonderful and blessed. And she was happy for it.

And she so desperately wanted to give him a son and make him happy too.

Brian's attitude shifted after his lengthy shower. Nancy could tell because he came out of the steamy room with a towel wrapped around his waist while and a cheery tune on his lips. Nancy pepped up at his adjustment and smiled wide when he said he wanted to go to the local diner for breakfast.

Quickly, she got up from the chair and scurried to the bathroom to get ready. The fogged-up mirror made it difficult for her to apply her makeup. Even when she wiped it down with the washcloth, the streaks of condensation made her reflection hard to discern. Her face appeared jagged too—like the wavy ripples of the ocean were cutting across the surface of her skin, and she scarcely recognized her own monstrous reflection. *Is this how he sees me all the time?* she thought. But before she could ponder her image any further, he was pounding on the door, begging her to hurry up. "I'm starving!" he whined with a playful tone.

She laughed at his eagerness to spend time with her. With a final dab of creamy pink rouge on her cheeks and a swipe of her lipstick across her mouth, she finally opened the door and smiled. "I'm ready! Let's go!"

The morning was like a dream—breakfast at the diner, then some window shopping in the town square. The hours seemed to fly by, and before they knew it, it was time to meet the tour bus at the depot. When they arrived, they noticed they were the only ones waiting in line, and Brian sighed his usual sigh of displeasure. "This better be good."

Nancy's stomach did a flip-flop at the sound of his annoyance. "Oh stop! It'll be great!" Nancy replied cheerily, hoping to stave off his negative attitude. "Besides, it'll be fun if we're the only ones."

"Fun? No, it'll be creepy."

"No! It'll be romantic. Like our own private tour."

Brian rolled his eyes and opened his mouth to say something, but the blue bus pulled up and stopped right in front of them. The words *Vineyard Voyages* were written in big yellow letters on the side. The bus door opened with a hiss, and Nancy grabbed on to the railing and meticulously climbed up the first step. She was extra careful so as to not trip over herself and make

Chapter Eleven

Brian embarrassed by her clumsiness 'cause Lord knew she had a tendency to be a little off balance (a flaw that Brian often pointed out.) With her eyes cast down, she ensured she was steady on her two feet, but the booming voice of the bus driver startled her, and she nearly tumbled backward into Brian's arms.

"Welcome!" the voice exclaimed.

Nancy gasped in surprise, shaken to her core.

"Welcome to Vineyard Voyages!" he continued.

She looked up and gasped again—this time more silently, to herself—when her gaze met the eyes of the handsome driver. She wanted to respond with a polite "hello," but something was wrong. Something felt … off. A strange sensation churned in the pit of her stomach, almost like a growl, as she took in the entirety of his presence. Nancy couldn't recall the last time she'd seen a man as striking as this one. He was almost too perfect, too flawless, as if he weren't entirely real. His short, jet-black hair framed a face that was both alluring and unsettling. But it was his eyes that captured her—peculiar, piercing gray eyes that seemed to hold her in place, as though they'd frozen time itself. She couldn't look away. Those eyes mesmerized her, hypnotized her, pulled her deeper and deeper. In their depths, she thought she saw something: a golden Ferris wheel, glowing brightly in the darkness, spinning endlessly. Round and round and round and round…

Brian gave her a little nudge on her backside, and she shook her head from her spellbound thoughts.

"I'm Trent," he continued. "And I'll be your *eyes* and ears throughout this tour." He emphasized the word *eyes* in a way that gave Nancy pause. Like he knew she had been staring at his. Like he was somehow able to read her mind.

"Hi, Trent," she replied, her voice shaking a little. "I'm Nancy. This is my husband Brian." Nancy hopped up the last step and made her way to the seat directly behind the driver with Brian following close behind.

Trent nodded at them both in the mirror and closed the bus door. "Brian. Nancy."

The way his voice sounded when he said her name sent goosebumps down Nancy's arms, causing every hair to stand at attention. His voice was soothing with a surreal-like quality, almost as if he weren't actually speaking out loud at all. Almost as if he were speaking directly to her—directly to her mind. But that was impossible because she knew Brian had heard him by the way he grunted an acknowledgment. Regardless, there was something both strange yet familiar about the sound of Trent's voice, and she was determined to figure out where she had heard it before.

"I detect a little accent?" Trent inquired.

Something in between Nancy's legs stirred, and the tips of her ears went hot with embarrassment. She smiled coyly. "New York. Is it *that* bad?"

Chapter Eleven

"Charming," Trent replied, and a gush of desire all but exploded in her panties. "So, what brings the lovely couple out to the Valley? Honeymoon? A little getaway from the kiddos at home?"

Nancy giggled nervously. "Oh no. We've been married almost what, hon? Three years now?"

Brian flatly answered, "What? Um, yeah. Three years." But Nancy didn't seem to care that he was not confident with his answer. In fact, Nancy hadn't really realized that Brian was there at all.

"Oh. That's wonderful. Any kids yet?" Trent pried.

A red-hot wave flooded Nancy's cheeks, and she cowered a little so Trent couldn't see it in the driver mirror. But when the side of his mouth curled up in a little smile, she knew he had seen. "Not yet, but we're working on it." She giggled again and nudged Brian's shoulder playfully.

"Nance..." Brian scolded.

"Well, it's true!" she squawked.

"Oh, Nancy," Trent said lightheartedly. "I honestly believe if you keep your good thoughts flowing and your actions to match, you can achieve anything your heart desires."

Nancy folded her arms across her chest. "Exactly!" she agreed, her eyes brimming with wonder and awe. "That's kinda what I keep trying to tell Brian here."

Trent huffed out a small laugh and revved the engine.

"Wait, Trent?" she asked, alarmed.

"Yes, dear Nancy?" he replied.

"Aren't there others? Is anyone else coming on the tour?"

"No, darling. Just you and the Mister!"

Brian sighed loudly. "Jesus Christ, Nance! I knew it!"

"No worries, Mr. Turner," Trent said. "I promise you're in for a real treat!" And as he pulled away, Nancy couldn't recall if she had told him their last name or not.

Trent spent the better part of two hours driving them around, offering a comprehensive tour of the area. He shared fascinating historical tidbits and detailed explanations about the intricate process of winemaking. Nancy was utterly enthralled. She clung to his every word, her curiosity bubbling over as she peppered him with questions like an eager schoolgirl hungry for knowledge. Trent was impressive. His depth of knowledge was admirable, and it didn't hurt that he was devilishly handsome. Nancy found herself hanging on to his every gesture and intonation, fully captivated. Brian, on the other hand, couldn't have cared less. History and technical details held no appeal for him—his sole focus was on reaching their destination and drinking to his heart's content.

Eventually, Trent dropped Nancy and Brian off at a vineyard, letting them know he'd pick

Chapter Eleven

them up later at the adjacent country club after supper. The two wandered leisurely through the grounds, exchanged small talk with other couples on similar tours, enjoyed a light lunch, and sampled every variety of wine the vineyard had to offer.

Nancy paced herself, savoring each sip, but Brian had no such restraint. He eagerly indulged in every offering, growing more unsteady with each glass. By the time they arrived at the country club, Brian could barely keep his head up at the dinner table.

After they ate, he stumbled off to the bar to continue drinking, leaving Nancy alone at their table. Her heart sank as she watched the other couples swaying together on the dance floor, their movements tender and intimate—exactly what she had hoped for that night.

Every so often, she glanced at the clock, counting down the minutes until Trent would return to take them home. The thought of him excited her—brought her out of her temporary misery and sent her nether region into a pulsating frenzy. She chastised herself for having such adulterous thoughts, but the more she told herself to stop thinking of Trent, the more the desire and curiosity grew. He seemed like the type of man who would take care of his woman—worship her like a goddess, give her everything she needed and wanted psychologically, emotionally, and physically...

Stop it! she scolded herself as her mind began to wander to unimaginable thoughts. And just when she had finally convinced herself to concentrate on something else, something more pressing like catching their plane the next day, the front door of the country club opened up, letting in a cool, early autumn breeze, and Trent stood on the threshold. She stiffened up like a child getting caught red-handed. He looked over at her and smiled when their eyes met and tapped on his wrist, indicating it was time to go. She nodded her head over to Brian who had passed out at the bar. Trent looked over at him and smirked, then he walked over to her. Nervously, Nancy tucked her brown hair behind her ear and ran her tongue over the fronts of her top teeth, subconsciously trying to clean them of any leftover dinner particles.

"Looks like the Mister has had his fill," Trent said when he reached her.

Nancy sighed. "Yeah. And we have to catch a plane tomorrow, and I have no idea how I'm going to…"

"No worries, Little Crow. I'll help you." He smiled again, and her heart seemed to thump harder against her chest.

Jesus, Nancy, she yelled at herself on the inside. *Get a grip and calm down!*

But it was no use. The glowing light in Trent's eyes drew her in again, and suddenly she felt a little detached—detached from the world and detached from herself.

Chapter Eleven

Maybe I had too much to drink, too?

"No. You're perfectly fine," he answered her inner thought and outstretched his hand.

Dumbfounded, Nancy muttered, "How did you..."

"Never mind that. You look like you need one last dance before you go back home." Trent wiggled his fingers, beckoning her to accept his hand and join him on the dance floor.

"Oh... no... no... I... I couldn't," she stammered. "I couldn't..."

Trent leaned down closer to her face. "I insist," he said firmly, but Nancy realized his words hadn't come out of his mouth. It was as if he had spoken directly to her mind. Entranced, Nancy hesitated no longer, took his hand, and let him guide her up from her chair. His touch was electric! Like little zaps of static prickling her fingers and palm. It startled her at first, and she instinctually pulled away, but Trent wouldn't allow it; instead, he held her hand tighter, forcing her to feel the tingles. After a few seconds, the warmth and fuzziness spread up her arm and down into her chest, sending waves of calm throughout her body.

When she moved onto the dancefloor with him, her legs wobbled for a moment as if she were more inebriated than she had originally thought. Trent moved a hand onto her waist to help steady her. "You okay?" he asked smoothly.

"Oh yeah. Fine, fine. I'm just a little bit of a klutz is all."

"I don't think so," he said smoothly. "I think you can handle yourself just fine." And with that, he led her to the dancefloor just as the song "Do You Believe in Magic" by the Lovin' Spoonful started to play.

And magic it was. Trent and Nancy danced for what felt like hours and hours. It was as if the world stopped, and only the two of them were animate beings in an inanimate world. The room shifted and changed, and she thought she saw stars sparkle around them every time he swung her around or smiled brightly at her. They talked all night without ever saying a word, and that nagging feeling of familiarity tugged at her heart. "I feel like I know you from somewhere," she said with her outside voice.

"Sure, Nancy," he answered. "I'm no stranger."

"But I can't remember from where. It almost feels like it was a dream."

"I can see that. But it wasn't."

"It's killing me that I feel like we've met before, but I just can't…"

"Does it matter, though? We're here now. And this is where we were always meant to be. This time. This place. Now. Here."

His voice was soothing, almost musical, wrapping around her thoughts like a melody. She found herself swaying, not just to the faint rhythm of the song playing in the country club but to the cadence of his words, which seemed to hum in perfect harmony with the air around them. The song from the speakers faded into

Chapter Eleven

the background, overtaken by something else entirely—Trent's voice. It felt like its own song, one meant just for her, a secret serenade that made her feel special, cherished, as if she were the only woman in the world.

"Nowhere," she whispered, her voice barely audible, carried away on the tide of his presence. He pulled her closer, and she let herself go, her eyes fluttering shut as she rested her head on his shoulder, losing herself in the moment.

"Ah, yes," he whispered as he pet the back of her head. "You're the only one who exists in the nowhere."

"Nowhere," she repeated dreamily.

"The now and here," he answered.

Nancy lifted her head and looked up at him, but she noticed that the room had somehow changed. They danced, but they weren't moving. They spoke, but they weren't talking. All around her, stars sparkled and glittered and asteroids raced across the vastness of open space. They were grounded on the country club dance floor, but they floated—weightless and hurtling in the great expanse. It reminded her of when her mother took her to the Hayden Planetarium in New York City when she was a kid. She remembered being amazed at what the cosmos looked like. And now she was there!

Now she was nowhere.

She gasped a little, and Trent tightened his grip on her waist. "It's okay, Little Crow. You're perfectly safe."

His touch put her at ease, and she looked up at him, locked eyes with him. There in the gray haze, she saw them dancing among the stars. The sky behind them began to open up, like something was tearing it apart from the other side. She heard a growl in her soul as the image of her and Trent spun around and around wildly. It made her dizzy to watch, but she couldn't look away.

"I *know* I know you," she said quietly, but she wasn't sure if she said it out loud or not.

"And I you," Trent answered. "I've known you for ages, Nancy. From the beginning of the World, to be exact. And you have no idea just how very special you are."

"I'm special?" she squeaked, her voice small and timid.

He placed a hand under her chin and tilted her head up slightly. "You will be the mother of a goddess one day. And she will do glorious things that will change the very fabric of this universe."

"I'm going to be a mother?" she questioned in disbelief. She had been trying for so long that hearing the words were like stepping into a dream.

Trent swung Nancy around, and her breath hitched as she caught sight of the sky. The opening above them was growing larger, a gaping tear spilling light into the night. Shooting stars rained down from the fissure, streaking across the darkness like firework trails, their brilliance both mesmerizing and ominous. The melody from beyond intensified, swelling with an otherworldly resonance that seemed to echo in her very bones. It

Chapter Eleven

wasn't just a sound—it was a force, pulling her closer to the unknown. She clung to Trent, her senses overwhelmed, as the world around them seemed to unravel into something entirely new.

Her eyes widened with utter fascination. "There are angels crying," she said sadly.

"Yes," he answered. "They're crying because they want to come home. All the angels. Their tears are falling stars that shimmer in the night sky. Together we can help them."

"It's so beautiful, though."

"Beautiful. And sad. Like you."

Nancy looked at him and furrowed her brow. "You think I'm beautiful?"

"Of course, Althea."

Nancy blinked her eyes rapidly with confusion. "Why do I know that name?"

Without another word, Trent bent down and kissed her gently on the mouth. She pulled back at first, but when his tongue began dancing with hers, her shoulders relaxed, and she accepted his kiss as he pressed into her stronger and deeper. Slowly, he ran his hand up the back of her neck and wove his fingers within her hair. She snaked her arms underneath his and clasped the tops of his shoulders as if she were holding on to him for dear life. Each kiss became more frenzied and wild and reckless as her passion burned between her legs—hot desire that saturated her pristine white panties and made her blush with deviant thoughts.

If you wanna fuck, just say it, Nance, she heard a voice in her head say. It was Trent's voice repeating Brian's words. Only this time, she wasn't repulsed by the rawness of the statement—she was quite the opposite.

"Yes," she moaned between chaotic kisses.

Trent lowered his arms and grabbed her backside, pulling her closer to him so she could feel his pulsating organ against her thigh. Her heart quickened at the thought of it—its girth and length—moving in and out of her, teasing the opening of her slick sex and then ramming her, furiously making her scream.

"Are you sure?" he asked, confirming her intentions.

"Oh, God yes," she sighed.

And when she opened her eyes again, they were no longer in the cosmos with the crying angels, no longer staring in space at a tear in the sky, and the song of the old ones was humming in her brain. They were in Nancy's hotel room, kissing frantically like their mouths couldn't get enough of each other. Like they both had a hunger that was so desperate to be fulfilled.

In their frenzied state, Trent propped her up on the edge of the little table in the room and reached up under Nancy's baby blue cotton dress. With one hand, he pulled her white panties to the side and with his other shoved two fingers inside of her. Her body shook with delight as he drove them hard and fast with upward strokes, ensuring he tickled her pleasure spot.

Chapter Eleven

Just when she was at the peak of desire, she scooted herself back to release his grip on her. Her panties snapped back in place as she leaned forward to unfasten the button of his uniform slacks. She unzipped the zipper and pulled both the trousers and boxers down in one fell swoop. His manhood made a tent out of his shirttails, but she lifted it up, revealing his cock. She licked her lips at the sight of him and spread her legs wide — an invitation to do as he pleased.

Trent took a step closer, placed one hand on her back to position himself, tore her panties to the side again, and drove himself deep inside. Nancy's body rose a little off the table like she was being impaled from below, and she cried out when he entered her. He kept her steady at arm's length as he pumped himself in and out, hard and fast, hard and deep, bringing them both to the edge of pleasure.

Nancy saw the stars again in her head as she exploded all over him. Her body tingled with static like every inch of her was numb. Never before had she experienced an orgasm from passionate sex, and she felt fuzzy and almost giddy.

It wasn't much longer after that Trent reached his pinnacle. Right before he came, he pulled her by the waist to bring her closer to him. He thrust quickly, and almost violently, but carefully making sure he wasn't pulling out too much. When he came, Nancy felt the heat burst inside of her and fill her up.

And then there was silence.

A waiter in the kitchen of the country club dropped a wine glass and the sound of it shattering on the marble tile startled Nancy from her daydream. She fluttered her eyes and adjusted to her surroundings, then looked down at the empty wine glasses on the table.

Oh boy! We drank way too much tonight! she thought as she rubbed the sides of her temples. She was confused. Startled. Unsure of her reality.

Suddenly, the front door of the country club opened up, letting in a cool, early autumn breeze, and Trent stood on the threshold.

Trent. Tour bus driver, Trent. The man I just… just… just had sex with, Trent? But that's impossible. That didn't happen…

He looked over at her and smirked a knowing smirk, and Nancy's ears immediately went hot. He tapped on his wrist, indicating it was time to go, and she nodded her head over to Brian who was passed out at the bar. Trent nodded and walked over to her. Nervously, Nancy tucked her brown hair behind her ear and ran her tongue over the fronts of her top teeth, subconsciously trying to clean them of any leftover dinner particles.

"Looks like the Mister has had his fill," Trent said when he reached her.

Nancy stammered. "Y… y… yeah. And we have to catch a plane tomorrow, and I have no idea how I'm going to…" She spoke quickly and nervously because images of their intense session kept rolling into her mind, and it was hard to concentrate on anything and…

Chapter Eleven

"No worries, Little Crow. I'll help you," he said. "We'll get you and the Mister back to your hotel safe and sound."

His smile immediately calmed her down and the song "Do You Believe in Magic" by the Lovin' Spoonful started to play in the club.

He reached for her hand to help her get up from the table. "I like this song," he said. "What about you?"

"Oh yeah. Yeah. It's catchy," she replied.

And as they walked over to the bar to retrieve a passed-out Brian, any inappropriate thoughts that Nancy may or may not have had quickly disintegrated from her memory, as if they had never been there in the first place.

Chapter Twelve

Friday, May 26th 1944
The Gentry Brothers' Wonders of the World Carnival
Tophat's Trailer
Glenmoor, Ohio
Early Morning of the Waxing Crescent Moon

I gripped the sides of the round table and shot up from the chair in a wild frenzy. "Don't you dare touch her!" I screamed. "I swear to God I will kill you if you even *look* at her!"

Tophat rose and scurried around the table to meet me, although it was in one swift motion that I scarcely saw him move. He fluttered. He glided. He floated. But he was fast about it and immediately materialized at my side. Placing his hand on my shoulder with his icy grip, I was locked in place and could not move (even though every cell in my body screamed at me to flee the carnival at once—to get Nancy from the trailer and steal off into the night). I was powerless against him.

Chapter Twelve

"You're everything *but* powerless, Jane," he said, his voice resonating throughout my inner core.

"You're a monster," I whispered, half hoping he didn't hear me.

"Ah, yes. I *am* a monster, admittedly. I'm just not *that* kind of monster. I would never do harm to a child. Not only is it wrong on so many different levels, but it is an offense punishable by death in my culture."

"But... but... Nancy!" I wailed, and he tightened his hold on me.

"She was a woman in that vision, Jane. A woman capable of her own thoughts and feelings and actions. A woman who created her own destiny."

"A woman, yes. But *you*? *You*? You were the same when I saw you there! The same! You should have had gray hair at least. Or wrinkles. Or *something*! But you were *you*. How could that be? I can't trust what I saw, sir. I can't believe it, either."

"Of course you can," he said gently, soothingly. "You believe in much, Jane. You've seen much in your years. You're not the one to deny what is above, below, and beyond. You only try to deceive yourself because your mother instinct is to protect."

I shook my head, slowly and deliberately, the only part of me I could manage to move. "No," I whispered hoarsely. "You lied to her. You deceived her." My voice cracked under the weight of my words, and tears began to pool in my eyes, threatening to spill over despite my best efforts to hold them back. But it was a losing battle. One by one, they slid down my chilled cheeks, hot streams cutting through the cold like steam on a frosted windowpane. Tophat leaned closer, his touch impossibly gentle as he swept his thumbs across my cheeks. With long, measured strokes, he wiped the tears away, his hands steady, almost soothing. The look in his eyes was soft, almost tender.

"Now, now. It's not deception if it's a fulfillment of a prophecy. Besides, you have your hand in the outcome as well."

"What? Why? What do you mean?" I stammered.

"It's all a matter of time, Jane," he said, his voice calm but edged with inevitability. "You saw it in the Augen deck—the future. In that future, you make it your mission to guide Nancy and her husband to the vineyard, fully aware that I'll be waiting for her. Fully aware of what must happen."

I froze at his words. My insides felt gutted and empty. *Madre Vuota.* "What has to happen?" I repeated as I stared into the flame of a lit candle on one of his shelves.

"You come from a long line of broken souls, a legacy that stretches far beyond the shadow of your murderous father, Albert Fish. It's a lineage tainted by darkness, but that stops with you. The cycle ends now. Your progeny—Nancy—she's the one who will restore balance, heal what's been shattered. Althea Aisling. She is the Healer

Chapter Twelve

of the Vision, the one who will guide us to the New Eden, the New World. She is destined to set things right. Through her, the world will witness an event more magnificent, more profound, than the resurrection of the Christian savior, for Nancy's child—*our* child—will bring the coming of a new era. The embodiment of the arch angel Jophiel, Nancy's daughter will be armed with a flaming sword and cast Adam and Eve out of Eden. Her role will ignite the dawn of a new age—the Dawn of the Blodheksa—one that will eclipse all that has come before it. This is our moment, our future, and it will be nothing short of glorious."

"Dawn of the Blood Witch," I whispered to myself.

Tophat reached forward and in one swift motion swooped up the cards of the Augen deck into a neat pile and placed them in my hands. My muscles loosened immediately, and my mobility returned. I shimmied away from his touch, creating some distance between us. "They are yours. They always have been. And they will serve you well. They will guide you and protect you."

"And Nancy?"

"Nancy most of all."

"And Aleister, Nancy's father? What about his people? They won't stop until…"

Tophat paused. He took a step forward and clasped my hands in his, so we were both channeling the power of the cards. Tiny shocks of electricity pricked my fingers and hands with a numbing sensation. He swayed his head in the air as if he were listening to someone whispering from beyond. "They're close," he said with his eyes closed. And the second he said it, I knew it was true because I too felt the words pulsing in my mind. "They're almost here."

Fear gripped me, and panic rose in my chest. It worked its way into my lungs and made it hard for me to breathe. I began to gulp for air, desperately struggling for the oxygen to keep me conscious and steady on my feet, but the thought of Christina Combs and the rest of the pack hot on our heels suffocated me. I was so naïve to think that I could evade them and just disappear into oblivion. I was so very stupid to think that I could be safe anywhere. The room began to spin just enough to make me feel sick in my stomach, and all I wanted to do was curl into a ball and cry, but I felt hollow on the inside. Hollow, defeated, alone...

His eyes flashed wide. "Oh, but you're not. And you are. Safe, that is," he said in response to my thoughts.

My face twisted in confusion. "How? How am I safe?" My words came out in hard, measured pants.

"Here. In the World. With us. I told you Jane, both you and Nancy are too important. There's no way I will allow anyone to do you harm."

A wave of peace crashed over me, and the lights in the room seemed to twinkle. I felt my heart steady, and my lungs slowly fill up with much needed oxygen. There was something

Chapter Twelve

soothing in Tophat's voice—in his words. They were genuine and rang true and put me at ease so that all panic released from my body, and I was suddenly comforted and calm. "They wish us harm," I whispered matter-of-factly.

"That and more," he confirmed.

"And you promise you won't allow it, right?" I reiterated.

"*We* won't allow it. They want the cards and the child, and they'll stop at nothing until they have both," he said, his voice steady but brimming with intensity.

I looked directly into his eyes, and what I saw within made me smile. Wild flames swirled, towering and ferocious, rising high enough to lick the clouds. Screams echoed in their depths—agonized, desperate. The acrid scent of burnt flesh filled the trailer, sharp and suffocating, stirring a sickening mix of disgust and strange exhilaration in me.

He smiled a slow, deliberate grin. "But we must wait," he said softly, almost mockingly. "Wait until they've arrived."

"And what about the sheriff? Tannehill McCrory? How are we to enact your plans if he's constantly sniffing around?"

"He's merely a thorn in my side. I can keep him at bay. *We* can keep him at bay."

"How?"

"Listen here, Jane. I need you to be my eyes and ears—my second set of eyes, if you will. You and Zora, you're the ones who'll help me make contact with the beyond, but I've got a hunch there's a rat in the room. Someone in this operation's been playing both sides, feeding information to McCrory, stirring up the shadowy rumors about the Shadow Man. We can't let this go unchecked. I'll need you to keep your head low but keep your eyes wide open. Watch every move, every word, like a hawk on a hunt. Someone's been cozying up to McCrory, and it's time we find out who. You and Zora are the ones I trust to make the right call."

"How do you know there's a rat? And isn't McCrory gonna get even more suspicious when you introduce me as the Witch from the *Shadowlands* of Endor."

"Yes. I completely anticipate that."

"And that doesn't worry you?" I crowed.

Tophat lowered his head and looked up at me from his furrowed brows as if to ask, "are you serious?"

I rolled my eyes and huffed knowingly. "Understood," I answered. "You need me to gather information."

"Use the Augen deck to guide you."

"And the other stuff?" I paused and inhaled, trying to choose my words wisely. "I've never ... *communed* with the spirits before. I've only been a spectator. I'm not sure I know how to. I'm not sure I can do what you need me to do and..."

"You have," he interrupted. "You have, and you can, and you will."

"But how will I know when..."

Chapter Twelve

"I'll call for you. You'll know. In the meantime, you are a performer. You will perform." He craned his head over in the direction of the snake tank. "All the World's a glamour, Jane. An illusion."

I leaned over his shoulder, my eyes locking onto Winnie. A soft white glow pulsed around her glass enclosure, enveloping it in an otherworldly haze. Her body seemed to flicker in and out of existence, like a light switch flipping on and off, and the low hum of static buzzed in my mind. In one moment, she was a harmless, languid python, coiled in lazy repose. In the next, she transformed into a menacing viper, baring her two-inch fangs with lethal intent. Both forms were real, yet neither was. Both belonged to this reality yet existed beyond it. She was—and wasn't—at the same time. Tophat's glamour was strong, but somehow I was able to see past it, through it, *beyond* it.

"And that's how we'll make contact with the other world, Jane," he said with finality.

In that moment, everything came full circle. The confusion that had gripped me while watching Winnie flicker between her two forms faded away. My eyes adjusted to the seamless fluidity of her transformation, and soon, it felt natural for her to exist in both states at once. Tophat's trailer began to change as well. The darkness from our reality seeped through the shimmering brightness of his glamour, the two forces colliding in a chaotic dance of flickering light and shadow. Everything around me pulsed and flashed, merging together until it settled into a single, cohesive image—one my mind could finally grasp. I sighed and relaxed, resigning to my new reality.

Tophat smiled. "I'll have Buster bring Winnie to your tent tonight. It'll be good for you to have her energy when you're working."

I gulped hard. "Tonight? Oh, but I don't think…"

"You're ready, Jane. There's no doubt in my mind that you're ready."

Buster and a handful of the other carnies had been at it all day, getting the Fortune Teller tent set up for me. Truth be told, it was the other men who did the real work—the hauling, the hammering, the sweat-streaked labor. Meanwhile, little ole Buster strutted around, barking out orders with the flair of the Carnival Barker he was, arms waving and voice booming like he was orchestrating the grandest show on earth. Classic Buster, always in charge, even if it was mostly for show.

Nancy was happier than in a pig in mud when she was told she was going to spend the evening with Zora's sister Elaine and her boys. I explained to her that she was going to have to go to work just like me. Elaine was just as excited to have a little girl in tow. She dressed her up in a wig and a fancy little dress and paraded her around like the bell of the carny ball. Of course, Nancy ate up all the attention and took her "duties" very seriously. Normally, I would have never let Nancy out of

Chapter Twelve

my sight, but there was something in Tophat's assurances that made me believe we were truly safe in the World.

The Fortune Teller tent was warm—more so than any of the other tents I had been in in the World. Maybe it was the thick, velvet drapes that hung along the sides of the canvas walls that held in the midday heat. Maybe it was the warmth from the incense burning and the candles that were lit up everywhere. I couldn't tell. When I surveyed the area, I took note of all the things within. A round table draped in an intricate lace cloth sat at the center. It was the same table from Tophat's trailer. Its surface was adorned with his crystal ball that refracted the candlelight into ghostly patterns against the burgundy and indigo tapestries. The Augen deck was next to the ball in a neat pile with their mysterious images face down. Winnie slithered languidly in her enclosure in one corner of the room. A tall mirror was perched against the tent rod in the opposite corner of Winnie. Surrounding it were all trinkets, lights, candles, and countless arcane objects that lent the space an undeniable air of mysticism.

But it was all a lie—a glamour—'cause the true magic turned on when I stepped inside. I don't know how I knew, but Tophat's voice whispered in my head when I breathed in the thickness of the air. And when I stepped in front of the mirror, Tophat's voice needled again against my temple, a slow hum that filled my ears with a muffled sound. "Madame Jane Crowe from the Shadowlands of

Endor," I heard, buried deep under the cacophony. "Madame Jane Crowe from the Shadowlands of Endor," Tophat repeated, more clearly the second time. "Madame Jane Crowe from the Shadowlands of Endor." His voice rang out clear as a bell, and I winced at how distinctly and how loudly it reverberated in my head.

I inhaled sharply, and taking his cue, I began to whisper to my reflection the words he spoke, "Madame Jane Crowe from the Shadowlands of Endor." And as if on command, my image in the mirror began to flicker in the same way Tophat's trailer flickered, the same way Winnie flickered in her enclosure from venomous viper to docile python.

I murmured the words, "Madame Jane Crowe from the Shadowlands of Endor," over and over, a rhythmic chant that seemed to pull the very air around me into a frenzy. Each repetition brought the flickering light to a fever pitch, the shadows and glimmers around me pulsating wildly, like a heartbeat made of fire and electricity. The tent seemed to shift, to breathe, as though it straddled two worlds—one grounded in reality, the other steeped in something far more mysterious.

Before my eyes, my clothing began to transform without so much as a tug or a tear. The cheerful yellow dress with its Peter Pan collar dissolved, replaced by a loose blouse embroidered with intricate patterns that seemed to tell stories of their own. A fringed shawl draped itself over my shoulders, and a long, flowing skirt brushed

Chapter Twelve

softly against my legs, whispering with every move. Around my neck, an assortment of charms and talismans caught the light: a crescent moon pendant, glimmering crystals, and a medallion engraved with arcane symbols. Yet amidst it all, the crow feather necklace remained, like a tether to my own reality, so that I wouldn't get lost in the glamouring. My hands, too, were transformed. Rings now adorned every finger, each one unique, their stones and metals shimmering in the dim light. As I moved, I jingled and jangled with the sound of a hundred tiny trinkets, like a gypsy conjured from the shadows of the night, alive with magic and mystery. For the first time, I felt like I belonged to both worlds, neither wholly here nor there but something entirely my own.

But it wasn't just my clothing that had transformed; the change ran deeper, more personal, as though the very essence of who I was had been reshaped. To my astonishment, my sandy blonde hair was no more. In its place cascaded long raven locks, dark as midnight, sculpted into thick waves that tumbled heavily down my back. Each curl seemed to shimmer in the dim light, full of life and mystery, a stark contrast to the girl I'd been mere moments before.

And my eyes! Gone was the icy blue color I'd known all my life. Now, they sparkled a sharp, almost metallic gray, so striking they felt like a piece of Tophat's soul staring back at me. Yet nestled within the gray, flecks of gold shimmered like sunlit embers, unmistakably Zora's. They weren't just my eyes anymore; they were something shared, something woven from all of us. They weren't mine, yet I knew in my heart they belonged to me just the same. They were *ours*, a connection, a bond forged in the strange glamour of that moment.

One of the canvas flaps of the tent flew open, and I quickly spun on my heels. There, in the makeshift doorway, my carnival friends stood with curious and prying eyes.

"Well, well!" Sis bellowed. "Looks like you are ready to work your magic... no pun intended!"

I laughed as she approached me. Vesper and Chickie circled around the tent, taking note of the décor. I could tell by their scrunched up faces they were feigning as if they were unimpressed with my setup, but I knew it was jealousy that oozed from them.

Sis held my arms out from side to side and inspected every aspect of my outfit. "Wow," she gushed. "Just... wow! I am absolutely blown away! I didn't think you'd be able to pull this off!" She ran her fingers through one side of my hair. "This wig! It's practically undetectable. Where did you get this? This wasn't in the storage tent!"

"Oh no," I lied. "Zora and I went into town this afternoon."

Chickie blew air from her lips, making them reverberate with a *pssh* sound. "Yeah, Janey. Your get-up's so good, I bet the people looking for you wouldn't even be able to tell."

My ears buzzed with her words, and a hot rage coursed through me, setting every nerve alight.

Chapter Twelve

Instinct clawed at me, screaming to snatch up the crystal ball from the table and slam it straight into her smug little face. I could see it clear as day in my mind—her delicate features crumpling like a cheap carnival flyer, those pretty eyes of hers sinking into the hollows where her pert nose used to be. There'd be nothing behind them, of course, just a hollow void, because if she'd had an ounce of sense, she'd have kept her trap shut about Aleister sniffing me out.

In the swirl of my dark thoughts, a bitter laugh bubbled up. *Oh, Tophat, forgive me for smearing Chickadee's brains all over your precious crystal ball,* I thought wryly. And then, as if conjured by the devil himself, I saw myself holding that bloodied ball up to Winnie's enclosure, letting her forked tongue flick and dart at the sticky mess like it was some macabre treat. The image was grotesque, but it didn't bother me one bit. In that moment, it almost felt ... right.

Time seemed to slip and twist in that moment, stretching seconds into something far longer. It couldn't have been more than a heartbeat or two between Chickie's sharp words and the sudden gust of wind that tore through the carnival grounds. The canvas opening of the tent fluttered violently, snapping like a whip as the wind roared past, pressing hard against the tent's sides. A low, eerie howl seeped in through every crack and gap, filling the space with an almost living sound.

Sis jolted at the noise, her nerves betraying her in a quick shudder that snapped me out of my dark thoughts. Thoughts so unlike me, so foreign, yet so vivid they felt like they belonged to someone else. The murderous and strangely curious idea lingered at the edges of my mind, reluctant to let go. I shook it off, tucking it away into the back of my head with a silent promise to revisit it later. *Zora will know what to make of this*, I thought, making a mental note to speak to her when the time was right.

Vesper took in a deep breath when the wind died down. "I see Tophat gave you his crystal ball."

"Didn't he make *you* get your own?" Chickie said to Vesper.

I peered over Sis's shoulder, ignoring her examination of every last item of my ensemble. "It's just temporary," I lied again. "Just until I can buy one for myself. Tophat says it's my first line of business when…"

"What are these cards?" Chickie whined as she picked up the Augen deck.

Quickly, I scurried passed Sis and swiped them out of Chickie's hands. "Yeah, embarrassing, I know. Tophat called it a Dummy Deck, just until…"

"You can buy your own," Sis said with a sigh. "I swear, that guy is good, but he sure does nickel and dime us!"

I wrung my hands together to release some of my nervous tension. "Sure does."

"Well, seems like Tophat set you up real nice over here," Chickie said, the contempt in her voice thick and bitter.

Chapter Twelve

Before I could respond, Vesper made a gasping noise, and I turned my head to see that she had noticed Winnie in the corner of the room. "What is *she* doing here?"

"Oh... um..." I stammered, fumbling for an answer.

"Oh yeah," Sis interjected, "Buster told me Tophat isn't replacing Tina. He doesn't want to take on another snake charmer, but he didn't want to get rid of Winnie, so he figured that putting her in the Fortune Teller act would be spooky enough."

Vesper's chest heaved with a silent sob.

"I'm sorry," I said. "I didn't know. I know Tina was your best friend. If you want Winnie, you can absolutely have her."

"*Is* my best friend!" she shot back at me. "We're going to find her good and well."

Sis moved over to her and draped her arm around Vesper's shoulder. "It's okay, hon. She's okay. I just know it."

"Yeah, Janey," Chickie drawled. "Maybe you can divine where Serpentina is. When you get your own deck, of course."

My stomach churned at her words, and an electric pulse, like the beginnings of a lightning storm, tingled in my fingertips. I sucked down my growing rage before it had a chance to manifest.

I knew Sis could feel the energy shift in the tent because her voice raised an octave, and her demeanor changed. "Well, Janey! Our new Madame of the World, we just stopped by to make sure you had everything you needed and to wish you good luck on your first night."

I straightened my back and composed myself as best I could. "Thank you," I muttered. "I appreciate that."

"Yeah, good luck," Vesper said flatly.

"Break a leg," Chickie sang sarcastically.

Sis gathered them both, one at each side, and whisked them out of the tent. The canvas of the entrance flapped with an echo as they disappeared into the night, their chatter fading into the hum of the carnival. When they were gone, I let out a long sigh.

I sank into the chair at my table. Slowly, I placed the cards back where they belonged, neatly stacked beside the crystal ball. My fingers found the lacey edge of the table covering, and I began to toy with it absentmindedly, twisting and smoothing it over and over.

The silence was heavy, yet oddly comforting, as if the tent itself were holding its breath. Suddenly, another sound boomed outside the tent, startling me from my vacant thoughts.

"Lady Jane? Are you in there?"

His voice smashed through the fabric of the tent, deep and unmistakable. Duke. A shiver ran down my spine, the sound of his voice sending tingles through my body before I could stop them.

"Come in. I'm here!" I said, perhaps a little too quickly, too eagerly.

There was a rustle at the entrance, and I watched as Duke bent his body low to slip into

Chapter Twelve

the tent, his broad shoulders scraping against the edges of the opening. Once inside, he straightened up, towering over me with a small, cheerful bouquet of dandelions in his hand. The sight of them — those simple, wild blooms — stirred something in me, and before I could stop myself, a smile spread across my face, wide and uncontrollable.

I stood to greet him, the warmth of his presence filling the space between us, like something magnetic that pulled me closer without any need for words.

"The tent was down. Not quite ready for business?" he asked with a gentle smirk.

I blushed. I couldn't help it. The warmth rushed to my cheeks, and I bowed my head with slight embarrassment. "No. Not quite. I was just doing some last-minute stuff."

He held out his arm and presented the flowers to me. "These are for you," he said.

The warmth intensified on my face, and I bit my lower lip. "Thank you," I gushed. "Did the kids pick them again?"

"No. *I* did," he replied sheepishly, and I think my heart melted at the words.

"Oh. You did? They're lovely."

"I just wanted to wish you luck on your first night. You're gonna be great, I know it."

"Thank you."

"You look beautiful, by the way. Different. You don't look like you, but I can tell it's you. Does that make sense?"

"Yes, it does. Thank you," I repeated. I felt like an idiot. There was so much more that I wanted to say, but the only words that croaked out were "thank you." I wanted to slap my face with my palm!

"Why don't you come out to the party tonight after the World shuts down?" he asked.

Friday nights after hours in the World were always a hullabaloo. The card games got rowdy, the music blared from every corner, and dancing spilled out onto the trailer porches. Folks whooped and hollered, cutting loose like they'd struck gold, because Friday meant the biggest take of the week. And really, any excuse to tie one on was good enough for the lot of them.

But me? I had never joined in the fun. I would set me and Nancy up in the trailer and listen to the ruckus outside. I know it was my protective nature getting the best of me. Besides, Momma always said that nothing good ever happened after midnight!

I dipped my head low. "I don't think so," I muttered.

He frowned, and I'll be damned if there was ever a sweeter frown on a man's face. It was the kind of look that could twist your heart into a pretzel if you weren't careful. "Aw, Jane!" he crooned, his voice all syrupy like a radio show announcer. "You never hang out with us."

My heart fluttered like a little school girl with a big crush. "Well, it's hard. With Nancy and all…"

Chapter Twelve

"Nancy's a great kid! Let her have some fun. Besides, she'll have been with Elaine's boys all night, eatin' all that sugary junk! She'll be so wired she won't know what to do with herself!"

I swished my foot across the dusty ground and hummed with hesitation.

"C'mon! We'll get into a game of Rummy. Or how about some poker? Maybe dance? You like to dance, don't you Jane?"

My ears went hot, and I knew the color pink was blooming all over my cheeks. "A little..."

"So, say you'll join me... I mean... us." He wiped his hands down the front of his trousers, and I giggled at his nervousness. "And I promise, no one's gonna cheat ya or anything. They save that business for the customers. Or we don't have to play cards. I mean, we could just..."

"Dance?" I interrupted.

"Or talk." The tips of his ears went red, and I didn't feel so bad about my own embarrassment.

"I'd like that," I whispered as I pressed the flowers to my face and inhaled.

Duke smiled wide and took a step forward closer to me. He paused and looked me deep in the eyes. The blackness of his reflected back a glimmering scene of stars dancing and swirling and circling around in a majestic wave. "I'd like that very much, Jane," he said and kissed me on my hot cheek.

He turned and left the tent.

"Hook the flap open," I called to him. "I'm ready now."

Chapter Thirteen

Friday, May 26th 1944
The Gentry Brothers' Wonders of the World Carnival
Madame Jane Crowe's Tent
Glenmoor, Ohio
Night of the Waxing Crescent Moon

The night turned out to be busier than I ever could've imagined. Truth be told, I didn't have a clue what to expect on my first night working the gig, but it sure wasn't the whirlwind that unfolded. At one point, Buster poked his round, shiny head into the tent, waving his pudgy hand with all five fingers spread wide like a starfish. "Five more minutes," his gesture hollered without a word. At first, I didn't get it. But then it hit me like a freight train—I peeked outside and saw a line, long as a Sunday sermon, snaking clear around the tent. My head spun. Was it because I was the new girl, fresh blood and all that jazz? Had Buster put a little too much razzle-dazzle in his spiel, spinning a tale that painted me as some sort of wonder? Or

Chapter Thirteen

maybe—just maybe—the whispers had started making the rounds, and folks were here because I was damn good at what I did.

Whatever the reason, I tightened my grip on the edge of the table, took a breath, and got ready to face the next curious face in line. What did I know? I used the Augen deck like Tophat had instructed, and I just kind of got swept away with each of the customers. There was a learning curve to it at first, and I admit, it took me some time to adjust to the cards—to the way they shifted and changed and danced before my eyes. It was funny, too, how them people in front of me had no idea the real magic that was laid before them. To their eyes, the cards were just the cards—static images painted on old, thick cardstock. But to me... Well, I saw something else, something dynamic. Something ... *more*.

Some folks took one look at the deck and turned their noses up, calling it too plain, too simple, as if the magic wasn't in the cards but in the frills around them. One gal, young and smug, claimed she was a bona fide expert in Tarot. She squinted at my cards, tilted her head this way and that, and finally huffed, saying she'd never seen a deck like mine before; of course, she hadn't. It needled her something fierce, enough that she insisted I ditch the cards and use the crystal ball instead.

That took us down another road altogether. The ball showed me stars aligning, the heavens splitting wide, and visions both beautiful and bone-chilling swirling in the glass. Her face went pale as milk as I spoke, and I couldn't help but wonder if she regretted asking for the "expert's" route.

Regardless, the Augen deck got the majority of my attention. It was nothing like the Thoth deck I kept hidden under my new mattress in Zora's trailer. While the Thoth deck was pretty enough and carried the clout of being from Crowley's design, the Augen deck spoke to me... literally.

At first, I had no idea what the cards were trying to tell me. Often, the images would change so fast, it was difficult for my mind to process the pictures and decipher a meaning all at the same time. Half the time I just winged it—praying to someone out there that the words I spoke made some kind of sense. Apparently, it must have because the line around my tent got longer and longer, and the hum of the crowd surrounding me got heavier and heavier.

After a while though, it just kind of *became*. I can't really explain how or when the shift in my brain happened, but things sort of *clicked*. Fell into place. I fell into a steady rhythm with the cards, and soon I could hear them whispering to me from beyond their plane of reality. It was surreal and gave me that drunk feeling—hence my obliviousness to time.

Buster came into the tent as I was finishing up with a client. An older woman had lost her cat and was hoping I could locate poor old Mr. Boots for her. I tried explaining that it didn't work like

Chapter Thirteen

that, but she was insistent that I tried. When I laid out the deck, trying frantically to wrack my brain for a half-believable story for the missing feline, the cards began to go wild. The images jumbled together with sharp edges that resembled cut marks from a knife. An angel appeared on the far-right card and raced across the deck over to the box on the left. By the time it reached the box, its wings had been torn off, and it appeared to be falling from the sky. My hands got clammy as all get out, and sweat started to coat the skin underneath the heavy fabrics of my glamoured costume.

"Amy," I heard a whisper in my head.

"Who's Amy?" I blurted out, and the woman's face fell to the floor. She was as still and silent as a statue, and her visage frightened me, for I thought she was having a heart attack.

And that's when Buster came in and said the normal Buster-like pleasantries—something about how Madame Crowe needed a short break to let the universe give her a recharge. Utter crap. He ushered the still speechless woman out of the tent and closed the flap behind him. He turned on his heels with a scowl on his little face.

"What's going on here, Jane?" he asked accusingly.

"What do you mean? I'm doing my job! Reading people's fortunes like I'm supposed to."

"Honey, you got a line that stretches all the way to Timbuktu! We can't have that. It's not good for business."

My tongue clicked on the roof of my mouth. "So, now I'm being chastised for doing a *good* job? I can't help it if every looney wants to see their future."

"You need to find a balance, or else Tophat's not gonna be happy with tonight's take," he said sternly. "That line isn't gonna wait all night for you."

"Fine! Then let those rubes get off and spend their money elsewhere."

"That ain't how this racket runs, Missy! The idea's to have 'em blow their dough fast and thick. If Old Lady Smithers only waits five minutes to get her reading, she's got time to toss her nickels at three games, catch Duke's act, and grab herself a plate of popcorn. But you stretch her wait out to twenty minutes, and suddenly she's only got time for a couple games and maybe a cold pop if she's lucky. We ain't lookin' to send folks home with pockets jingling, Crowe—we want those purse strings snapped shut by the time they hit the exit!"

"So... you don't want me to do my job," I said indignantly.

"That's not what I said. Do your job, of course. Just don't do it so fucking well. Fudge some stuff, Janey. Not everyone can get a miracle. Especially here."

I rolled my eyes and opened my mouth to respond, but he interrupted me before I could get a chance to speak.

"Ya know that Vesper broad? Wasn't the best of Fortune Tellers, but she did have an eye for

Chapter Thirteen

business. She kept a small hour glass that held sand for ten minutes and used it as part of her shtick. Ask her for it. She don't need it no more, and you sure as hell do."

I let out a huff as Buster slipped out of the tent. With a practiced motion, he hitched up the canvas flap, letting the waiting crowd catch sight of the dim glow inside. "Alright, folks, settle down now," he barked, clapping his hands together for effect. "Madame Jane's back in action! She's recharged, reconnected, and ready to commune with the great beyond. It's not an easy gig. Talking to the spirits can be draining work, ya know."

The line of patrons let out a collective chuckle that rang out in the night. I inhaled deeply, readying myself for my next client. "Come in! Come in! I bid thee welcome," I called from where I sat, and when I looked up to see who had entered my tent, I nearly fainted. My face went white as a sheet, and I thought, *You must look like Mr. Boots's owner right now.*

Sheriff Tannehill McCrory.

He loomed in the threshold, a giant of a man in his sheriff uniform and cowboy hat. He put one hand on his hip, and the motion of it pulled his sheriff jacket to the side and revealed his service weapon. I damn near froze at the site of him cause with McCrory around, I knew that spelled trouble not just for the carnival but for me as well. Some moments passed by, and he cleared his throat at my lack of a greeting. "Excuse me!"

His deep, rumbly voice snapped me out of my frozen fear.

I shook my head, and trying to muster up as much sweetness and pleasantries as I could, I sang out, "Oh, how rude of me, Sherriff! Please, do come in."

He took a step inside and unfastened the tent canvas door, and it flopped down with an ominous *thud*.

"Oh, that's not necessary, Sheriff," I said, trying to mask my uneasiness of being alone with him. "The others stand far enough back that they can't hear anything from our session."

He took a lumbering step forward, his boots scuffing against the canvas floor, and before I could even blink, he was at my table. His movements were like a predator closing in on its prey. With a measured hand, he pulled off his cowboy hat, ran his fingers through his hair, and slicked it back in one fluid motion.

The man sitting before me was not the same McCrory I'd seen at the Big Tent. There was a ruggedness to him now—a shadow of stubble on his jaw that hadn't been there before, peppered with silver like ashes left after a fire. His eyes were heavy with something sharper—anger, exhaustion, maybe both. He didn't look like the lusty rogue who'd pawed at Serpentina. This McCrory was a man on a mission, and that look of determination made my blood run colder than the spring night outside. I felt my senses heighten, every nerve in me braced for what I knew was coming.

Chapter Thirteen

"I'm afraid there ain't gonna be a session," he said matter-of-factly.

I knew he wasn't here for a reading. I wasn't dumb, but I knew in order to preserve my safety and the safety of my girl, I had to pretend like I was. "Oh? That's unfortunate."

He dug into the inner chest pocket of his jacket and pulled out a small notepad and pen. "You're new here, aren't you?" he asked as he flipped to a blank page and clicked the top of the pen.

"Yessir," I answered politely, remembering how Momma had taught me my manners when it came to Johnny Law.

"Madame Jane Crowe?" he questioned as he stared at me with his crystal blue eyes. "What's your real name, darling?"

The side of my mouth twitched uncontrollably. I couldn't help it; it was a natural reflex or something. But I knew he picked up on the slight gesture because his eyes flashed, and he put the pen to the paper.

"Jane Crowe," I croaked.

"You sure about that?" he sneered.

I puffed air from my lips with a *psh* sound—anything to mask the mounting nerves in my body. "With all due respect, Sheriff, I think I would know my own name."

He paused to glare at me, then scribbled on his notepad. "Uh huh. And just how long have you been with the carnival, Madame Jane?" The sound of my name from his lips was like a hot iron poker branding a bull with the emblem of its owner. There was no doubt in my mind he was on to me.

My thoughts shot off like fireworks, each one more frantic than the last. I was the greenhorn, the new girl who barely knew Serpentina or any of the others. I hadn't been around long enough to cozy up to anyone, let alone know their secrets. This little interrogation—because that's what it felt like—had to be about Aleister and his crew. My palms grew slick with sweat, the damp fabric of my dress offering little relief as I wiped them down once, then again. I was conscious of every gesture, every facial expression, every cross and re-cross of my legs, and I knew McCrory was scrutinizing my every move. "Less than a fortnight, sir. My daughter and I arrived on the night of the fifteenth."

McCrory's eyes shot open with surprise. "Daughter? The Cooch girl didn't say anything about you having a daughter!"

I think my face contorted in a way that matched his sentiment. "Pardon? Cooch girl?" Thoughts of Chickie and Vesper turning me in to the sheriff raced in my mind, and it was getting harder and harder to hide my expression, my anger, my utter rage at the thought of them betraying me. Immediately, I envisioned myself running from the tent, swooping up Nancy, and hightailing it outta there! But not before I stopped at the Cooch Tent and beat Chickie and Vesper's faces bloody!

Chapter Thirteen

"I'm sure you know I'm running an investigation, Miss Jane. I was just at the adult entertainment tent, and the very fair and kind ladies told me I should speak to you—you being a psychic and all." He turned his head around in a semicircle, looking for something. "They never said you had a kid. Where is the scamp now?"

A little sigh escaped my lips. "She's with the sitter," I said, relieved. "So I could work."

"I see, I see," he hummed. "Well, ya see, I don't like missing girls on my watch, Miss Jane. So, if there's anything you can tell me about the snake charmer—the one they called Serpentina—it would be very helpful to me."

"I didn't know her well," I replied.

"But you *did* know her," he shot back quickly. "Why else would you have her serpent in your tent?" He pointed to Winnie's enclosure.

I looked over my shoulder, and Winnie's head bobbed languidly up to the screen top of the cage. Her image in my head had stopped flashing long ago, and all I could see was her true form—the docile python. "Oh, I... um..." I stammered. "The Boss gave the snake to me. Said it added mystery to the Fortune Teller gig. Said he wasn't going to take on another snake charmer."

"That's a dangerous creature," he commented and wrote something in his notepad. "Mr. Solwood wouldn't give it to you if you didn't know how to handle it, now would he?"

It hit me that McCrory only saw the deadly viper in the tank, and I was at a loss for words. Struck dumb like a mute.

"Tell me, when was the last time you saw her?" McCrory asked.

"Saw who, sir?"

McCrory let out a low, disgruntled huff, his thick fingers fiddling with the oversized gold buckle on his belt. The way he slid it back and forth over his protruding belly made an irritating swishing noise against his cotton shirt—a sound that set my teeth on edge. He shifted in his seat, his hard-set eyes narrowing. "The snake charmer," he said, his voice gruff and gravelly. "Serpentina."

I didn't need time to chew on that one. I knew exactly what he wanted to hear, but I also knew my answer wouldn't sit well with him. If he was already hot under the collar, this was bound to tip the scales. I locked eyes with him, steady and sharp. "The last time I saw Tina," I said, pausing just long enough to let my words hang heavy in the air, "was when she performed in the Big Tent..." My gaze didn't waver as I added, "for you."

McCrory stiffened in the chair. He clicked the pen closed and put it and the notepad back in his front jacket pocket. "The other ladies said you might be able to help my investigation with your sixth sense and all."

It was my turn to stiffen. The nerves welled inside me something awful, and I instinctively picked up the cards of the Augen deck and began

Chapter Thirteen

shuffling them mindlessly. I knew what had happened to Tina. I mean, I didn't *know*, but I knew enough that she was never coming back, but I needed to keep my breathing steady and keep my emotions in check so as to not tip off McCrory. "It doesn't work that way, Sheriff."

"Oh no? Then how does it work? Or does it not work at all? Do I need to charge this establishment with fraud? That's a very serious offense, Miss Jane. A hefty fine. Loss of your job. Possible jail time. But if you have something of substance I can work with—a name, something you saw that seemed suspicious, anything that could be construed as out of the ordinary, then maybe I can letcha off the hook here." His voice echoed his threats, and my heart began to flutter with anxiety.

I dared not look up to meet McCrory's eyes; instead, I kept my gaze on the cards. They pulsated against my palms and sent electric shocks to my fingers as I gingerly weaved them in and out and back and forth against each other. They seemed to sing out to me in my head, like they were begging for me to lay them down on the table so they could reveal to me a spectacular image. Each card flick, each hand twist, each swish of the cardboard swiping against each other made the power of the deck increase, seep into my wrists, travel into my arms, and send a surge of warmth into my body. Soon, I felt weightless, as if I was floating above the table and looking down on the sinister man before me. And when the power inside reached a sweltering pinnacle, I finally spoke. "I can read your fortune, Sheriff, and only *your* fortune," I said with stern voice and placed the cards back on the table faced down.

Something changed in his aura, like something hovering around him. A dark shadow hugged his shoulders, and when I blinked my eyes to get a better look, I think it *smiled* at me.

"I wish I could help you find Tina," I continued, "and whoever else you're looking for, but like I said, it doesn't work that way."

McCrory's eyes darkened with a glint of defeat, and the shadow glided away from his shoulders and over to Winnie's enclosure. He stood up, placed his hat back on and tipped his head in my direction. "Thank you, Madame," he said, his demeanor completely changing. "I'll let you get back to work now. But if something does cross your mind, please make sure you let me know."

"Will do, Sheriff," I said politely, and he turned around and walked out.

I let out a shaky breath, the sound louder than I intended. It was then I realized my fingers were curled tight around the edge of the table, my knuckles white as bone. For all the nerve I'd mustered up to stare him down, there was no denying it—something about Tannehill McCrory set my skin crawling. He didn't just unnerve me; he lingered in the air, like the faint stink of a cigar long snuffed out but still clinging to the room.

Chapter Thirteen

The night dragged on, with me shuffling cards and peering into the crystal ball until the Ferris Wheel's lights flickered their final spin. At closing time, Buster's round face appeared through the tent flap. He flashed his "five-finger salute," the universal sign that time was up and proceeded to escort the last stragglers out of the World with a bark and a wave.

After his earlier scolding, I'd picked up the pace—spinning more hurried fortunes than thoughtful ones, tossing out broad predictions when, with a little care, I could've conjured something truly spellbinding. But for the sake of Buster, Tophat, and the lifeblood of the World, I bit my tongue, swallowed my pride, and hustled through the crowd like a good little cog in the carnival machine. Still, I knew deep down that when the earnings were tallied, Buster was bound to be sour about the haul from my first night. He'd probably threaten to have me sacked if I didn't increase my revenue, but I knew what he said didn't ultimately matter. At the end of the day, it was Tophat who called the shots, and I knew he wanted to keep me close to his chest.

The back lot of the World was alive as everyone gathered in celebration. Bendy Bella, the contortionist, provided everyone with her famous homemade moonshine. Vesper and Chickie sat on the front porch of one of the trailers with mason jars filled with the stuff—their feet dangled off the side while their flapper-girl dresses hung low off their shoulders. They were arm in arm, singing loudly and drunkenly to the songs on the Victrola from inside. Vesper snorted in drunken delight and chastised Chickie (who was equally intoxicated) for singing the wrong verse of the song. And they laughed and laughed. And laughed even harder when I walked by.

"Hell-ooooo, Janey May!" Chickie sang out.

I grimaced and gave a slight wave.

Vesper elbowed her. "That's not her name, silly! She's Jane Crowe. Madame Jane Crowe. Show some respect." By the way their voices lilted up an octave, it was obvious they were, in fact, both intoxicated already.

"Yeah, yeah," Chickie slurred. "She's the new you. The new Vesper. *I* should be the new Vesper."

"Oh, honey. No one can be the new me. There's only one me."

"Ain't that the truth!" Chickie exclaimed, and they clinked their jars.

"Hey, Jane!" Vesper called out to me. "I can't tell which I like better: the costume or the real you."

I smiled a fake smile at them as I hustled by. I hadn't even realized that the glamour had worn off the second I stepped outside of the tent. My hair was back to its normal ashy blonde color, and my clothes had transformed back to what I had on before I began reading fortunes. I looked down to see my yellow dress flitting at my ankles and when I reached up to smooth the Peter Pan collar down at the sides, all the jewelry that had jingled and jangled on my fingers and wrists were no longer there.

Chapter Thirteen

And I had never physically taken them off.

Finally, I reached one of the rickety wooden benches we used for eating quarters. There, under the glow of a swaying lantern, Sis was holding court as the dealer in a lively card game. Zora, Razor, and Elaine were perched around the table, their cards clutched tight and expressions as sharp as a knife's edge. At the far end, Duke sat with Nancy nestled in his lap, the little imp holding a fan of cards just below her eyes. Duke leaned close, whispering something in her ear that made her giggle, her laughter bubbling softly over the din of the night.

"Hey!" I exclaimed as I raced over to them. "Someone wanna tell me what's going on?"

"Poke-uh, Mommy," Nancy replied, not once taking her eyes off her cards.

"Excuse me?" I wailed at Duke. "You're teaching my three-year-old *poker*?"

Duke laughed heartily. "Well, they gotta learn sometime, right?"

I put my hand on my hip and bounced up and down on my leg. "Not at three!"

Duke slipped the cards out of Nancy's hand and set her on the ground as he stood up. She flung her arms around my legs in a tight embrace, and I patted the top of her head. "She's a smart kid. Fast learner. I was up five bucks."

"Stop it! You kid!"

"Kid you not. Scout's honor."

I bent down and picked Nancy up. "I didn't know you were a Boy Scout," I said to him.

"There's lots you don't know," he said with a sly grin.

His charming demeanor made my stomach do flipflops, but I just readjusted Nancy at my waist and smiled back. "You helped Mr. Duke win some money?" I asked her.

"Yep!" she replied with a strong nod, her hair bouncing around her face.

"That was very sweet of you, Nancy. I'm sure Mr. Duke will buy you something special as a reward."

Duke glared at me with a side smile.

"Popcorn!" Nancy exclaimed.

"No, no!" I retorted. "I'm willing to bet Miss Nancy had quite her fair share of sweets to last a lifetime! Did you have fun with Miss Elaine and the boys tonight?" I asked her.

She nodded. "They my fends, Mommy."

I pulled her in closer to me, inhaled her sweet sugary scent, and kissed the top of her head. "I'm so happy for you. It's so good to have friends."

The music swelled to an old ragtime song. The trumpets and horns and drums blared with frenetic energy. "How 'bout that dance, Miss Crowe?" Duke said, and he reached out his hand toward Nancy.

My face twisted slightly, and Duke gave me a quick wink. "You too, of course, Madame."

Nancy's tiny finger curled tightly around one of Duke's sturdy digits, and before I knew it, we were scampering off like a couple of mischievous kids chasing the sound of the music. The

Chapter Thirteen

air buzzed with laughter and the stomp of feet as a sea of folks swirled and shimmied around us, hootin' and hollerin' like they didn't have a care in the world. The music had a kind of magic to it, lifting us off our feet and spinning us into a whirl of wonder that only the World could conjure.

For those precious moments, Nancy and I were untouchable—free as the wind, far from the shadows of enemies near and far. I danced like I hadn't a single worry, the rhythm shaking loose every ounce of tension I'd carried.

Even Buster, that crusty little lecher, shuffled his way into the crowd, his smile wide enough to rival the moon. He caught my eye, tipped his hat, and threw me a thumbs up. "Good first night," he said, his voice loud enough to cut through the music.

I nearly stumbled out of sheer surprise. Of all the things I'd expected, a compliment from Buster sure wasn't one of them.

When the music died down and the night began to slowly unravel, it didn't truly end—not for me, anyway. In my head, the beat rolled on, a wild symphony of drums and voices, echoing from somewhere beyond the veil. The melodies weren't of this world, sung in tongues I couldn't name yet somehow understood deep in the marrow of my being.

The rhythm pulsed through me—an intoxicating rush that made me stagger as if I'd drunk too much of Bella's moonshine, yet I hadn't touched a drop. I thought, *This must be how Vesper and Chickie are feeling right now.*

Duke helped me settle Nancy into bed later on. Once she was sound asleep, we drifted to the couch in the main room, the soft light from the oil lamp casting warm shadows on the walls. We talked for hours, just like he'd said we would—stories, laughter, and shared secrets filling the space between us.

Zora never made it back to the trailer that night. Duke and I surmised she'd decided to stay with Razor. It was better that way, really. The idea of her walking in on us—sitting close, heads bent together, voices hushed—might've made things awkward. Especially when the talking turned to giggling, and the giggling turned to whispering, and the whispering turned to kissing.

Chapter Fourteen

Thursday, June 1st 1944
West 5th Street
Downtown East Liverpool, Ohio
Afternoon of the Waxing Gibbous Moon

Duke and I had fallen into a routine rather quickly. More quickly than I had ever anticipated a relationship to form. After that night we spent dancing and laughing and talking and heavily petting like stereotypical crush-sick teenagers, things heated up real fast. Zora unofficially moved out of the trailer and in with Razor, and Duke ended up staying with me and Nancy (unbeknownst to Buster and Tophat, of course). And while we shared a bed, we didn't *share* a bed. Duke was the perfect gentleman in that respect. Being sexual was not on the top of my to-do list. I mean, fooling around was one thing, but the actual deed was another. But Duke said he would wait for as long as I needed, and I thought that was just swell.

I liked Duke. A lot. He was sweet and kind and gentle and all those other mushy-gushy words.

There was no denying that he was nice to look at, and his body structure was godly—beyond compare in every way, but he was good to Nancy, and that's what counted the most. He treated her like a father should treat his daughter, and that was the biggest reason why I was so attracted to Duke.

The thought gnawed at me, and my chest ached as I sat there watching Duke make silly faces to coax a giggle from Nancy. It was how I had dreamed Aleister might have been with her—a gentle, doting father, present in ways that mattered. How blind had I been? Blind and stupid, spellbound by his charm, his power, and the allure of his teachings.

The signs had been there all along, glaring and undeniable. The cryptic lessons he insisted I study, the way he held court among the others in our so-called "community" back in England, the whispers of prophecy he shared only with me in the still of night. Nancy wasn't supposed to be a child to him—she was supposed to be his legacy, his strength, his rebirth. The vessel for his ambitions, the anchor to an aging man desperate to outwit mortality. She wasn't his daughter. She was his revival. His grand experiment.

And then they called her empty. *Vuota*. And that was the end of that; I knew I had to flee and flee quickly. But Aleister wasn't the sort of man to accept an ending. He would stop at nothing to get her back, to shape her into what he needed for his dark conjurings, his rituals, his *awakening of the Beast*.

Chapter Fourteen

Because as long as Aleister breathed, we weren't safe.

But with Duke around, it seemed like I had a fighting chance—he was automatic protection, and I knew being by his side would bring Nancy and me an extra layer of safety. Duke played the role of protector and companion much like Momma's loyal shepherds.

That morning at breakfast, the usual crew sat on the benches chatting and eating what the cooks considered a nutritious meal.

"Not this runny stuff again," Sis complained as the eggs dripped off her fork.

Nancy laughed, and Sis exaggerated just for her by scrunching up her nose. Nancy mimicked Sis's gesture.

"Did Tophat bring on new cooks that we just don't know about?" Vesper asked.

"Maybe the World's going belly-up!" Chickie exclaimed. "Maybe they can't afford to feed us no more, and we'll be shutting our doors soon!"

I rolled my eyes and bounced Nancy on my knee. Chickie's dramatics wore on me. We hadn't really spoken much since I was made the Fortune Teller, and she got sent to the Cooch. I knew she was jealous because I had gotten the job she wanted. And I knew she was jealous because gossip in the World spread quickly, and Chickie definitely got wind of the fact that Duke and I were an item, which seemed weird to me because she supposedly had that pen-pal fella of hers. Regardless, if she really had been my friend, she would have been happy for me instead of being green with envy. Besides, she had betrayed my trust and had made some questionable comments in passing, so… I guess we weren't really friends to begin with anyway. Which, to be quite honest, was a-okay with me.

"Now you just hold your horses there, Sassafras! The World ain't going nowhere!" Buster growled with his high-pitched voice.

"Jesus Christ, Buster!" Sis squealed. "You gave us a start!"

"Yeah, Buster!" Vesper chimed. "Your sneaky ways nearly scared all the best performers to death!"

The table erupted with laughter. Buster was not amused. "Aw! Quit your squawking and listen up." He took a little notepad from his front jacket pocket, and it reminded me of the one McCrory had on him the other night. Buster flipped it open and tore out a page. "The Boss says we need to go on a supply run."

"'Bout time!" Sis exclaimed and held up her fork full of slime. "You see this? This isn't considered edible in seven countries…"

"Nine," Chickie interjected sarcastically.

"Nine," Sis agreed. "Yet the cook is passing this off as *eggs*. Let me ask you, Buster, what did *you* have for breakfast this morning?"

"Oh, you never mind that, Savoy," Buster answered.

Sis dropped the fork onto her plate. "See! Just as I suspected. Favoritism in its purest form."

The table gave a collective grumble.

Chapter Fourteen

"Now, now! Quit your bellyaching!" Buster groaned. "The Boss was real specific about this supply run. Sassafras and St. Clair," he said as he handed the page to Vesper. "This is what Tophat wants from you."

Vesper studied the paper then handed it to Chickie.

"Okay," Chickie said. "No big deal."

Then Buster tore out another page, but this one he folded up and gave to Zora. "Heart and Crowe," he said. "This one is for you."

Zora opened it gently, as if she were peeking at a top secret spy mission. She pursed her lips together and nodded her head. I narrowed my eyes at her as if to ask, "What's that about?" but her reaction let me know she would fill me in later.

"Janey," Buster began, "you're to drop the rugrat off with Elaine. We're going to East Liverpool in ten minutes, people. Sis, you're driving!"

The drive to East Liverpool wasn't long—fifteen minutes, give or take—but Sis made sure it felt like a thrill ride. She had a lead foot, and you could feel every ounce of it pressing that gas pedal. Buster, ever the nervous Nellie, sat shotgun, barking out warnings like he was getting paid by the word. "Be careful! Slow down! If you wreck Tophat's car, he's gonna wreck you!" he shrieked, his hands gripping the dashboard for dear life. That only egged Sis on. The more he panicked, the harder she pushed. Chickie, perched beside him, tried to stifle her giggles but wasn't doing a great job of it.

In the backseat, I was wedged between Zora and Vesper, a tight squeeze thanks to the car's cozy size. Every time the coarse denim of my overalls brushed against Vesper's bare knee, she huffed like a cat whose tail had been stepped on. She'd shift, pulling her leg away like I'd done it on purpose. "Sorry," I muttered the first couple of times, but by the third or fourth bump, I decided she could just deal with it. Her grumbling grew louder, but it didn't bother me any. Zora caught my eye and smirked, and I couldn't help but grin back. The car rattled along, a little too fast, with laughter and grumbles filling the air as we tore down the road like a pack of unruly kids.

When we reached the downtown area, we all hopped out of the car except for Sis. Buster had torn out another piece of his notebook paper and folded it up. "Sis," he said, "you stay here with the car until we all get back. Everyone's got their orders. But don't take too long. We got a show to do tonight."

"Thursday nights are the worst, Buster!" Chickie complained.

"Yeah, we hardly make no money!" Vesper added.

"Yeah, well, we don't make nothing on Wednesdays, and Tuesdays, and Mondays neither, so I don't know what you're getting at." Then he handed both Vesper and me an envelope with money in it. "Spend it wisely and bring back any change."

"Such a cheapskate!" Chickie complained.

Chapter Fourteen

"Well, you said yourself we have slow nights. Maybe if you showed those titties more, Chickadee, you'd pull in some more dough."

Chickie stuck out her tongue, and I stifled a giggle.

"You really want me to stay in the car?" Sis asked, her voice rife with aggravation. "There ain't nothing else Tophat needs me to do?"

"Just follow them orders, Sister," Buster said, and he winked at her. "Okay, ladies, I'm off," he announced. "Like I said, don't be too long. Get what's on your list and be back in a jiff."

"What about you, Buster?" I asked.

He waved his paper in the air. "I got my orders, too!" he said and hobbled down the street with his cane.

"Ugh!" Vesper sighed. "I guess we should split up."

"What does Tophat have you two doing anyway?" Chickie asked Zora.

"Oh, we gotta pick up some new props. Get Jane more things to get settled," she answered nonchalantly.

"Not fair! You guys get to do the fun stuff," Chickie whined.

"Yeah, but we're getting food, so we'll get to pick out what *we* like!" Vesper replied. "C'mon, Chick, let's go."

"Wait! I wanna call home first!"

"Yeah! Good idea. We'll find a booth on our way to the grocer. Bye, gals." And they took off in the opposite direction of Buster.

"That's actually a good idea," I said. "I'd like to call my mom if you don't mind."

"Sure. Not a problem," Zora said.

"What about you? You have anyone to call?"

"Nope. I got my sister and my man back at the World. Don't need to talk to anyone else."

I paused and eyed the folded paper in her hand. "We're not really getting new props, are we?"

Zora shook her head. "Better." She smiled, and her eyes twinkled with a thousand glittering yellow stars.

When we found a payphone on one of the street corners, I used the trick that Sis taught me when I first came to the World. "Hello, Operator?" I said when the cheery voice on the other end answered with a "Hello?"

"How may I help you?" she replied.

"I'd like to place a collect call to New York."

"Certainly," she said. "May I have the number?"

My nerves made my arms itch. I was afraid I had forgotten Momma's phone number, but finally I stammered, "TO5-6456. Alice Baker."

"And who may I say is calling?"

"Kay. Kay Fabe."

"Thank you, Miss Fabe. Please hold while I connect the call."

I looked to Zora as I heard Momma's phone line buzzing on the other end. As each ring passed without a pickup, my mind started to fear the worst: *Aleister got to her. She's dead on the kitchen floor with her entrails spilled all around her. The dogs haven't eaten in days, and they have no other choice*

Chapter Fourteen

but to feast upon Momma's fresh dead corpse in order to prolong their own survival a little while longer. Blood has matted her hair, and I just know the coroner is going to have one heck of a time brushing it out and making her look presentable for the funeral.

As the scene unfolded in my head, the expression on my face must have grown grimmer because Zora mouthed to me, "Are you okay?"

A police car slowly drove down West 5th Street. Zora tugged at my overalls to get my attention, but the phone clicked on Momma's end, and I heard her sweet voice answer, "Hello?"

My body twirled in delight to hear her alive and well.

"Hello, Ms. Baker? I have a collect call for you from Miss Kay Fabe in Ohio. Will you accept the charges?"

Momma's sigh floated through the line like a soft breeze, full of relief and that warm, quiet joy only she could carry. I could hear the smile tugging at her lips, and for a fleeting moment, I wished she could hear the one on mine. "Oh, no, sugar. Not today," she said, her voice gentle as ever. "But thank you for asking."

There was a pause—just long enough to be more than silence. It wasn't hesitation; it was love, stretching out and lingering between us for that brief moment. Then, faint but unmistakable, I heard it: a kiss, pressed tenderly to the receiver as if she were sending it over the miles, a little piece of her to hold onto.

The line went quiet, but I didn't feel alone. I was okay, and so was she. The relief swelled in my chest, warm and steady. It was the kind of comfort that needed no words—just the knowing.

"I'm sorry, Miss Fabe," the operator said. "She disconnected her line."

"Oh, that's alright. Thank you anyway." And I hung up.

Kay Fabe—it wasn't just carny lingo; it was a lifeline. A clever little trick we used to reach out to our loved ones without dropping a dime on a call. It was our way of saying, "I'm alive, I'm okay," without saying much at all. Especially for me and Momma, it was a godsend. With me on the run and her most likely under watchful eyes, a regular phone call was out of the question.

Kay Fabe let us keep that connection, even when the show eventually barreled down the road to the next town. A little coded message in the static of the line, a way to let her know I was still kicking without putting either of us at risk. It wasn't perfect, but it worked. And in our world, sometimes good enough was all we could hope for.

"We need to get a move on," Zora said, the worry starting to rise in her voice.

"What's the matter?" I asked.

She groaned low in her throat. "A sheriff's car just drove by, and I could have sworn it was McCrory."

"McCrory?" I exclaimed. "What's he doing out here in East Liverpool?"

Chapter Fourteen

"I don't know," she said, looking over her shoulder.

"Was it even really him?"

"I don't know," she repeated. "But I'm not willing to stick around and find out."

"You think he followed us or something?"

"I don't know."

I waved my hand carelessly in the air and breathed out. "Well, who cares? No big deal. We're on a supply run," I said. "If Johnny Law ain't got anything better to do but follow us into town..."

"*They're* on a supply run," she interrupted.

I looked at her with daggers coming from my eyes, and my mouth went round. "Vesper and Chickie."

She nodded, and her golden eyes seemed to get dim. "C'mon," she said and grabbed my arm again.

Zora and I kept our heads turned to the side to so that anyone driving on the main drag wouldn't be able to see our faces easily. When we came to the second or third crosswalk, she nudged my arm to turn to the left instead of going straight. I didn't hesitate and went with how her body guided me. The second we turned the corner, the scene of the city shifted, and I was overwhelmed with an ominous feeling that made me feel uneasy. I had been in seedy cities before; heck, my own neighborhood back in New York was about as suspect as they get, but this was different. There was something off about Jackson

Street. Something in the way the wind whipped up in my face for just a second. Something in the way the trees stood where the sidewalk met the curb. Something in the way a hushed silence fell all around us as the sounds from West 5th Street faded into the background, leaving behind an eerie hush that wrapped around us like a shroud.

Jackson Street. We made a left at Jackson Street. It felt important for me to commit to memory. Like, I needed to be grounded in my surroundings so I would be able to remember how to get back to Sis and the car and ultimately back to Nancy at the World. Jackson Street felt as though it was a giant mouth waiting to swallow us up, and if I let it consume me, I'd never get back to my girl.

We finally reached a little house at the end of the block, the kind of place you'd walk right past if you weren't looking for it. It was no wider than a single room with paint that had long since given up the fight and a roof that sagged like a tired old man. The whole place had an air about it, like it wasn't quite tethered to the same world as the rest of us. Without so much as a knock or a ring, Zora pushed the door open and stepped inside like she owned the joint.

A wave of incense hit me the second the door creaked open, a heady mix of earthiness and sweetness with a sharp, metallic bite underneath. Dried herbs hung from the low ceiling in bunches, their brittle leaves swaying just a little, though there wasn't a draft to speak of. Colored glass lanterns hung from hooks here and there, throwing

Chapter Fourteen

fractured rainbows across the walls and floors, though the dim light only made the shadows seem deeper—darker. The way they pooled in the corners, you'd swear they were alive, biding their time.

I stopped just inside the doorway and took it all in, my eyes darting from one strange object to the next. It felt like I'd walked into a whole other world, one that didn't play by the same rules as ours. And just like that, the normalcy of the street outside felt a million miles away.

"The world beyond the World," I mumbled, and Zora gave me a side smirk. She removed her black silken head scarf, revealing the tattooed runes on her hairless head. The lamplight gave the appearance that the runes were glowing on her skin, and I squinted my eyes to get a better look, but every time my sight came into focus, everything shifted and changed again, like the atmosphere itself was in constant, tangible motion. There was no doubt the house on Jackson Street was one that held great power. I smirked in spite of myself with the thought that Aleister had never experienced even a sliver of this kind of magick.

Beaded curtains at the far end of the hallway clanked together, and a woman floated out and greeted us. She was short with auburn hair swept up in a bun at the top of her head, and she gave a small grimace when she saw Zora. By the way her forehead crinkled with displeasure, I surmised she was a little older than us.

Zora placed a hand on my shoulder. "She's with me," she said. "Gideon's new Fortune Teller."

The woman's dark eyes went wide, and she smiled at me. "Welcome," she said.

I lowered my eyes, nodding to acknowledge the woman's greeting, but when I raised my head again, something strange washed over me. My gaze locked onto her face, and suddenly, a bright red X seemed to materialize across it, vivid and sharp, as though a spotlight had suddenly been cast right between her eyes. The X danced, pulsating with an eerie intensity, as though it were alive. I blinked furiously, willing the vision away, but when I looked up again, it was gone. The woman's face was as serene and calm as before.

"He's ready for it," Zora said, her voice strong and commanding.

"Of course," the woman said and headed back to the room behind the beaded curtain.

"What's Tophat ready for?" I whispered from the side of my mouth. "And why does she call him Gideon?"

Zora nudged me to be quiet. "What did you see?"

"What?" I asked, lowering my voice as low as it could go.

"Did you see something? On Dareza? *In* Dareza?"

"Who's Dareza?" I asked.

"*Her*, silly! Quick! Did you see anything?"

"A... a... a red X," I muttered. "On her forehead."

Chapter Fourteen

Zora nodded in confirmation. "Okay. Okay. This is good."

"What are you talking about? Who is she? What are we doing here? What is Tophat ready for?"

Before Zora could answer, the beaded curtain rustled again, and Dareza reappeared in the doorway, her hands outstretched, holding a vial. The glass was a light violet color, and inside it was filled to the rim with what looked to be some type of ashy substance. It was delicate, the kind of thing you could break with a single wrong move. Zora took the fragile glass gently in her hands and smiled. "Thank you," she said to her. "I'm sure he will be pleased."

"Good," Dareza said, beaming with pride.

The gold flames in Zora's eyes flashed with intensity as she held the vial up to her face. She unscrewed the little wooden cork and dipped the tip of her forefinger in it.

"It's taken me a while to get it just as he instructed, but I think it's perfect now," Dareza said.

"Hmmm," Zora hummed, inspecting the substance on her finger. "Only one way to find out." And with that, she rubbed her forefinger along the side of her hairless head—outlining the area around her right ear, up and around it and down the side of her neck. The ashy contents coated some of her rune tattoos, and as she swiped her finger away, Zora gasped, and her body went rigid. Her eyes fluttered to the back of her head, and she made a small moaning sound in her chest—a sound that only came from the depths of someone in the throes of passion. With her eyes rolled back, mouth agape, and the heavy inhales with the short moaning exhales, it was clear that whatever was in that vial sent Zora head-first into a fit of lustful ecstasy. I watched her intently until her golden pupils fluttered back open, and her entire body relaxed.

"Oh," she said as she regained her bearings, "he'll definitely be pleased."

Dareza smiled proudly. The apples of her pale cheeks flushed with pink, and every freckle on her face seemed to disappear as her face scrunched up into a wrinkly ball. Then she curiously pointed at the crow's feather around my neck, then to Zora's chest. "She has your feather?" she asked.

I looked down at the necklace I wore with confusion.

"Oh, yes," Zora said matter-of-factly.

Dareza reached down her blouse and lifted out a similar necklace. She dangled her feather in the air to show me. Its colors changed with every movement of her hand—from green to black to purple to gold, like how an oil slick changed color in the sunlight. "Zora gave me one, too," she said. "Plucked from her crow's back." Then she used the feather to point at Zora's black bird tattoos that sat right underneath her collarbone.

Before I could take a step closer to inspect it and compare it to mine, she quickly tucked it back under her shirt.

"Say..." Zora said, stretching out the syllable of the word. "I'm sure Gideon will want to thank

Chapter Fourteen

you personally for this." She gingerly held up the vial. "I mean, it surpasses all expectations."

Dareza blushed. "Oh, you know that's not my scene."

"Yes, but he is absolutely going to want to compensate you for all you've done and..."

"He can send Buster with payment like he always does, Zora," Dareza interjected.

Zora placed a hand on her hip and sighed. "For *this*? No. That's too impersonal. Besides, when was the last time you came out to the World?"

"Oh, jeez," Dareza said, her eyes looking upward as they darted back and forth across the ceiling. "It's been..."

"Forever?"

Dareza sighed. "Feels that way."

"You should come out and see us," Zora said. "Gideon is planning a string of big shows."

Dareza fidgeted. She clasped her hands together and rotated her wrists back and forth. "Oh, Zora. You know that scene isn't for me."

"I know, but it'll be fun. Let Gideon thank you proper. And Jane here is the real deal. The genuine article, Dareza. The three of us can talk shop, swap stories..."

I heard Zora saying the words to Dareza, but I heard their true meaning underneath. Tophat didn't make us come to East Liverpool for a vial. Tophat made us come out for *Dareza*...

"I'll even give you a reading," I said, picking up on Zora's vibe. "Half-off."

Dareza scoffed. "Ah! You carnies and your tricks! I know you'll tell me half-off then tell me a double-than-normal price so I'm none the wiser. Besides, honey, there's only one person I let read my cards, and it's not you."

Thinking quickly, I said, "I have a deck, though. A deck unlike any other. A deck you've never seen before."

Dareza lowered her chin with derision. "Honey, I've seen all the decks this side of the Ohio River. I highly doubt…"

"It's the Thoth Deck," I blurted. "From Lady Freida. She designed it for…"

Dareza's eyes went wide with curiosity and a hint of jealousy. "*The Beast*? I know all about them. Crowley's reputation is legendary, but that deck is just a rumor. It can't be true."

The flames in Zora's eyes rose so high, I thought they would leap out of her sockets and burn the whole shack down. "Jane studied under Crowley for years," she added.

Dareza was left dumbstruck at what she was hearing, and again, a faint red X began to flash on her forehead. "Oh… well… then…" she stammered, "I suppose I could find a way to get out there tomorrow. It would be nice to spend some time with like-minded people."

We got back to the car, and the rest of them were already there waiting for us.

Chapter Fourteen

"I was just about to send the search party out for ya!" Buster wailed when he saw us in the distance.

"Yeah, yeah!" Zora said, waving her hand in the air dismissively.

We hopped into the back seat with Vesper, and Sis started the engine. Chickie draped her arm around the top of the seat cushion and craned her neck to look at us. "So! How was your run? Get everything you needed?"

"Eh," Zora feigned indifference. "Didn't really see anything we liked. What about you?"

Vesper held up the brown paper bag in her lap and smiled. "I think we're good now!" she beamed.

That was odd. One brown bag of food? That's what Tophat called a food run? That doesn't make sense. The more logical explanation was that their food run was a ruse, a cover for something else just like ours.

"Okay, people," Sis announced, "let's blow this popsicle stand!" And just as she was about to pull out, the same police car that we saw before drove slowly by again.

Zora twisted her head and followed it through every window. "C'mon, Sis. Get a move on. I think McCrory is here following us or something."

"He's not following us, Zora!" Chickie sang. "He's here on police business."

"Wait!" she screeched. "That actually *is* him? He's in East Liverpool right now?" We eyed each other suspiciously, and Buster shifted in the front seat but didn't say a word.

"He saw us at the grocer," Vesper said. "Talked to us for a few minutes, told us to have a nice day, and left."

"You talked to him?" I repeated in disbelief.

Chickie laughed. "Of course, silly! Hill's a harmless goober. You know he can't resist us girls from the Cooch!"

"So, what exactly did McCrory talk to y'all about?" Zora asked, the suspicion pouring from her lips.

"Oh, nothing really. I mean, yeah, but…" Chickie started.

"He's still looking for Tina, bless his soul!" Vesper exclaimed.

"He's such a good and noble man," Chickie gushed and Vesper half-rolled her eyes.

"Oh yeah, does he have any leads?" I asked.

"Nothing he can really talk about," Vesper answered, "but he assured us he's going to do everything in his power to find out what happened to her."

"Hmmm…" Chickie mused thoughtfully. "But what can he really do without a *body*? He's got those dead girls he's investigating, and their corpses left evidence so…"

"Hush!" Vesper scolded. "I'm okay without a body! That means Tina ain't dead!"

"Yeah, and you know the last thing McCrory wants is to raise his body count," Sis said flatly from the front seat.

"Stop it, guys! Tina is *not* a body!"

Chapter Fourteen

"Yet," Sis mumbled under her breath, but I don't think anyone heard her but me.

"Well, guess that means we'll have to keep McCrory happy in the meantime. I mean, if he's going to remain invested in the body-less investigation," Chickie said with a subtle chuckle.

Vesper stuck out her tongue. "That's on *you*, woman. Tina wanted nothing to do with that man, so I'll follow suit. I'll accept his help in finding her, but that's about it. That's where I draw the line."

"Awww, c'mon, V! Hill's kinda hunky!" Chickie gushed.

"I guess. If you like that sort of thing."

"Jane knows. She likes big, muscular guys. Don't ya, Janey?"

I didn't answer her snide comment, as Zora and I raised our eyebrows at each other. In that unspoken moment, I knew that Zora knew that *I* knew whose ashes were in Dareza's magic vial. Buster and Sis remained silent the entire ride back.

Chapter Fifteen

Friday, June 2nd 1944
The Gentry Brothers' Wonders of the World Carnival
Tophat's Trailer
Glenmoor, Ohio
Night of the Waxing Gibbous Moon

The night had been gloriously rife with action. I hadn't seen a longer line wrapped around my tent since I started. I had eased into a steady rhythm of quasi-real readings so as to keep up the pace like Buster had instructed. Once in a while, I would be overcome with something from beyond the boundaries of our human understanding. Sometimes I would hear that ancient sounding music playing way off in the distance, and a voice would whisper sweet nothings in my head, and I would be compelled to speak truth to the customer. But most of the time, my ruse was so well structured, so well-crafted, that everyone believed whatever it was I had to tell them. Maybe because they were so desperate for answers or self-validation, or maybe they just

Chapter Fifteen

needed to hold on to their last threads of faith. The world was a hard and unforgiving place, and the World served as a much-needed escape for many of them—a place where they weren't under the confines of their financial and social limitations, nor were they scrutinized by their Bible-thumping peers. At the carnival, and especially in *my* tent, they were free.

Carnivale.

Farewell to the flesh.

So, it truly made no difference if what I said was bogus or legit because all that mattered was that the illusion was there and in full effect, which in turn, caused the money to flow like wine. Every now and then, Buster would pop his head into the tent's opening to see my reaction to how the night was faring. Every one of my *thumbs-ups* made him giddy with dollar signs flashing in his eyes. I'm sure his little Johnson was just as excited, too, cause on more than one occasion, he hobbled away a little more oddly than usual. Like there was something *extra* in his pants.

When it was time to shut up shop, Zora came sauntering into the tent with Dareza in tow. I heard her shoo away the last few customers in line. A couple of them grumbled and protested, stating they had been waiting just to see me for quite some time. She placated them by saying if they came tomorrow and said, "Zora sent me," I would give them ten percent off their reading. That shut them up real fast.

"Carny tricks," Dareza scoffed and turned up her nose when she entered my tent. I don't think Dareza liked anything about the carnival, like it was somehow beneath her or something. She stared disapprovingly at Winnie in her cage, and as she squinted, I got the feeling she was able to see beneath the glamour—that she was able to see Winnie for the docile python she truly was. "Look at all this pretend," Dareza huffed.

"Now, now," Zora gently scolded, "you know it's not pretend. It's all business. We all gotta eat, right?"

Dareza huffed again with displeasure.

"I'll tell you what's *not* pretend," Zora said as she motioned for Dareza to sit at my table.

Dareza complied, and I took the seat across from her. She crinkled her nose as she inspected my setup and pointed at the Tarot cards next to the crystal ball. "That's Gideon's deck, isn't it?" she said unimpressed. "I've seen that already." But by the tone in her voice, I understood that to mean that she had seen the Augen deck, but she hadn't really *seen* the Augen deck because if she had, her reaction wouldn't have been so lackluster, so *dismissive*.

Quickly, I scooped up the Augen cards and placed them in the right-side pocket of my apron. Then I reached into the left-side pocket and procured the other cards. "I came into possession of *these*," I said and Dareza's eyes narrowed as I spread them across the table. "Lady Freida

Chapter Fifteen

designed them—based on Aleister's instructions, of course."

Dareza's mouth hung open in surprise. "She's the artist," she whispered, but it was loud enough for me to hear.

"Yes. And his faithful disciple."

I hadn't breathed a word of my secret to anyone else at the World, and yet here I was, teetering on the edge of spilling the beans to a sorceress I'd only met just yesterday. My nerves got the better of me, and I cast a quick, uncertain glance at Zora, hoping for some kind of guidance. She gave me a curt nod, and I found myself nodding right along with her, as though her confidence had somehow willed mine into existence.

Dareza's face lit up at my gesture, and she hovered her hand over the cards. "May I?" she asked.

I nodded again. She picked them up, admiring the beautifully painted images of symbols and swords, cups and chariots, gods and goddesses—all intricately designed and crafted by hand. I noticed her hand slightly shake with excitement and anticipation as she shuffled them, gently moving the cards back and forth and in and out. She smiled with delight as each one passed through her fingers.

"They're beautiful, aren't they?" I said as I became entranced with the way they flew in her hands. The colors seemed to blend together in a whirl, and I could hear the sounds they made like the echoes of a carousel—each voice singing as it whizzed by in the darkness. "They sing so sweetly," I mused, remembering why I took them in the first place, remembering the peace and comfort they brought me just to look upon their faces, remembering how I felt an intense need to possess them.

But suddenly she stopped and set them back on the table. Her face darkened, and she tilted her head toward them as if listening to something.

"Dareza?" Zora questioned. "Are you okay?"

Dareza looked up at me with a look of consternation. "No. They're *not* singing, Jane."

"Beg pardon?"

"They're crying. They cry because they are not a complete set. They are trapped, in limbo, unable to perform the duties that they were created for."

"I know," I replied shamefully.

She stopped, closed her eyes, and tilted her head up. "No. You shouldn't have them. You have to give them back."

With that, she made a move to pick them back up from the table, but I was quick enough to beat her to it and shoved them back in my front pocket. I could feel Zora tense up beside me.

"Jane," Dareza admonished, "this is wrong. You shouldn't have them. They're not for you."

"You're right," I answered. "They're not for me. They're for Althea," I blurted mindlessly, and as if on instinct, I clapped my hand over my mouth the second Nancy's real name escaped it. I froze with terror. I had been so good with concealing it, so careful with not slipping up, so cautious with keeping that name so close to my chest, that

Chapter Fifteen

I wanted to pull Winnie from her enclosure and let her squeeze the life from my neck. Of course, Dareza had no idea who I was talking about, but I suspected Zora did. Just saying her name out loud exposed her to the cosmos and left us vulnerable.

Stupid, stupid, stupid girl!

Zora immediately sensed my discomfort and moved over to Dareza. "I think it's time we get moving over to Gideon's trailer. He's waiting for us."

Dareza stood up and smoothed her hands down the front of her pinafore. "Yes. Yes, of course. Did you give him the vial?"

Zora nodded. "Yes."

"And?"

"I told you it was going to exceed his expectations. He is beyond words."

Dareza's smile widened, and for a moment, I think she forgot all about the Thoth Deck and the forbidden name I had uttered. True magicians, after all, take immense pride in their craft, and the mere mention of Tophat's approval seemed to send her soaring to cloud nine. Whatever this concoction was, it had clearly been a labor of love—and a touch of ego. I wouldn't know, though, because Zora hadn't breathed a word about it since our trip to East Liverpool.

Once again, Tophat's trailer was nothing like I remembered it. Zora eased the door open, and the moment we stepped inside, a chill slapped us across the face like an unwelcome stranger.

The walls weren't walls anymore—they looked like jagged rock, cold and unfeeling, and the air smelled damp, like something ancient and untouched. In the center of the room—or whatever this was—a fire roared, its flames casting long, flickering shadows. Around it, a careful circle of white salt glimmered faintly in the firelight, its purpose clear to anyone who knew their way around the arcane. But this wasn't just a trailer anymore. No, this was something else entirely. A cave, yawning wide and stretching deep, far beyond what any trailer could ever hold. The cramped, dingy space I'd expected had vanished, replaced by a cavern that seemed to defy all logic. It was like we'd stepped out of this world and into another—another time, another place, one where the rules we knew didn't mean a thing.

"What is this?" Dareza asked, mystified.

"This is all Gideon," Zora said proudly. "His illusions know no bounds."

"Illusions?" His voice echoed, and suddenly he appeared from behind one of the shadowy rock walls. He wore a white tunic shirt and brown doeskin pants. I found it odd—out of character, so very un-Tophat-like to not have his top hat! He smirked at me, and I immediately knew he had read my thoughts, so I tucked my hair behind my ears and cast my eyes to the granite floor.

He approached and gave us all customary kisses on the cheeks. "You don't need your glamour here," he whispered in my ear as he pulled back from his greeting kiss. I looked down

Chapter Fifteen

at myself as he stepped away from me, and to my surprise, my Fortune Teller costume had melted back into my *plain-Jane* attire.

Tophat then reached for Dareza's hands and held them out in front of her, as if he were absorbing every bit of her face. "I cannot thank you enough, gifted one," he said to her lovingly, and his voice bounced off the gray rocks of the cave and reverberated in my head.

"I'm so sorry it took me so long to…" she began.

"No apologies, my dear. We both know these things can't be rushed."

"I hope it's…" she squeaked, and I noticed her voice sounded normal and small. It didn't boom in the cave like his did. And that's when I realized Dareza was on a different plane from us. She was not *in* Tophat's cave. She was in the trailer. Yes, she saw the cave and the fire and the salt and the smoke, but to her, it was an illusion, a glamour. To *us*, we had stepped into a different level of reality.

"Come," he said and guided her across the salt circle and next to the fire. "I want you to witness just how magnificent your artistry is."

Zora took my hand, and we joined them in the circle. Tophat held the vial up, so the light of the fire glinted off the subtle violet hue of the glass. We were all mesmerized by the way the glass gave off kaleidoscope colors and shapes. The rainbows danced like spotlights shining in the cave and in Tophat's eyes. His gray eyes turned dark and refracted each color individually and together all at once. It was dizzying and made my head spin.

"The ashes of the dead are powerful," he said as he opened the cork of the vial. "And you have given me a most precious gift."

Dareza blushed at Tophat's admiration. Her cheeks glowed pink from the warmth of the fire and the feeling of pride from within. "Like I said, it was…"

"Don't sell yourself short," he interrupted, and I suddenly realized every time she spoke, he seemed to cut her off, like he didn't want her voice in his space. Like he didn't want her to hear the sound of her own words. Like he didn't want her to be cognizant that she was *elsewhere*. Dareza was powerful, that much I could sense. And her power caused Tophat to be cautious in a way that was palpable.

"There is only one way I can repay you for your faithful service," he said. "You've been loyal to me, to the World, for quite some time, Daritshka."

Her eyes widened, and she smiled so brightly, so innocently, when he called her that pet name.

Tophat dipped his thumb inside the vial and coated the tip of it with the ashes. The crunch echoed in the cave, and the flames of the fire in the center of the circle bent as if a rush of wind had entered.

But there was no wind.

"Come, my loyal friend, and be anointed in the ways of the Old Ones."

Chapter Fifteen

Dareza closed her eyes and bowed her head in supplication. Tophat ran his thumb across her forehead, spreading the ashes on her face. And as he did this, he chanted in that ancient language. It was the language of the runes, the words of old. And they came out of his mouth and screamed from the inside of his brain. They sang from his soul—delightful music with bells and chimes and wind and rain and the sea lapping up against a rocky shore. I heard sounds of the forest—of trees swaying and crows cawing. A crow with inky black feathers that shimmered iridescent green and purple and gold perched upon a mass of dried leaves and branches guarding a bloody treasure underneath. It looked like the feather around my neck. Like the one around Dareza's neck. *"A hunk of meat. An unfinished dissection of flesh. A mass of unrecognizable decomposition,"* a voice whispered in my head.

"They screamed a thousand times," Tophat said in that strange tongue, but that's not what Dareza heard because that's not what Tophat actually said. But he did. But he didn't. But he did. I was in that double world again—the one where the glamour was blinking the truth from the truth and the world was flashing with the concealment of the World.

Dareza smiled as Tophat continued to dip his thumb in the ash and gently draw symbols on her cheeks and up and around her ears. His feather-like touches tickled her and sent her in a series of soft giggles that she so desperately tried to contain. Then he marked her chin on both sides and dragged his thumb down the center of her neck, right over her throat. "Remember, Daritshka, keep your good thoughts flowing and your actions to match."

She smiled faintly, as if caught in the last threads of a dream, but that peace shattered the moment her eyes flew open. A look of pure terror consumed her face, and a sound rose from her throat. It wasn't a scream, not even a gasp, but a croak, dry and raw, like something was lodged deep inside her, strangling her from within. Her lips parted, trembling, as she fought desperately to pull air into her lungs. *Croak. Croak. Croak.* Each sound grew more frantic, more strained, as though invisible hands were wrapped tight around her neck.

Dareza's body convulsed slightly, but she couldn't move beyond that. She was frozen, trapped within the circle of salt, unable to clutch at her throat or flail her arms in desperation. Her wide, terrified eyes darted between me and Zora, pleading silently for salvation.

"Please," her gaze seemed to cry, "Help me!"

But neither of us moved. I swallowed hard, my hands trembling as I reached into my pocket and gripped the Augen Deck, but Zora remained as steady as stone. Her expression was unreadable, her eyes locked on Dareza with a sharp, unyielding focus.

And then, Zora raised her hands, slowly pulling away the scarf that covered her head. The

Chapter Fifteen

glow of the firelight caught the intricate runes tattooed across her scalp, their curves and angles suddenly alive with motion. They shimmered faintly at first, a soft orange light that seemed to pulse in time with the croaking sounds coming from Dareza's throat. With every labored croak, the glow intensified, building from a gentle simmer to a fierce blaze. The runes throbbed with an eerie rhythm.

Until soon, the croaking stopped, and Zora's runes were bright and glowing and filled the cave with a glorious light. Dareza's lifeless body slumped over, and my heart jumped in its cage at the sound of the body hitting the granite. Tophat quickly straightened her out; Death had yet to fully engulf her as she looked as if she was sleeping.

"The cards," Tophat instructed me.

I fumbled with the Augen Deck, my hands trembling as I knelt and laid six cards face-up on the ground inside the circle. But as I stared at them, my heart sank into my stomach.

The cards were blank.

No runes, no illustrations, not even a hint of the vibrant, intricate designs that once marked their surface. Just an abyss of black, empty and endless, staring back at me like a void.

"I... I... I can't..." The words stumbled out of my mouth, shaky and frantic. My fingers hovered over the lifeless cards, as though willing the images to reappear through sheer desperation. "I don't understand... They're supposed to..."

I looked to Zora, panic seizing my chest. "They're blank!" I whispered, my voice cracking. "They're completely blank!"

Her glowing runes pulsed in response.

"You can," Zora said, her voice cutting through the air like the crack of a whip. She didn't look at me, her eyes fixed firmly on Dareza's motionless body. "They're not blank. You're not seeing."

"But there's nothing!" I snapped, my fear bubbling into frustration. "How am I supposed to..."

Tophat pointed to Zora. "Read."

Zora tipped her head forward, beckoning me to read the runes on her skull. I squinted my eyes, and this time the words came into focus. They were no longer symbols, and the sharp lines of the runes began to curve and take shape. They twisted and melded into words—English words that were known to me.

And I began to read her out loud.

"In the beginning, in the land veiled by ice and bound by frost, there were the Three. And the Three were united, their paths lit by the wisdom of she who was called Blodwyn. And the Three found joy in their unity, for their purpose was one, and their hearts beat as one. And the Three, under Blodwyn's guidance, set forth upon the sacred task: to unseal the gates of the Old Ones and restore the world to the life that had been, as it was in the days of their forebears. And so, the Three labored, their spirits unwavering, their cause divine, for they sought not their own glory but the rebirth of what had been lost."

Chapter Fifteen

An image on the card on the far left began to glimmer to life. An image of three beautiful women dancing in a circle in the frozen tundra came into vision: one with white hair, one with red hair, one with black hair. They danced around a fire and chanted and laughed and kissed and sang ancient songs in an ancient tongue.

"In the days of sorrow and rejoicing, the mother of the three was taken by the hand of death, and in her stead came forth the babe, a new life born unto them. This union of loss and birth became the crux upon which their destinies turned, shaping the hearts and minds of the Three in ways unforeseen. The path before them, once steady and clear, twisted into one of trials and secrets, leading them to a purpose that would alter the course of their fates. For it was this path that would sow the seeds of discord and give rise to the ultimate betrayal of Sorcia, whose heart wavered in the shadow of temptation. And thus, the threads of trust were severed, and the bond of the three was tested as the wheels of destiny turned ever forward, fulfilling what was written in the stars."

The next card fluttered on the ground, and the scene showed me the red-haired woman rocking a white-haired baby in her arms as the white-haired woman looked on lovingly. Behind them, the black-haired woman stood with arms folded over her chest with a scowl on her face. Suddenly, her image began to fade from the card, and she eventually disappeared from the background.

"Blodwyn was the One, anointed and set apart, for her works were mighty and her power unmatched.

Witch of the Midnight Shadow

She touched the lame, and they walked; she placed her hands upon the blind, and they saw the light of the world once more. From the veil of death, she summoned the mother, restoring her breath and life, for her will was beyond the grasp of mortality. In the fullness of time, Blodwyn laid herself upon the altar, a sacrifice for the Conduit, that the greater purpose might be fulfilled. But death could not bind her, for she returned, transformed, born anew in another form, to walk among her brethren once again. Aizel and Trond, the devoted keepers of her name, bore her legacy through the ages, that her memory might never fade. Aizel, wise and inspired, forged the sacred tools: the cards of divination, the books of wisdom, and the pendants of power. And these artifacts became vessels of her essence, that her truth might echo through the generations and her light guide those who sought the path."

The third card hummed, and the image took form. The red-haired woman sat in a cave just like the one we were in and feverishly wrote in an ancient book. The Blodheksa book. And then the image changed to show her forging a necklace that looked like an eye, but it wasn't an eye. It was a locust. I didn't know how I knew that, but the voices in the air had whispered it to me, and I got the feeling that there was a funny joke behind it that had made the woman laugh in spite of herself.

"And Aizel, steadfast and unwavering, labored through the sands of time and the void of space, bound by the sacred covenant sworn in the days of old. Her heart, resolute and her hands tireless, she journeyed

Chapter Fifteen

across the lands and seas, seeking the fragments of purpose scattered across creation. Through trial and solitude, she forged onward, her focus unbroken, her resolve undiminished. And with her own hands, she crafted the tools of her destiny: the sacred cards, the hallowed books, and the pendants of power, each infused with the essence of the covenant. Thus, her labor bore fruit, and the tools of the eternal purpose were set into the world, that the covenant might be fulfilled and the balance restored."

The fourth card flashed with a white light, and when I looked down at it, an image of an ancient hourglass came into focus. The purple sand inside the top portion quickly trickled down until it filled the bottom portion. When the last grain of sand fell, a red X faintly pulsed over the card.

"And through the endless stretch of ages, as the fruits of her labor ripened, Aizel's heart stirred with the knowledge of what awaited her. She, the steadfast and dutiful one, knew the final task lay ahead. Her mission—one that would shape the dawning of a new world—was to aid in the birth of the Blodsøster and Blodbrødre, the sacred siblings, to walk the earth again. For Aizel, this was the last step, the last breath of her eternal purpose. She had served her covenant, but the culmination would come with her final sacrifice. Her mortal body, though, was destined for the flames. The fire would come—fueled by the rage of an angry mob who could not understand the magnitude of what she had begun. But Aizel, the eternal, was not to be claimed by death. Though her body turned to ash, her soul would rise anew, untethered and unbroken. For

she was Aizel, blood of the old ones, and though her mortal form perished, her essence, her spirit, would remain—alive and thriving in the currents of time, ready to fulfill her destiny, undaunted by the flames."

Smoke began to rise from the fifth card, and the image that appeared was that of an old woman tied to a stake being burnt alive. The card screamed and sang, and the woman laughed as the flames licked her feet. The fire completely engulfed her until the stake fell to the ground in a heap of ash. The smoke billowed up to the top of the card, collecting there as if it was ready to be released. The tattoos on Zora's head stopped glowing, and I blinked my eyes back to reality.

"That's it," I said, bewildered. "There's nothing more."

Tophat smiled. "Oh yes, Jane. There is." He pointed to the cards. "Say her name. Call her forth."

I don't know how. I don't know why. But I did as I was told. I did what I felt in my heart. I did what spoke to my soul. I did what felt *right*. And for a split second, I realized that everything I had ever attempted in Aleister's camp had never felt right. Not like this.

I said her name.

I called her.

"Aizel. I beckon you to join us now. Bless us with your presence, oh ancient one."

And in that moment, the smoke from the fifth card rose from the top and into the cold air of the cave. It danced around me in a smoky vortex and tickled my noise with feather-like kisses. Then it

Chapter Fifteen

swirled together into a thick band and hovered over Dareza's lifeless body before it dove into her open mouth.

The silent seconds felt like hours as the three of us waited with bated breath to see if anything would happen. Then suddenly, Dareza's fingers twitched. It was subtle, and I almost missed it. Tophat was on it in an instant, though. Quickly, he knelt beside Dareza's body as her chest began to heave with shallow breath. Her head turned, her eyes snapping open, but they weren't hers. They were bright green, brilliant and glowing. They could only be the eyes of Aizel.

Zora and I exchanged a surprised, yet relieved glance, and she reached her hand out to hold mine.

Tophat removed the feather necklace from around Dareza's neck and handed it to me. "Yours," he commanded, and I put it on. Then he leaned in close to Dareza's face, his ear against her lips. I watched as the lips moved and listened as the groaning, guttural sounds made their way from her throat. It was the croaking noise of Dareza's last living breath, but Tophat smiled at what he heard. He was more than pleased. At one point, I heard the croaking voice whisper a name, "Alessandra," but I couldn't be sure. Regardless, Tophat hovered over the face of the dead woman, listening to what she had to say, smiling with every new piece of information he received. It was obvious he had gotten what he wanted.

Chapter Sixteen

Friday, June 2nd 1944
The Gentry Brothers' Wonders of the World Carnival
Jane's Trailer
Glenmoor, Ohio
Late Night of the Waxing Gibbous Moon

Tophat told me to leave after the ritual was completed. He asked that Zora stay behind to help wrap things up. I didn't ask any questions, but it was obvious that Tophat was over the moon with how everything had turned out. He kissed my forehead and smoothed my hair down my mid-back and told me something to the effect of how grateful he was to finally have the key. I didn't know what that meant. I didn't know what any of it meant. And again, I kept my mouth shut good because I was still on the fence whether or not I actually wanted to know the score. Besides, I was feeling drunk, not quite myself, and I thought it best to just trot on back to my trailer like nothing happened. I knew I had *supernatural proclivities*, as Aleister used to

Chapter Sixteen

say, but nothing like this. Nothing like what happened in Tophat's trailer. No. That was something beyond my scope of reason and logic. But one thing was certain. One thing I could say with one hundred percent confidence — *I rather enjoyed the way it made me feel.*

The cave was cold, and Dareza's dead body even colder, but the runes on Zora's skull were warm and inviting. Saying them out loud, reading the words of the ancient story filled me with such delight that my lips tingled when each word passed them. It was electric, and it filled me with a light so bright, it felt as though the sun was blinding my human vision and granting me a second sight. I remembered a part of the story tattooed on Zora. It said that Blodwyn had made a blind man see, and that's how I felt — like I was seeing something else, something otherworldly, something beyond. Like the time Tophat had summoned me to his trailer to tell me I was his Witch of Endor. His necromancer. I saw everything for what it truly is and was and ever will be. I was the truth and the light and the way, and by my sheer will, the dead spoke through the dead.

My head raced — the thoughts flowed through me in a disconnected stream of consciousness. Every time I felt as if I was fixated on one particular reflection, my train of thought shifted to something different. I felt confused, and at times lost, but I always felt whole. It didn't make any sense — none of it did, but it did at that moment, so I guess that's all that mattered.

My heart throbbed—like echoes in my chest, each beat reverberating through my ribs and into the hollow silence surrounding me. The rhythm was uneven, frantic, as if trying to outpace the thoughts racing through my mind. Each pulse seemed louder than the last, a deafening reminder that I was alive, yet Dareza and the one called Aizel were not. And that reminder of what transpired—of what Tophat did to the sorceress—made my heart beat even faster and harder until I could hear the blood rushing in my ears.

My body tingled—warm pin pricks, like when my hands fell asleep, took over every inch of my flesh, radiating from the tips of my fingers to the soles of my feet. It was the kind of sensation that made me hyperaware of my own existence, as if my body wasn't entirely my own. The tingling grew more intense, almost electric, as if I were a conduit for something unseen, something powerful. It left me feeling untethered, suspended between the physical and something far beyond my understanding. Something that hovered in Tophat's ancient cave. Something that allowed me to pull out a voice from the cosmos and breathe it into the body of a dead woman. *Her* body didn't tingle, didn't feel, but mine sure did. And as I approached my trailer in the dead of night, I realized something *else* was tingling between my legs. And for the first time in a very, very long time, I was fully aware of my womanly desires.

The trailer door creaked open, and I held my breath as I crept inside. All was dark within, and

Chapter Sixteen

I tiptoed around trying not to wake Nancy. The second the door latch clicked, the lamp in the living area snapped on and Duke sat on the couch looking concerned.

"Who's there?" he whispered with a stern voice.

"Just me," I whispered back.

"Oh, oh good," he said, his volume back at normal level.

"Shhh... isn't Nancy sleeping?" I admonished.

"No. No. She stayed over at Elaine's. The kids tuckered themselves out, and Elaine asked if she could just keep her there for the night and..."

The sound of his voice fueled my already inebriated feeling. The words danced in my head and brought me into focus—made my head clear, but my heart thumped harder, and my nether region throbbed ferociously. I inhaled, reached my hand behind my back to untie my apron, and flung it across the room. Then I bent over slightly with one hand against a cabinet and removed my boots. I flung them across the room as well.

This startled him. Quickly, he stood up and took a tentative step toward me, maybe in hopes of calming me down. "I thought it was okay," he said. "She was already asleep when I went to get her after the party, and I figured why disturb her. I'm sorry. I thought you would be okay with it."

I took a step back and surveyed the mountain of a man before me. I scanned his entire face—his brown eyes, his slightly crooked nose, and his square jaw that made his cheekbones jut out in sharp angles when he clenched his perfect teeth.

Then my eyes roamed down his chest, and across his arms, and I could see the strength in his body and the way his muscles shifted beneath his shirt with every small movement.

I wanted him. No, I *needed* him. I ached for him. The magick high I was riding could only be sated with one thing. The magnetic pull between us was undeniable, and my breath hitched as his gaze caught mine.

"Janey? You're not mad, are ya?"

I closed the distance between us in a single bold stride. My hands found his chest. The solid warmth of him beneath my fingers made my pulse quicken, and I thought my head was going to explode. He grabbed my wrists and gazed deeply into my eyes. "I'm *definitely* not mad," I cooed.

Without thinking, without breathing, I stretched up on my toes and pressed my lips to his. The kiss was urgent—passionate and uncontrolled. His muscular arms wrapped around me, pulling me into him, and for a moment, I melted into his chest as the world around us disappeared.

I shuffled my legs, guiding us to the back room. The bed that we shared was beyond the black curtain divider—the bed we shared but had yet to *share*. Duke nearly stumbled over the threshold and collapsed into the sea of soft blankets. We both giggled between our vigorous kisses as I straddled my legs around his waist. He was gigantic—a hulking human specimen, and I felt so small against his body. So small and fragile, like he could toss me around like a ragdoll if he

Chapter Sixteen

wanted to—if I'd let him. But I knew he wouldn't, and that was my power over him. He was gentle and sweet and kind, and I was safe. With him.

His hands were on me in a flash, rough and eager, trailing up my stomach until they found the soft swell of my bosom. A breath hitched in my throat as he took his claim, fingers kneading with a hunger that sent a delicious shiver racing down my spine. I turned my head, pressing my lips to his neck, teasing his skin with feather-light kisses. I felt him sigh against me, his breath warm, his body taut with anticipation. A slow smile curled on my lips—I had him right where I wanted him.

With one swift motion, I grasped the hem of his tee and pulled it over his head, tossing it aside without a second thought. My hands traveled over his chest, still slick with oil from his show. My fingers glided over his firm, heated skin. Every muscle was cut from stone, shifting beneath my touch like the ebb and flow of the tide. I let my fingers linger, grazing his nipples, giving them the faintest pinch, just to see how he'd react. He jerked beneath me, a low sound escaping his lips—half a gasp, half a groan.

When he could no longer stand my teasing, he grabbed my waist and pulled me back down onto him as his mouth once again found mine with a flurry of kisses. Our tongues danced in wild rhythm, and I wondered if he too could hear the music outside. Because *I* certainly could. I had been hearing it ever since I got to the World. I don't think it ever stopped, either. It just got softer and louder depending on the moment.

And right now, it was loud.

The drums pounded in time with our furious tongues lashing in each other's mouths. The song swelled in time with the hunger between my legs. The discordant harmonies echoed in the trailer as I reached a free hand down to his waist and unbuckled the belt on his trousers. With one of *his* free hands, he helped me shimmy them down around his ankles until he was fully exposed to me in all of his erect glory. I looked down to get the full view of his raging manhood and thought, *If God were a man, he would have blessed himself with this exact thing of beauty.*

I sighed at the sight of its length and girth and bulging snake-like veins pulsing on the surface of the thin skin.

"Nothing you haven't seen before," he joked.

Yes, that was true. I'd seen his mighty rod on more than one occasion, but this was different. Something in me had shifted, something deep in the marrow of my bones. Maybe it was the violet vial, laced with the ashes of the dead, that had snuffed the sorceress right before my eyes. Maybe it was the moon, casting its inky shadow over the raw edges of my soul. Maybe it was the way Zora's runes shimmered like glowing embers, whispering an ancient tale upon her brow. Or the way the Tarot cards spun in the air, wreathed in ghostly smoke. Or the voice—that deep, guttural

Chapter Sixteen

voice—that crawled from beyond the veil, calling itself Aizel.

The night played over and over in my mind, a fever dream I couldn't wake from. And somewhere in the thick of it, my body betrayed me. My crevice ached—an ache that ran deep, curling around my spine, tightening low in my belly. I burned for him, to feel the weight of him upon me, to feel the force and power of him plunging deep inside me, to feel him thrusting his mighty self into the very pit of my stomach! I ached to be filled with the root of a god. My god. My Iron Giant.

Quickly, I lifted the bottom of my pinafore dress and laid it across his chest so that my bare skin rubbed up against him. I rocked my body back and forth, cradling his manhood on the outskirts of my flower, but not letting it penetrate the opening. I moved up and down, coating his shaft with my slickness as my petals brushed up against him with gentle kisses. He moaned again, and I knew he was going mad with desire—mad with anticipation. I rotated my hips, and he sighed every time the tip of his manhood slid closer and closer to the ultimate pinnacle of desire.

The same feeling of anticipation rose higher in my own chest, and the music in the arena grew louder and more frantic. Like the heartbeat of a rabbit racing a mile a minute. And when I could stand it no longer, I brought my body upward a little bit, positioned my legs so as to brace for his entry, and slid my hips down onto his shaft as far as my insides would allow him to go.

In an instant, a white light exploded in my head. It rocked me like how the roar of a jet engine shakes the entire plane on lift off. *I* was on lift off—my insides shook and spasmed with unnatural jerking movements. Every inch of my body twitched and shuddered like I was having a pleasure seizure. I think I might have cried out, but the music in my head and in the air had gotten so loud that it drowned out any bit of noise. I rode on top of him for a few seconds, but the seconds felt like hours. My hips rose at a snail's pace, and they slammed back down on him like sand descending in an hour glass. I enjoyed every inch of him all over me, every ridge of his manhood, every throbbing vein from his shaft pulsating like a second heartbeat against the walls of my sacred cavern (not like Tophat's cavern, but sacred in its own right). Every thrust, every movement, every push and pull and moan and groan happened in slow motion. But my conscious mind knew that couldn't be true, that in the real world, Duke and I were lovers enjoying the heated frenzy of our passionate time together. And yet there was a part of me that was no longer in the real world. There was a part of me that had somehow traveled up, out, and beyond—to the world beyond the World.

My vision swam in a flood of white light, washing over everything like the flash of a camera bulb. When I looked around—at the room, at Duke—something strange happened. The world

Chapter Sixteen

as I knew it began to waver, the walls of the trailer rippling like heat rising off asphalt. Then, like ink bleeding through thin paper, images pressed through the veil of reality, through the smoky shadows.

I could still see the trailer, but it was slipping, melting away into something else. The pictures came in hazy at first, shifting and flickering like an old newsreel, before sharpening into crystal-clear scenes. Things happening in real time—things I shouldn't have been able to see. It was as if I were watching a moving picture show, only this one was projected straight into my mind, and there was no turning it off.

Tophat and Zora wrapping Dareza's body in a linen cloth and tying rope around her four, five, six times. The World's car pulls up. Buster at the wheel. Sis gets out of the front seat and makes her way into Tophat's trailer. Zora leaves and walks away to the backlot of the World. Sis and Tophat drag the body into the backseat of the car, and they drive away.

Then the picture faded away.

Sis is in on it? I thought. I mean, I had vaguely suspected Buster was "in the know," but what I had just witnessed gave me proof that Sis was involved as well.

Duke's slow-motion thrusts continued, and my eyes rolled into the back of my head with a wave of ecstasy as another picture materialized in the room.

A car pulling up to the entrance of the World—the wooden structure that resembles an archway. A man gets out from the backseat and walks over to the sign in red block letters that reads CARNIVALE. "This is the place," he calls to the driver and passenger in the front. I can't see their faces.

Suddenly, Buster peels up to the entrance from the opposite side. He slows the car down to a humming throttle and says, "Carnival's closed, folks."

The man nods. "We know. Just checking it out."

"Well, there's nothing to check out right now," Buster says, and the irritation in his voice is palpable.

Sis glares at the intruders.

The person driving the car leans over the passenger next to her, and as she cranes her neck out the window, I catch a glimpse of her face. I see who has rolled up to the World. My heart sinks to my stomach when I realize it's Christina Combs, Aleister's underling.

I closed my eyes, trying to stop from seeing the vision, but it was no use. Even with my eyes closed, I could see. "Oh god, they're coming!" I cried out, and I know Duke must have thought I had misspoken.

"Come for me, baby," he moaned in response.

"Sir," Christina calls to Buster, "what time does the show start tomorrow?"

"Seven o'clock on the dot," he sneers. "Why, who wants to know?"

"We're just really excited to catch up with an old friend of ours and her little squirt!"

Christina and the man laugh. Buster huffs and gives the horn a tap. "Yeah, yeah, get going now. You're on private property after hours."

Chapter Sixteen

The vision faded, and reality changed back to normal. I scarcely had time to process the panic that had begun to work its way into my chest because I blinked my eyes and was back in the room on top of Duke. His pace quickened, and he grunted with each passionate thrust inside of me, but my attention was no longer on the sex. I was still reeling from what I had seen—breathless that I was so close to being discovered, panic-stricken that Nancy was no longer safe.

"They're coming," I squeaked, somewhere between a whisper and a moan. "Now."

And with one final upward thrust, and an excited cry, so did Duke.

Chapter Seventeen

Saturday, June 3rd 1944
The Gentry Brothers' Wonders of the World Carnival
Jane's Trailer
Glenmoor, Ohio
Early morning of the Waxing Gibbous Moon

And so, I laid there in the crook of Duke's arm, my head swirling with a million thoughts. Like the stereotypical portrait of the stereotypical couple, Duke had cocked his head back against the pillow, raised him arm up, caught me in his post-coital embrace, and fallen fast asleep. But there was no rest for me. My immediate reaction was to jump off of him during the act, run to Elaine's trailer, wake Nancy up from her sleep, and run. Run. Run. Well, thank god for Duke's rod inside of me because the act of getting up and cleaning up and actually breathing again helped me to get my head on straight and think things through. I mean, logistically, there was nowhere to run *to*. So, I laid next to snoring Duke and tried

Chapter Seventeen

every which way to compose myself and walk myself through the entire scenario.

Which is not to say that my heart didn't feel like it was going to explode out of my chest because it did. And then suddenly, I had a desperate feeling like I needed Momma at that very moment. I longed for her comfort and protection (and maybe the backing of her six large German shepherds). She always knew how to make things better, and I thought, *Maybe if we leave right now, we could get a few hours on Christina Combs and her ragtag group and make it back to Momma after all.* So dumb.

I couldn't help it, though. No matter what kind of solution popped into my mind, I reasoned it away in the very next thought. I couldn't focus on anything viable or tangible and was starting to think I was shit outta luck. Zora would know. Tophat would know. But the two of them were currently indisposed—disposing of certain things I dare not even remember. I knew it wouldn't have been so nerve wracking if Nancy were with me. At least I'd be able to relax a little with her in my sights.

The restless night dragged on. Duke's snoring intensified for a few hours then calmed to a low, grumble sound from his upper chest. If I managed to steal five minutes of shut-eye here or ten there, I'd have called myself lucky. But luck wasn't in the cards tonight. Somewhere in the long stretch of sleepless hours, I stopped wrestling with the problem gnawing at my mind and let my thoughts drift to my sweet baby girl. My Nancy. My darling. My little one. I spoke to her in the quiet of my thoughts, hoping somehow, somewhere, she could hear me. The memory of her smiling face soothed the ache in my chest. And though sleep never came to claim me, at least, for a little while, I found some peace.

At the first rays of sunlight, when the world was still a shadowy shade of blue, a pounding on the trailer door jolted me from my deepest thoughts. I sat up in the bed with a fright, and Duke huffed away his last strangling snore.

"W... w... what was that?" he stammered awake.

"The door. Let me go see," I practically whispered and shot up from the bed.

When I pulled open the door, my heart near about split in two. There stood Zora, cradling Nancy's half-sleeping little body in her arms, holding her close like she was the most precious thing in the world. I stepped aside without a word, and the second Zora passed her to me, I pulled my baby tight against my chest. I buried my face in her soft blonde hair, breathing her in, trying to capture every bit of her warmth, every trace of her scent. She squirmed against me, restless, but I didn't loosen my hold. I couldn't. Didn't matter if I was squeezing her too tightly. Didn't matter if she wriggled in protest. I could hear her breath, smell it, feel it warm against my skin. And if those were the last breaths she ever took, I could live with knowing they were spent right here, in my

Chapter Seventeen

arms. "Morning, my baby," I whispered, my lips brushing her ear.

"I not a baby," she gurgled in a froggy voice.

I chuckled, squeezed her one last time, kissed her forehead, and placed her on the couch. "Rest, my big girl." She smiled at me and fluttered her eyes back into her dreamland. I turned to see Zora staring with a look of consternation.

I searched Zora's face for an answer, a sign. "What's wrong?" I blurted.

She seized my wrists and yanked me toward her, fingers rough, grip unyielding. "Jane," she said, her voice urgent.

Her hands were filthy, caked with grime. A layer of dirt masked the tattoos on her hands, making them look like black inky splotches. The scent of kerosene clung to her clothes and dark circles framed her eyes—hollows carved from a sleepless night.

Her intensity heightened my senses, and I stared deeply into her eyes. "What? Tell me what happened."

"Last night..."

I relaxed my shoulders. "I know. I saw."

Her face twisted with confusion. "Huh? What do you mean you..."

"Janey? You okay out there?" Duke called from the bedroom.

"It's just Zora," I answered.

Zora raised her eyebrows and smirked. Her forehead wrinkled up and it pushed her head scarf up a little over the top where her hairline should have been revealing some of the runes. Although, when I caught a glimpse of them, they weren't runes, per se. They were no longer mysterious symbols that I couldn't decipher. They were now words... actual words that I could read and understand, but for some reason, the story had changed! Just hours ago, I read Zora's tattoos like a book, committing every part of the story to memory. But at that moment, the line across the top of her head said something different, something that wasn't there before. "You're different," I commented in disbelief.

"As are you," she replied as she glanced over her shoulder, acknowledging Duke in the bedroom.

I smirked back at her.

"What did you see?" she continued. "You had a vision?"

"I think so. You could say that. I saw you and Buster and Sis with..."

She raised her hand up to silence me, and I stopped and paused. "And then that group of people hanging around the entrance. They're here for us." I jutted my chin in Nancy's direction. "Those were Crowley's people."

"They're coming back tonight," she said.

I made my way to the edge of the couch and gingerly sat down so as not to disturb Nancy, but she shifted her body and made a cooing noise. I ran my hand lovingly across her back, petting her like one of Momma's shepherds. "Tophat's glamour was lifted," I said. "I don't know how or why or for how long, but Crowley and his people

Chapter Seventeen

are powerful in their own right, so whatever happened... what we *summoned* in Tophat's trailer..."

"Left something open," she finished for me.

"Exactly. It allowed them to see *through*, just like I was able to see through, somehow."

"And *in*."

I nodded.

"How were you able to do that, by the way?" she asked.

Just then, Duke appeared in the threshold, rubbing his eye with one closed fist and raising his other arm above his head in a stretch that made his spine crack loudly. His bicep flexed as he made the gesture, and it looked like a basketball had been placed just under his skin.

I glared at Zora and raised an eyebrow. She smirked back knowingly.

"Morning, ladies," Duke mused when his full body stretch was complete.

"Duke," Zora acknowledged slyly.

"So now what? I know I have to leave. Like, now. But where do I go? What do I do?" I continued saying to Zora.

"Leave?" Nancy squeaked into a pillow, and I gave her back a little swat.

"You hush now," I admonished. "The grownups are talking."

"Um... you're not going anywhere," Duke said as he knelt down beside me.

I sighed, letting the air fill my lungs so deeply that my chest puffed out.

He kissed the top of one of my knees. "You think the strong man is gonna let anyone hurt you or the tyke?"

"How much did you hear?" I asked, bewildered.

"Enough," he said.

"I not a tyke!" Nancy said into the pillow again.

I let out a nervous laugh. "I said *shush*, you," I scolded her playfully. "You don't even know what a tyke is!"

"Duke's right, Jane," Zora said. "I think there may be a way around this."

"A way around it? Not sure about that."

Zora put her hand on her hip and gazed out the window. The sky was getting brighter as the sun rose higher in the sky.

I put a hand on Duke's shoulder. "I'm sorry you're tangled up in my craziness," I apologized.

"No need to say it. I guess that's what I get for falling head over heels for a witchy woman and her witchy kiddo."

"I not a witchy kiddo!" Nancy exclaimed.

Duke and I both burst out with laughter, but when I looked over at Zora to see if she had heard Nancy's innocent remark, Zora's eyes had rolled into the back of her head, and the line of runes at the crown of her head glowed faintly under her silky scarf. I was glad that Nancy was tucked away headfirst into the depths of the couch because if seeing Zora made *me* feel uncomfortable, I could only imagine how it would have frightened a three year old.

Chapter Seventeen

And to cast out your enemies, you must work in the shadows, I read to myself. But those words hadn't been there before. I didn't read that sentence during the ritual. It was new. Fresh. Like Zora was conjuring something from beyond. Something only *she* could hear and see. I nudged Duke on the shoulder, beckoning him to look at Zora, and when he did, his mouth nearly fell to the floor.

"And to cast out your enemies, you must work in the shadows," I said aloud, and my words brought Zora out of her trance. Her eyes flipped back to normal, and she blinked a few times to catch her bearings.

"We're going to breakfast," she said. "Like usual. We're to gather some of the others and let them know what's going on. Buster is on alert and knows not to let anyone on the property."

"Wait... what just happened?" Duke stammered.

Zora ignored him and looked out the window for a moment as if she was hearing something in the distance. She cocked her head to one side and furrowed her brow. "McCrory," she said like she was relaying a message. "He'll be here tonight, too. Someone in East Liverpool reported a shopkeeper missing."

"Already!" I exclaimed in disbelief.

Zora pursed her lips together and nodded with woeful confirmation.

"Can someone explain to me what's..." Duke began, but I put a finger on his lips to silence him.

"Witch stuff, dear," I said playfully.

That seemed to placate him because he took my finger into his mouth and sucked on it seductively. It sent shivers down my spine and flooded my mind with the passion we shared from hours ago. My stomach fluttered for a second, but I quickly turned my attention back to Zora.

"Tophat," she said answering Duke, but her gaze cut straight through me. There was no mistaking it—she'd come with orders straight from the Carny Boss himself. Tophat had called her an acolyte, and I supposed that meant more than just blind devotion. There was something between them, an unspoken current, a knowing. "Not always," she said, as if plucking the thought right out of my head. "But this—this is about you and Nancy. And priority number one is keeping her out of harm's way."

Upon hearing that, Nancy shot straight up from the couch with a look of panic on her face. Quickly, I reached for her and cradled her in my lap. Her little rabbit heart beat frantically against my thighs, and I rocked gently in hopes of calming her nerves.

"You're okay, Little Crow," Duke said to her in a higher pitched voice, and she looked up and smiled at him. "It's gonna be okay, Momma Crow," he said to me, and it was my turn to smile.

Zora tilted her head to the side again and squinted. "Come on, it's time to go."

Chapter Seventeen

Acting on her instructions from Tophat, Zora rounded up Vesper, Chickie, Sis, Razor, and her sister Elaine at the cookhouse. The urgency in her voice conveyed just how dire the situation was and how instrumental everyone would be in thwarting the people who had finally caught up with Madame Jane Crowe. She doled out orders like a general commanding an army—Tophat's army, and surprisingly, everyone complied without a song or a dance (which I had fully expected from at least Chickie).

"Tophat needs Janey tonight. She'll stay with him in his trailer," Zora murmured, her voice hushed but firm.

Duke's gaze flicked to me, and a hint of something darker curled at the corner of his mouth. Jealousy, maybe. I could see the questions forming in his head before he even spoke them. I reached for his hand, giving it a quick, reassuring squeeze, shaking my head ever so slightly. Whatever he was thinking—whatever notion had crept into his mind—it wasn't that. There was no funny business between me and Tophat. That fate belonged to Nancy, much further down the line, though that part I kept to myself.

"We're dealing with two women and one man. They'll be on the hunt for both me and Nancy. They probably have our pictures, so they'll be flashing them around all over the World for sure," I said in a low voice. "The head of the operation is Christina Combs. But she'll probably be using an alias."

"But we also have a McCrory problem," Zora continued. "There's no doubt he'll be on the prowl tonight, what with the new missing woman's report from East Liverpool."

Vesper's face tightened, and I knew she must have been thinking about Tina. I wanted to grab her hand and tell her that Tina was never coming back. That Tophat had used the ashes of her dead body in order to kill the sorceress Dareza so the spirit of an ancient heksa could come through and speak to him.

Zora shot me a crooked look, and I shut my thoughts down right quick. "So, with McCrory on the case, and the cultists on the hunt…"

"Cultists?" Chickie cried out, and everyone in our circle *shushed* her.

"We need to shake up the game plan for tonight," Zora went on. "Chickie, you're stepping in as Madame Jane. Hit wardrobe, find yourself something with a little mystique, and set up shop in the Fortune Teller's tent."

Chickie's eyes sparkled, her red lips stretching wide in a grin she couldn't contain. She bounced her knee up and down, jittery with excitement, like a dame who'd just hit the jackpot at the races. I'd never seen her so downright giddy, like she was sitting on top of the world and didn't have a care to spare.

"Vesper, Sis, Razor, Duke—this is where you come in. McCrory knows Chickie from the Cooch.

Chapter Seventeen

If he gets into the Fortune Teller tent and sees her in Jane's place, he's going to get suspicious..."

"He already *is* suspicious!" Sis exclaimed.

"Right, but we don't want him snooping harder than normal. In fact, we don't want him and the cultists to cross paths at all."

"Cultists," Nancy mindlessly repeated under her breath. Chickie heard her and nodded at her in agreement. Child to child. I just rolled my eyes.

"So," Zora continued, "do your jobs and do them well. Create a diversion any way you can. We're all actors here, and we all play our roles to a tee. Ramp it up. Extra."

"And Nancy?" Elaine asked.

"They're looking for a little girl," I said. "But we don't have a girl at the World, do we?"

Sis clapped her hands together in excitement. "Oh, honey! I know what you're about to say!"

Elaine's face twisted in confusion. I mean, did she *not* know that Sis was truly a man?

"Nancy will be your son tonight," I said.

Nancy's head popped up from my chest and she scowled. "I not a son! I a daughter!"

Zora reached her arm and touched Nancy's shoulder. "Just for tonight, sweetie. It's pretend. Make-believe. You like it here at the carnival, don't you?"

Nancy nodded begrudgingly.

"So, you know how your Mommy dresses up and goes to work and how you hang out with Auntie Elaine and your cousins every night?" Sis said.

Nancy nodded again, her hair bouncing up and around her cherubic face.

"It's like that, honey," I said softly, convincingly. "Just for one night, I promise. You're going to pretend to be one of the boys. To play a trick on the people. To make them laugh."

"I don't like tricks with stinky flowers," she grumbled.

We all chuckled at the innocence of her words. "No. Nothing like that." My words satisfied her enough, and she eased back into my lap.

Elaine stood up and bent over to take Nancy from me. "What do you want me to do to her?" she asked.

"Dress her in one of the boys' outfits. Cut her hair. Short. Maybe a hat, too. Black-eye makeup? Anything to distort her features."

"I have black hair dye," Elaine suggested.

"I'm okay with that," I agreed.

"And call her something else. Ya know… a *boy* name," Duke emphasized, his brows knitting on his forehead.

Elaine's eyes widened as inspiration struck. "Silas! I'll call her Silas!"

I scrunched my nose with slight disgust. "Why that?"

"I always liked it. If I ever have another boy, that's what I'd name him!"

"Well, whatever it is," Zora cut in waving a dismissive hand at her sister, "you take Silas and the other boys and have a great night."

Chapter Seventeen

I kissed Nancy on the forehead before Elaine pulled her completely away. "Have fun with your brothers tonight, *Silas!*" I teased and nuzzled my nose against hers.

Nancy giggled and Elaine whisked her away.

Tophat's trailer wasn't normal by any stretch of the word, but when I stepped inside that night, it felt a little ... *less*. There was no strong glamour to make the inside resemble an ancient cavern or have sunlight shining right through the walls. It just felt *normal*. Like stepping into anyone else's ole trailer.

But I didn't need normal. I needed the illusion—the concealment of a glamour—more than ever, and I was a little unnerved that Tophat's defenses were seemingly down.

"Why do you doubt me, Jane?" he purred from his table.

My heart jumped in my chest when he spoke, and a gasp escaped my lips.

He chuckled. "Sorry! Didn't mean to frighten."

I took a step farther into the trailer. "No. It's not you. I'm just a little on edge is all."

Tophat rubbed the thin layer of hair on his chin thoughtfully. He was dressed all in black—black button-down shirt with a silken red bowtie, and even though he was seated, I could see him having on nothing but black slacks. His long frock coat was draped over a coat rack in the corner of the trailer and his famous hat was nestled at the top. Then he ran his fingers freely through his shaggy black hair. "You need not worry. We'll get this all taken care of." His voice was lyrical. Musical. It had layers to it that overlapped itself and created a harmonious song. His words were luminous, and the candles throughout the trailer increased their light with every word he spoke. *That sounds so ridiculous,* I thought to myself, and then I realized I no longer had my own, inner private thoughts. Tophat was privy to all of them.

"Only your good ones and only when they flow freely," he answered.

I smiled and nodded at him, letting him know I had caught on to the playful remastering of his catch phrase.

"Sit," he commanded, and I obliged, taking the seat across from him at the table.

An ancient book was open in front of him, and I glanced over at the runes on the pages. "Is that the Blodheksa book?" I asked, recognizing the familiar symbols.

"Mmmhmm," he hummed.

"It's old," I remarked.

"Very old," he answered as he flipped a page over. "I'm sure you have no trouble reading…"

I craned my neck across the table. "No problem at all," I interjected. "I can read them just fine, like how I can read Zora's tattoos. I don't know how, but I can." I paused, reading a line from the page. The name Blodwyn was written there, and I remembered having said it during the ritual. A

Chapter Seventeen

ponderous name. Blodwyn. It sounded ancient and almost powerful. I mouthed the name to myself wondering to whom it belonged. *Blodwyn.* Like the name of an angel. Like the name of a supreme being who no longer walked this Earth but was very much still alive today. I don't know why I thought that. Although, I can't really say it was much of a thought than it was a feeling deep in my gut. "Who was Blodwyn, anyway?"

He looked up at me sharply with eyes that scolded for even saying the name aloud. "Blodwyn is my sister," he replied.

My face contorted like Bendy Bella on stage. "*Is*? But she must be..."

"Ancient," he replied.

"And that would make you..."

"Seventeen years less ancient," he said with a chuckle.

"But what we did last night..." I began. "What did she tell you?"

He lifted a hand up to silence me. "What we did last night was more important than you'll ever know."

"But I called forth a different name. *Aizel.* Not Blodwyn. Wouldn't you have wanted to reach out to your kin?"

"Necromancers call upon the dead, Jane. You know that. They don't contact the *living*."

My chest constricted as if Winnie had been wrapped around my body. There was so much I still didn't know or understand.

"That's okay, Jane. You don't have to understand everything. But what we do need is to protect you and Nancy from what's about to set foot in the World."

"I know," I said in a low voice.

"You brought them both? The Augen and the Thoth?"

I reached into my apron, fished out the two decks, and set them on the table next to the Blodheksa book.

"Good. Read them."

I gulped. "The Thoth Deck?" I crowed. "I've never read them before. I don't know how…"

"Why haven't you?" he asked, but it was more like he was probing me. Like he already knew the answer to the questions and was only asking them so that I would come to some grand revelation. Momma used to do that to me all the time, and I kinda hated it.

"I was afraid," I said meekly.

"Afraid of what?" he replied.

"Afraid Aleister would somehow sense them being used, and his people would be able to find us."

"And yet, that's exactly what happened, isn't it? The Deck was a calling card. A beacon. Having them in your very possession drew them to you."

"I know," I agreed shamefully.

"So, if you knew, why did you take them in the first place?"

"I don't know," I whispered.

"But you do, Jane. You do."

Chapter Seventeen

He was right. I did. I knew exactly why I took them. But in my defense, it was more of an instinctual thing than anything else. I knew my time at the compound was coming to an end. I knew I had to somehow get out of there because I had heard the chatter of their plans. Christina was the ringleader, that's for sure. I think she was driven by jealousy. Not that she was jealous that I was the mother of the Beast's child because I don't suspect she had any interest in Aleister that way, but she was jealous of my high position—a student elevated to a supreme role as the life giver of our leader's progeny. I was well respected in the compound, in our group, in the hierarchy of Crowley's system. I was in the top tier.

Christina had been involved in Crowley's magick longer than most, but she never got the attention I did, making her dangerous. So, when she planted the notion in the congregation's minds—that Nancy was *empty*—I knew it was trouble. *Vuota*.

The real kicker? She wasn't wrong.

Nancy *was* empty. I'd known it since before she ever took her first breath. Even in the womb, she was quiet, unresponsive. I'd rest my hands on my belly, hum lullabies, speak words of power from the divine texts of Aleister himself—nothing. No stirrings, no restless kicks. Just silence. The only thing I ever got in return was a nasty case of heartburn or a wave of exhaustion that sent me straight to bed. No vivid dreams. No celestial glow. Nothing but a creeping certainty that the child growing inside me was ... ordinary.

So, when Nancy finally opened those tiny eyes and cooed up at me, I knew it for sure. She was just a baby—no great spark, no grand design. And deep down, I always figured it was only a matter of time before someone else put the pieces together, too. And Christina was gunnin' for me hard—gunnin' for my little girl. God knows what they were going to ultimately do to my sweet one.

Lady Frieda, one of Aleister's closest friends and confidantes, had been helping him to design the Thoth Deck. She had been away on a retreat and left the unfinished prototype at the compound. One afternoon, I was walking through the hallway when I heard a crow cawing its fool head off, like it was in distress or something. The sound was coming from the study, and it was so loud I thought it had gotten in the window somehow. But when I got there, there was no crow in the room. I investigated. The windows were shut tightly; everything was in its place. But the crow kept cawing, like it was trying to get my attention or something, so I just listened. Eventually the caws turned into whispers, and the whispers turned into words. Words in another language. I couldn't understand them at first, but the more I listened, the more I was able to decipher what they said: *The cards will protect her.* And when I looked down at the secretary desk in the middle of the room, the Thoth Deck was laid out before me. That was all the sign I needed.

Chapter Seventeen

"Was that so hard to come to terms with?" Trent asked.

I sighed, realizing he had once again been rooting around in my head.

"You just misinterpreted the message. It's a common mistake. Sometimes the signs aren't clear, and we think we know what they're saying. Trust me. I've been there myself. There are no absolutes when you're dealing with the other realms. Everything is fluid, and everything has a tendency to change."

I knitted my brow. "So, what exactly did I misinterpret?"

"Well," he said thoughtfully, "you thought the Thoth Deck was going to protect Nancy, but in fact, it simply lead your enemies straight to you. However, had you not taken them, you would not have ended up here at the World where you have received the deck you were meant to have. *The cards that will protect her.*"

My eyes widened when he repeated my words, for I realized that it was Trent's voice I had heard when the crow cawed in the study. "How… I don't…" I stammered, but he spread out the cards of the Augen deck, and the pictures started to spring to life.

I see in the first card the man who had accompanied Christina sitting in the Cooch tent as Vesper danced wildly around him. He paid extra for a private session, and while he was titillated by her tits and other assets, he held up a picture of me and Aleister side by side with Nancy in front of us. Like a picture-perfect family.

"Have you seen them? Do you know them?" he asks her.

Vesper circles him, moving her hands all around his chest in order to distract him. "No, sugar. Can't say I have."

"They may be in disguise. Matilda and Althea, but they're probably using aliases."

She hums. "Hmmm... nope. Not familiar at all. The lady is awful pretty though. I could see why you're looking for her!" *Vesper moves in close to his ear and whispers.* "She an ex-sweetie, sweetie?"

The man's face turns as red as a tomato. "No. Nothing like that."

"Bet you'd like to have the both of us at once, wouldn't you?" *she purrs.*

His eyes flutter into the back of his head, and he drops the picture to the ground.

In the trailer, Tophat handed me two of the Thoth cards. "To the flame," he instructed, and I held them over the candle. They caught fire in a flash, nearly exploding in my hand. When I looked back at the Augen card, Vesper was straddled over the man, and he bucked wildly into her in the throes of passion. The image on the card gradually faded away, and the second card rattled to life.

I see in the second card the woman who was with them. She roams the Midway, stopping everyone she can as she holds up my picture and asks if they recognize me. She crosses paths with Elaine and the Creed boys—my Silas included. Nancy sure does look the part in one of the boys' outfits. Her hair is jet black and short, just as we had discussed, and Elaine even

Chapter Seventeen

put some black eyeshadow around Nancy's right eye to make her look like she had a little boy shiner. When the woman kneels down in Nancy's face and holds up my picture, something flickers in Nancy's eyes. The flicker of recognition. The woman's mouth curls into a smile like she's just hit the jackpot.

Quickly, I extended my hand, and Tophat gave me two more cards to burn, and we held them together as they ignited. When they were reduced to ash, the Augen card showed the woman suddenly standing up with a confused look on her face, like she had suddenly forgotten what she was doing. Elaine scolded her for talking to her children, then ushered the kids away to the games as that image faded as well.

In the third card, I see Christina Combs prowling the sideshow alley, her eyes sharp, her jaw set. She's hunting. She doesn't need a photograph or a name—just her gut, her instincts, and the pull of something unseen. She sweeps through the tents with a scowl, pushing past flaps and peering inside. First Sis's tent, then Razor's. She barges into Duke's space, only to spin on her heels, unsatisfied. But when she reaches Zora's tent, her fingers curl around the curtain, and without hesitation, she pulls it back. A flood of light engulfs her. Zora stands at the center, bare as the day she was born, arms spread wide. Every inch of inked skin glows, the symbols alive, pulsing like the heartbeat of the universe itself. The light fills the space, bright as the inferno in Tophat's trailer that day. Then Zora's eyes—yellow, burning—lock onto Christina's. And just like that, she stops cold. Frozen.

I burned another two Thoth cards, and when the ashes fell on top of the Blodheksa book, Christina blinked her eyes, unable to comprehend what she had witnessed. Unable to remember why she was there in the first place.

"That's it. Those were the last of them," I said.

Tophat pointed to the fourth Augen card. "There's more, though."

The fourth card flashed to life, and I was taken aback for the image was something I had not anticipated. Tannehill McCrory in the Fortune Teller's tent—my tent—talking with none other than Chickadee Sassafras. They were arm in arm, like how she would have been familiar with him in the Cooch. Chickie's face was real close to his, lips practically touching, and she was whispering something I couldn't make out. Red X's flashed on both their foreheads, and my hands vibrated with violent tremors.

"It's... it's *Chickie!*" I exclaimed. "With McCrory!"

Tophat swiped the card up from the table and mumbled something under his breath. The energy in the trailer shifted so dramatically that the floor beneath us shook. I stared into the blackness of the fifth Augen card until it started to twinkle. Twinkle, twinkle lights. And the twinkling of the lights made my fingers tingle, and my toes tingle. Like an orgasm with Duke. I felt fuzzy and put my hand in front of my face, but I could see through my hand! It was translucent with a white film over the shape of my palm and fingers. Static.

Chapter Seventeen

I started to fade. And the card started to get brighter. And the trailer shook with a violent jerking motion. And Tophat chanted. Chanted something about a spell and a word and fire and a woman and Silas and I gripped the feather necklace and opened my mouth to cry out...

Then the shaking stopped, and I was gone.
Gone.
Just *gone.*

No longer in the trailer or in this realm of existence. I blinked, and I had catapulted to another time and place. The trailer didn't exist. The World didn't exist. Everything around me was covered in a layer of dark haze, and I was in the sky, in the cosmos. In that place, I saw Nancy and Trent. There was a tear in the sky, and a growling sound coming from a line of pulsing stars. Something eager to get out. Something crying to get out. I knew I needed to help it, so I shut my eyes tight, propelled my body into the ether, and thrust myself into the line of stars. Because I could fly. I was not me, but I was me. I was a bird—large and black with oil-slick colored feathers, and my beak protruded in front of my face. *Jane Crow*, I thought, *in the flesh and feathers.*

On the other side of the cosmos, there was a tree in the forest. I crashed down on one of the low hanging branches, and beneath me, Tophat stood with a woman I had never seen before. Against the tree, there was an outline of a shadowy body. Another man.

The woman said, "I think I know her, too," and pointed at me.

"I do as well," Tophat said.

I tried to call out to them, but I couldn't speak. My voice was tangled in my throat, and only foreign noises came out from my mouth, my beak. Caws, like a crow. Caws, like a crow choking on its feathers.

I cawed and cawed and cawed, frustrated that they couldn't understand what I was saying. "Death. Death. Death," I fervently repeated, but the words of my human self only rang in my head when all that was really being said from my beak was, "Caw, caw, caw."

I cawed so desperately. I cawed my fool-crow head off. And then finally the woman said, "I am death." And I stopped and sighed, like a weight had been lifted off my chest. Like the feathers were no longer strangling my throat.

"We are death," Tophat responded, and it felt like *finally* they had understood me.

Then I flew off the branch and over to the shadow man against the tree. I plucked out his eyes with my crow's beak. I don't know why, but it felt like something I had to do. And when I took them from his face and gulped them down hard, a light swelled up inside me, and the atmosphere around me grew much, much brighter. I could see even more than ever before! The man screamed in agony as Tophat and the woman watched, and I flew away back into the line of stars.

Chapter Eighteen

Monday, June 5th 1944
The Gentry Brothers' Wonders of the World Carnival
Jane's Trailer
Glenmoor, Ohio
Morning of the Waxing Gibbous Moon

Everything changed after that night. Time seemed to slow down and speed up all at once. I felt different—changed. I felt as if I had transformed into something above and beyond myself. Something not human and not of this Earth and yet somehow connected to it and the World all at the same time. When I walked, I could scarcely feel my feet touching the ground beneath me. I floated a few centimeters just outside gravity's reach, like a bird hovering over its prey, like a crow gliding among the trees in the other worldly plane, like a shadow dancing underneath the moonlight—the shape of it varying with each step and flicker. The shape of me changing and becoming more and more distorted. *Farewell to the flesh.*

Witch of the Midnight Shadow

I woke up in my bed in my trailer without knowing how I had gotten there or when I had left Tophat's place. Curiously, someone had put Winnie's snake enclosure in my room, yet I couldn't remember if that had been me. A vague notion swept over me like a fragment of a dream of me leaving Tophat's trailer, going to my psychic tent, and carrying Winnie back to my place, but it was hazy and disjointed and flickered in my head with a red dream-like haze. *Like the red eyes of my crow-self.* Winnie's thick body had indicated that she had recently fed, and I propped myself on my elbows to get a better look at her. She nudged her head against the glass tank, and her body rippled with slow domino-like undulations. Against her taut skin, the impression of five thick human fingers pressed up against her from the inside and then slowly faded into itself as she languidly shifted her position. I shuddered at the sight and blinked my eyes rapidly to eliminate it from my memory.

And yet, deep down in my gut, I knew the particulars of me leaving Tophat's trailer, fetching Winnie, and crawling back into bed didn't amount to a hill of beans. Not when there were bigger fish to fry. For one, my lungs weren't hitching with every breath—I could breathe easy, real easy, and not just in the literal sense. There was a lightness in my chest, a freedom I hadn't felt in longer than I cared to admit. And I knew, without a shadow of a doubt, that I wouldn't be haunted anymore by the specter of... of... hell's bells, it took a

Chapter Eighteen

second for my brain to catch up—Aleister. With the Thoth Deck burned to cinders, he no longer had a beacon leading him straight to me. And whatever hex Tophat and I had cooked up, well, it had thrown Christina and her pack of wolves off the scent. They were stumbling blind now, lost in the trees, stranded in the dark of the other world, where my crow-self could swoop down and pluck out their eyes, too.

Then, there was the matter of Chickie and her betrayal.

Her betrayal.

Jesus Christ, the thought of her siding up to McCrory from word jump made my skin crawl, made my throat reflexes gag. It felt slimy and icky and gross... and so damn obvious! Because when I went back and replayed all the instances in my head, I want to smack myself in the face for being so blind. For someone who is supposed to be gifted with sight beyond sight, I surely was blind to what was right in front of me. But I remember, Chickie said on the train to Ohio that she had an older gentleman she had been writing letters to. Chickie was overly dramatic when the others told us about McCrory's unsolveds and the legend of the Shadow Man, but in retrospect, she knew it all, didn't she? She knew who he was the second he strode into the Big Tent to see Serpentina's performance. I remember how Chickie commented on his good looks. And then when he just magically showed up in town on our supply run? I wonder how many business lap-dances she gave him? Was she really upset about having to work the Cooch, or was it just an act that she was upset for not being named Madame? What did she tell him about me? About Nancy? She was McCrory's mole all along. She had been feeding him all of our carny secrets from the get-go.

Winnie slinked again in her cage, and I realized that the flashing glamour had been completely lifted. No longer did she blink in and out of reality in my mind. Anyone who walked into my room now would be able to see her for what she was — a lazy albino Burmese python and not a deadly viper. Quickly, I hopped up out of the bed, threw on a robe, and marched straight to the line of trailers where Zora and Nancy would be.

But when I stepped outside, I could feel in the air that things changed. There was a different feel, a different vibe to it all, and it wasn't just the early grip of summer rearing its head above the early morning horizon. I spun my head around in a circular motion, and I noticed the dust from the ground was unsettled and loose. There had been movement in the World — lots of it. And as my eyes took in the entirety of the back lot, it quickly dawned upon me that the movement was happening *everywhere*. My stomach dropped when it hit me.

The carnival is closing up shop.

I put some pep in my step and jogged as fast as I could to Zora's. Without knocking, I burst through the door, ready to bombard her ears with a slew of questions that were perched eagerly

Chapter Eighteen

on my tongue, but when I stepped inside, Zora was gliding back and forth across the floor, gathering all the items and incidentals in her trailer and placing them in large cardboard boxes. "Was wondering when you were gonna get up," she sang without looking at me.

"What are you talking about? What do you mean?"

"Janey, Janey! We're packing up and heading out. Buster gave the order last night."

I clicked my tongue on the roof of my mouth. "The order? What do you mean we're heading out?"

"The World. Trent says it's time to hit up a new town. We've spent enough time here. Exhausted our cashflow."

"Tophat said that? When did he say that? When did he tell Buster to…" I stopped to think, and a searing pain came above my left eyelid. Furiously, I rubbed the offending area.

Zora stopped packing and stared at me with concern. Her black silk scarf was wrapped tightly around her head, concealing her rune tattoos.

"That's impossible, Zora! I was just with Tophat last night. We…"

She narrowed her eyes. "Are you sure about that, Jane?"

"Of course I'm sure! It's…" I paused again and looked outside the small window of her trailer. A group of rugged roustabouts trudged through the dirt with bundles of wooden planks that looked like the deconstructed archways to Bendy Bella's tent. They spit into the dust and cursed that they had to make many trips to get the one display broken apart. "What day *is* it, Zora?" I said, my voice barely audible above their groaning.

"It's Monday," she responded matter-of-factly. "Monday the 5th of June."

I think my heart seized in my chest, and my jaw dropped to the floor.

I've been asleep that long? I thought.

"Nancy!" I managed to screech. "Where's..."

Zora put her hands on my shoulders and locked me into place. "She's right as rain, Janey girl. Nancy's with Elaine and the boys. Apparently she's really playing into her Silas persona." She chuckled.

I sighed, and my chest deflated like a dead balloon at a birthday party. "Duke?"

"Working his ass off with Razor and the rousties to get this place in tip-top for Tophat." She rolled her eyes and huffed. "Buster and his stupid sayings. I swear that little man gets on my very last nerve. It boggles my mind how Trent has put so much faith and trust in him."

Just then, there was a small knock at the door, but before Zora could yell, "Come in," it opened quietly and Tophat poked his head within, surveying the scene. He smiled when his eyes landed on me and stepped fully inside to reveal Nancy bouncing gently on his hip.

Her eyes lit up like a Christmas tree when she saw me, and I rushed over to them and swooped her from his arms. I pressed my face deep into her

Chapter Eighteen

neck and inhaled her sweet scent, committing the smell to my memory.

I will never forget the way she smells in this very moment—like almond cake and ocean water.

"Too tight, Mommy!" she squealed, and I could feel her nose crinkle up against the side of my face.

"Sorry, baby," I apologized and eased up.

"Trent," Zora greeted him with a curt nod to which he nodded back in kind.

"We're almost done wrapping things up here," he said to me. "I figured you wouldn't need very long to get yourself organized, so I let you rest."

I clutched Nancy tighter and turned my body defensively from him. Nancy winced. "Sorry, baby," I whispered again to her. "Let me rest?" I said to him.

"Did you tell her what's going on?" he asked Zora.

She shook her head. "Didn't get a chance to."

Tophat nodded, reached into his tailcoat pocket, and pulled out the Augen deck. "These are yours. They always have been and always will be." He handed them to me. "I told you they will protect her."

I looked down at them. The faces were blank, absent of any image, like they were waiting for me to conjure something up. "How do you know that?"

"Aizel told me. It was one of the many things she told me that night."

"So where are we going now?" I asked.

He motioned his thumb from his chest to Zora. "*We* are going farther west," he replied. "There's nothing left for us here. The magic is drained from this place."

I glared at Zora suspiciously. She looked down and shuffled her feet. Then I set my gaze back on Tophat. "Okay," I said drawing out the last syllable of the word obnoxiously. "But what about McCrory? What about the investigation? What about what I saw with Chickie and…"

"Just like *I* helped *you* take care of *your* problem," he began.

"The people from across the pond?" I said in code.

He nodded. "*You* helped *me* take care of *my* problem."

"McCrory? What did I…? What did we…?"

"Sis is going to take you to the bus depot in East Liverpool. Take the 9:45 to the train station in Cleveland. There, you'll get on the Mercury line to Grand Central Station."

"Wait! *Me*? You're sending *me* back to New York?"

"With Nancy, of course. And Duke. He wants to be with you, Jane. He's a good man, and he'll be a good father for Nancy."

My head swirled. Tophat's words hovered in the air around me, and I had trouble stringing them together to make cohesive sentences.

"We go see doggies again, Mommy?" Nancy asked against my chest. Her hot breath seeped through the fabric of my pinafore and blossomed

Chapter Eighteen

on the skin of my upper chest, warming the very center of the thin bones just beneath the fleshy surface.

I patted her hair and kissed the top of her head. "You would like that? You wanna see Bear and Lady and Moose and the others?"

She nodded fervently.

"A pack to protect the pack," Zora said.

Tophat took a step closer to me, and my eyes got lost in his. There, images swirled like a gray tornado, and I could only catch on to bits and pieces of them. They made me feel nauseous and dizzy.

"You don't want me to come with you?" I asked, and the words sounded so pathetic, so desperately childlike.

He flashed that wolfish grin, the kind that could warm a soul or set it on edge, depending on the tilt of his mood. "But of course I do, Madame Jane Crowe, Witch of Endor. Imagine, if you will, all the unholy wonders the two of us could conjure. In another life, doll, we might've ruled the whole damn world. But that ain't the hand we were dealt with. Not this time. I need you to skedaddle on back to New York, back to your mother, and carve out somethin' real for yourself, for Duke, for that little girl of yours. Give her a childhood worth having—one filled with sunshine, not shadows. Not yet, at least. Break the chain, Janey. The one *your* old man forged, the one *her* father tried to reinforce. Keep her safe. Keep her clear of the dark. Because one day, when the time's right, the dark's gonna come callin' for her. And when it does, she'll have a role to play—one she was born for, and she'll be filled with the light and the life to pave the way for the New Eden. *Vuota* no more."

"You're staying?" I said to Zora.

She nodded.

"I told you," Trent said. "We all have our roles to play. Zora's not quite finished being my associate."

"Everything is still fuzzy, though. I feel like I've lost time."

"When you're settled and on your way, look to the Deck. Things will become clear."

I sighed and rocked Nancy in my arms. Zora walked over and embraced the two of us. "Thank you," she said. "I'm going to miss you very much." She kissed me on the cheek, and her lips felt hot against my skin, like how Nancy's breath ignited my chest. Underneath her black silk scarf, her tattoos glowed orange for a flash of a second. "You'll always have family at the World."

"Thank you," I whispered back.

She stepped aside as Tophat placed his hand on Nancy's shoulder. She turned her head and looked at him—wide-eyed with innocence and awe.

"Now, Little Crow. You be sure to take care of your Mommy here. Promise me you'll make sure *she's* safe."

Nancy giggled and tucked her chin into her chest.

Chapter Eighteen

"You and I will see each other again someday, Little Crow. But until then, keep your good thoughts flowing and your actions to match."

She giggled again. "Okay."

Tophat put his other hand on my shoulder. "Sis'll be leaving soon. You're not going to want to miss your ride."

I nodded and looked into his gray eyes one last time. There was a forest, and the setting sun cast shadows of the tree limbs across the leaf-littered floor. That familiar music played in the distance—the drums, the flutes, the voices of the angels singing discordantly in their foreign tongue. A murder of crows swooped low beneath the branches, cawing in refrain to the song, but in that moment, I heard it all, I understood it all, I knew it all. "You are death," they sang to me. And instead of feeling a sense of dread or despair, I was comforted and at peace. I may have been death, but for now, we were safe. Nancy was safe. And we were going home.

Monday, June 5th 1944
The Mercury Line Train
Leaving out of Cleveland, Ohio
Afternoon of the Waxing Gibbous Moon

Duke rested his hand on my knee and gave it a reassuring squeeze as the train pulled from the station. I smiled at him before resting my head into the crook of his arm. He gave the top of my head a little peck, and Nancy, her squirrely self barely still in my lap, giggled her fool head off at the open display of affection.

"Oh?" he teased. "What's so funny about a little smooch-a-roo?"

"Nuffin'," she cooed.

"Oh yeah? Nuffin'?" he joked and reached out his hand to tickle under her arms.

She laughed and laughed and begged him to stop until I twisted my body in the seat, pulling her out of his reach. He gave me a questioning look, and I rolled my eyes. "She's digging into my hips," I mumbled.

He smiled. "Sorry."

I couldn't help but smile back. He was just too easy on the eyes to *not* get a smile out of me.

"Come here, kiddo," he said and stretched his hands out for Nancy to climb into his lap. "Give your mother a little break and sit still for a few minutes."

Nancy obeyed, scurrying straight into Duke's waiting arms. My smile stretched wider at the sight of them—like true father and daughter. Something deep inside me stirred, something warm and whole, like a missing piece sliding into place. A sense of fulfillment settled over me. Full circle. That's what it felt like. Everything I had ever longed for, everything I had fought for, was right there—wrapped up in the laughter of my little girl as she bounced in Duke's grip, the steady strength of his arms holding her close. And soon,

Chapter Eighteen

that *everything* would be rattling down the tracks, back to Momma. Back where I belonged.

Tophat was right. This is a good thing.

And yet, despite the overwhelming joy I felt, I still felt unsettled. Unnerved. My exit from the World was rather abrupt, and I couldn't understand why. Tophat had insisted we leave as quickly as possible with no goodbyes of any sort. Heck, I didn't even get a chance to say goodbye to Winnie and wave goodbye to the five fat fingers dissolving in her gut.

McCrory's fingers, I assume.

A red light flickered behind my eyes, and a sharp pain stabbed me above my eyebrow when the thought of Sheriff Tannehill McCrory popped into my mind. And suddenly, I had a dreadful feeling that something terrible had happened to the mean ole sheriff and that I was responsible for it.

I reached in my front apron pocket, pulled out the six cards of the Augen Deck, and laid them out on the dinner tray table in front of me.

"Mommy's cards!" Nancy declared, and Duke raised an eyebrow.

"Yep," I chirped. "Mommy's cards." I looked at him. "I just need to see one thing." And he nodded, bidding me to do my business.

I hovered my hands steadily over them as the roar from the engine filled my head. Subtly, in the background of it all, the music played—the rhythmic crunching of gears and hissing of pistons combined together to form a mechanical song that instantly lulled me. It was beautiful! Whistles and motors and rumbles from underneath the seat made my body sway to and fro. And soon all the metallic sounds transformed — blended, meshed, became the voices. They were the voices that sang to me and for me.

A magnetic sensation stirred in the space between my hands. I closed my eyes and inhaled as a wave of white light began to swirl in the void. Images began to appear on the once blank cards — pictures that flickered like a film reel out of control telling the story of what I felt in my heart...

A young man walking alone on the streets of East Liverpool in the dim morning light. He smelled of sweat and steel, the night shift at the mill still clinging to his clothes. The bus had left him at Mulberry, and his boots scuffed against the cracked pavement of State Street.

Then — a pause. A shape in the weeds. A flash of bare feet peeking from tangled green blankets. A moment of hesitation before he moved closer to see the body of a young woman. He can hardly catch his breath. He's never seen a dead body before. The blood drains from his face.

She was laid out on her back, cradled in the overgrown grass like a forgotten doll. Her dark brown hair spilled over her shoulders. There were tiny strands of gold and white on the undersides, and her hair was fine and feathery. It reminded me of the down of a baby chick.

Chickadee.

Chapter Eighteen

Only her countenance wasn't hers. It was as if a wavy mirror had been placed over her face like a mask. A strong glamour had welded itself to her, and I remembered that Tophat had said that the magic was drained from the World. I came to understand it had been drained because it was now concentrated within the dead body of my once friend, Chickadee Sassafras, who would remain nameless forevermore.

A pink slip clung to her body, torn at the strap, slipping down over her shoulder where a dark bruise bloomed at the base of her neck. Curious, he pressed fingers to her skin. Warm. Still warm. Death had come only hours before. A death that my soul screamed that I had a hand in bringing.

One of images in the Augen Cards billowed with dark black smoke, but I refused to look at it. I was okay with not remembering my role in her demise.

I blinked, and the cards began to fade, but the image of the woman remained. Forgotten in the weeds. Waiting to be named. Forever to be labeled the Carnival Girl.

I picked up the cards and returned them to my apron pocket. Duke nodded at me and said, "Find what you needed?"

I nodded back.

"Can I play with your cards, Mommy?" Nancy playfully asked.

"No, sweetie, not this time. Maybe when you're a little bit older."

"Okay," she relented.

"You sure you're okay?" Duke asked again.

"Yeah, yeah. I'm fine," I responded with the images of Chickie's body still swirling in my mind.

"Still thinking about that midnight shadow?"

My ears perked up at his choice of words. "Huh?"

"Well, Madame Jane, whatever you were seeing in those cards must have been pretty wild."

"How so?"

"You just looked different. Like it was you, but it wasn't."

"There was a shadow on your face, Mommy. A big gray *spot!*" Nancy chimed.

"Oh, you hush, you," I admonished. "Forget about all that silly stuff and the carnival and those people there. It was probably just smoke from the train's engine coming in through the vents."

"Can't deny it, though, Jane. It was like you were one with the shadow," Duke whispered from the corner of his mouth.

"I am the Shadow," I whispered back, and he nodded knowingly.

I am the Witch of the Midnight Shadow.

Book Club Questions

1. What role does motherhood play in Jane's story?

2. Jane states that the fiddle is the devil's favorite instrument. Why do you think that is?

3. How does the setting of the story add to the sense of mystery and the unknown associated with witches?

4. Jane often feels a bolt of electricity between her and Tophat. What do you think it means?

5. Whose fortune does Jane see in the Tarot Cards when she first talks to Tophat in the trailer? How do you know that?

6. Why do you think the carnies call Trent "Tophat" instead of his real name?

7. Zora says in Chapter 9, "The carnival life sometimes just does stuff to people and makes them do things that might seem out of character." Explain what she means.

8. Explain the significance of the name *Crowe*.

9. What does faith mean to Tophat? And Jane? How is that similar or different to what faith means to you?

10. Of all the songs to play while Nancy and Trent dance, why "Do You Believe in Magic"?

11. Discuss the similarities and differences between religion and witchcraft.

12. What is the significance of the music Jane hears constantly throughout the book?

13. Why is young Nancy considered *vuota* (empty)? Why does that matter?

14. Compare and contrast Aleister and Tophat.

15. What is the gray spot on Jane's face at the end of the novel? What is the midnight shadow?

Author Bio

Maria DeVivo writes horror and dark fantasy for both YA and adult audiences. Each of her series has been Amazon best-sellers and has won multiple awards since 2012. A lover of all things dark and demented, the worlds she creates are fantastical and immersive. Get swept away in the lands of elves, zombies, angels, demons, and witches (but not all in the same place). Maria takes great pleasure in warping the comfort factor in her readers' minds—just when you think you've reached a safe space in her stories, she snaps you back into her twisted reality.

Discover more at
4HorsemenPublications.com

10% off using HORSEMEN10

www.ingramcontent.com/pod-product-compliance
Lightning Source LLC
LaVergne TN
LVHW041746060526
838201LV00046B/917